T

Four Islands

the story of
Four Islands

CRAWFORD IVIN

Cross Publishing

The writings of historian John Medland
are quoted freely

Image of author © Chris Bamber
www.atlasimages.co.uk
Cover picture ©

ISBN: 978-1-873295-37-3

Published by Cross Publishing
Chale, Isle of Wight

Operation PLUTO was a remarkable feat of British engineering, distinguished in its originality, pursued with tenacity and crowned by complete success. This creative energy helped win the war.

WINSTON CHURCHILL

My deepest thanks to Pat and Bernard. Without their hard work and guidance this undertaking would never have been possible.

Also to Elizabeth for her advice and proof reading, and finally to my wife for her encouragement and patience throughout.

Prologue

The Isle of Wight. South Coast
of England. Summer 1943

There was no moon that night. The air was still, heavy even. The gentle south westerly which had been caressing the island for most of the day had all but died out leaving the islanders to a humid, sleepless night.

To the west of the island, not far from St. Catherine's Point along the cliff top from Blackgang Chine, a lone member of the Home Guard leisurely patrolled the worn footpath. Tom Wallace, a fisherman by day, whose forebears had trodden the same path laden with smuggled contraband, was dreaming of Alice, the girl he'd met at the village dance. Had he concentrated more on his duties and not dwelt on the taste of Alice's lips, he might just have heard a sudden yet definite gurgling surge of water not far out to sea as a submarine broke surface. A German submarine. But the sound was quietly lost to the regular beating surf.

As Tom strolled on, a rubber dingy landed on the stony beach and right away gentle popping sounds were audible, in the still air, as a lethal blade punctured the thin skin again and again forcing air out. The redundant dingy was quietly rolled up and hidden behind some rocks. It would be days, weeks even, before it would be discovered and by then the lonely figure, who had already merged with the darkness, would be miles away.

Tom failed to catch the third and final important sound of the night, as hissing high pressured air was expelled from the submarine's tanks before it slipped from view beneath the waves.

Chapter One

The man looked at his hands, slowly rotating them until the full horror of the palms was before him. Deep cracks stared back. Swollen, red, encrusted with dirt. Blisters oozed pus; nails broken and bleeding. Surprisingly there was no pain but inside he died another death.

He had never seen hands like it. Certainly not his own, and he gingerly rubbed them together, imagining warm running water and a soothing balm. No chance of that. Not here.

"You!" The word came like the bark of a dog. "942! Keep working." 942 dismissed concern for his hands and quickly raised the heavy steel bar before he could feel the sting of the overseer's lash, and drove the point deep into the rock above his head, dislodging a large chunk which fell to the floor of the tunnel with a thud. But the noise was lost. Lost amongst a hundred other sounds of men working the length of granite rock face in semi darkness, wielding pickaxes, breaking rocks into manageable pieces for other workers to shovel into trolleys mounted on makeshift rails, ready to be pushed and hauled to the surface over 33 metres above their heads. This was the most dangerous time. The dust had only just settled after the rock had been dynamited. Cave-ins were common. One minute you could be working next to someone, the next they would be dead. Crushed, buried, or worse, injured. Their cries and screams echoing throughout the network of tunnels as they were dragged away, never to be seen again.

To have to listen to the pitiful cries of young men was worse. Teenagers, boys as young as fourteen, screaming for mercy, calling for their mothers. Sounds that haunted your sleep for weeks. And old men. Men too old for conscription, but good for a few months of twelve hours a day hard labour before they dropped dead of exhaustion. Poles, Spanish Republicans, Ukrainians, French and Russians. But it was the Russian workers who bore the full extent of Nazi brutality, especially after the suffering they had inflicted on Hitler's 6th Army during the battle of Stalingrad. The life expectancy of a Russian slave worker was six months.

This was Ho8. Hohlgangsanlage 8. A vast underground network of tunnels carved out of solid rock on the German occupied island of Jersey, the largest of the English Channel Islands. Built as a bomb proof, gas proof, artillery repair facility and barracks store, (although later to be used as an underground hospital).

Over 5,000 slave workers, mostly Eastern European, were brought to Jersey by 'Organisation Todt' (O.T.), to lay railway track, build anti-tank walls and bunkers, dig trenches and gun emplacements, widen roads and excavate tunnels. All in a bid to turn the island into an impregnable fortress as part of Hitler's 'Atlantic Wall' defences. The Channel Islands became the most heavily fortified area in Western Europe.

Yet, the harshest of these building programmes were the tunnels. Here, in the claustrophobic confines, it was impossible to distinguish between day or night. Where the back-breaking work continued around the clock, seven days a week. Where chest infections, tuberculosis, lice, eye infections and diseases of the skin were rampant amongst a workforce kept hovering between life and the hereafter on starvation rations, with nothing to wear, regardless of the weather, but the clothes they had on when snatched from villages, homes and loved ones.

Whatever the conditions on the surface, here, deep underground, the permanent cold ate into emaciated bodies, sucking a man's energy and will to survive. Gnawing his hopes, his dreams, until eventually he had nothing but death to live for.

942 was from Poland and had worked on the tunnels long enough to know by the change of guards that his shift was drawing to an end. It had been a bad day. Three rock falls, one dead, two injured.

He had tried to make a grab for the dead man's jacket before he had been taken away, but someone beat him to it.

It was customary that as soon as a worker fell he would immediately be replaced by another of the same nationality, so that there could at least be some fundamental communications and understanding. But as soon as the dead Pole had been removed, an elderly Russian worker arrived. It was obvious he was Russian, not by anything he said, or his lack of reaction to intimidation and threats of the overseers to which, in time, all workers developed a degree of immunity, but by his appearance. His clothes were reduced to rags like all the Russians. Rags upon rags.

He had bound strips of material around his legs and arms, and his chest gave the impression of being held together by layers of various fabrics tied with pieces of string. In place of shoes, long since worn through, he had made sole shaped pieces of wood held to his feet by strips of cloth. On his head a turban of mixed and brightly coloured cloths sat precariously in place to cushion the pain of falling rocks. But, apart from all that, which was a common enough sight in the tunnels, and the strong scent of stale sweat - for no-one was able to wash regularly - it was his face which 942 particularly noticed. It was the face of an aristocrat.

Delicate, pallid skin was stretched tight across high set cheek bones and a large, hooked nose. The thick, grey-white beard held a definite shape and the ends of his moustache had been given a defiant twist. In the gloom it was impossible to determine the colour of the stranger's eyes, but, from the way they protruded under the intelligent forehead, already damp with perspiration, blood shot and exhausted, it was evident that here was a face, well born perhaps, but this was also the face of a very sick man.

The sharp sound of a whistle suddenly pierced the noise of work. The night shift was over. Everyone immediately stopped what they were doing. The next gang of labourers could already be heard crunching their way down the tunnel towards them.

942 dropped the metal bar and joined the lines along with the other men in a well rehearsed routine, ready to be marched to the surface. He fell in beside the Russian as a roll-call was taken. The man called his number in Polish as 596.

The two columns moved forward passing the incoming shift, heads and shoulders sagging at the prospect of another twelve gruelling hours.

Further along the complex of tunnels conditions improved. Walls and floors were being lined with reinforced concrete, and electricity lit the way ahead.

Islanders were encouraged with reichmarks and extra rations to work for the Germans. Builders, plumbers, electricians were given the better and less dangerous jobs and could earn a reasonable living. In many cases necessity drove them to collaborate with their new masters, or starve. One or two of the Jersey men looked up from their work as the columns passed, their eyes full of compassion for the foreigners without hope.

942 glanced at the Russian. "You speak Polish?" he asked. For a moment he thought the man hadn't heard or didn't want to talk. Then the rag covered head slowly turned.

"That's why they put me with Poles." The voice was dry with rock dust.

"Where are you from?"

"Why?"

"No reason."

The man's tired eyes held the Pole for a moment. Tired and sad.

"I came from old St. Petersburgh", he spoke slowly, as if he hadn't heard the words himself for a long time. "Born in the halcyon days of the century long before the revolution. My brother and I were in Smoensk when the Nazis took us. He is already dead."

Suddenly the Russian doubled over and started to cough. Falling against the wall of the tunnel. A rasping, hollow cough from deep within his lungs. 942 moved to help him as the column passed by unconcerned.

"Keep up there!" shouted a guard. The two men tagged on to the column tail.

"Why do you risk helping me 942?" he asked,

when he had regained his breath.

"Why should I not?"

"This is why not." The Russian spat into the palm of his hand and held it between them. Even in the poor light of the tunnel it was not difficult to recognize the distinctive colour of blood. He wiped it on his sleeve. "Tomorrow," he said, "or maybe the next day, I shall die."

"How can you be so sure?"

"I know. Don't waste your energy on me, 942. Look out for yourself."

They had almost reached the entrance to the complex. The light of a spring dawn illuminating the tunnel mouth at the top of the final slope, where a fine drizzle and fresh, warmer air greeted the emerging slave labourers.

Without exception every man raised his face heavenwards and breathed deeply, thankful his shift was at an end. It would be another twelve hours before they had to return. The Poles were taken off to their vermin infested Lagers or compounds nearby, the Russian to his. 942 could hear the man coughing as he walked away.

That evening, at 1800 hours precisely, the efficient German war machine had assembled the night shift to descend underground once more, amidst a lot of shouting and swearing from sadistic guards addicted to the sight of human suffering. The men were careful not to make eye contact. No-one wanted a slap or a rifle butt in the stomach. Their stomachs were almost empty, having eaten only meagre portions of bread and water together with a few rancid vegetables, and the pain left by a rifle butt could last for hours seriously restricting the ability to work. If you couldn't work you would be sure to feel the lash. Again and again.

The final head count was almost completed when the Russian, 596 appeared. He was being goaded forward at the point of a Nazi steel bayonet. The more the Russian stumbled the more the soldier laughed.

The Unteroffizier conducting the count was furious at having to restart, and lashed out at the man, bringing the back of his hand sharply across the Russian's face, before pushing him in line beside the nearest worker, 942.

Eventually, they moved down into the cold and dripping dampness of the tunnels.

"The cough?" He asked quietly, noticing a patch of congealed blood in the corner of the man's mouth.

"I told you not to care. What are you, a doctor?"

"Dentist."

"A dentist! I can believe that," he said, taking in the younger man's unusually dark eyes. "You have an astute air. I suppose we all have a past we've left behind."

"What about you? What did you do?"

"Me? I had a book shop. Nothing elaborate, but it was mine. I loved my books."

"Have you family?"

"Have, or had, I don't know which. Perhaps it's better I don't know. A wife and son. But I doubt if they would have survived. What do you care? Why so many questions?"

They were passing the lines of day shift labourers. Their clothes and faces stiff and pale beneath layers of rock dust.

"You interest me. There's something about you. What's your name?"

"Why do you want to know my name?" he asked, assuming some ulterior motive. But then his face lined with the beginnings of a thought. "I've been in this annex of Hell for over five months. You're the first person to extend the hand of friendship."

"My name's Jan," the Pole told him.

"By rights you should call me Count Ronofsky. But," he flourished a hand, "in view of the current order and informal surroundings I'd be more than pleased if you were to call me Pasha."

"Pasha it shall be."

They had reached the semi darkness of the work tunnel and were instructed to collect their tools. All conversation ceased. Pasha broke into a bout of coughing and spat heavily into the dust. A whistle sounded. Work commenced.

It was hours before the men were allowed a five minute water break. Water in and water out.

Jan followed the sound of coughing and went to sit next to Pasha who had distanced himself from the other men, sitting on a boulder, alone.

"How are you feeling?"

"You must get away from here," he whispered, making sure there were no guards listening nearby. "Or you will die like they all do eventually."

"Ha! What hope is there of that?"

"But you must try. You are still a young man. You have your whole life before you."

"I'd never get off the island."

"You say you're a dentist?"

"Yes."

"Then there is a way."

"However can my being a dentist help me to escape?" The old man was sounding ridiculous.

"Shush! Keep your voice down! Trust me. There is a way. The guards don't know I'm fluent in German. I know what they get up to. They're all open to bribery."

"Polish, German, a Russian Count. I knew there was something about you."

"French too. My brother and I had private tutors. We ..... ." Pasha Ronofsky didn't finish the sentence, but instead broke into a fit of coughing that was agonizing to listen to.

The order came to resume work.

"We must talk further," he said, forcing himself erect. "We must".

At the conclusion of the twelve hour shift the two exhausted men made sure they were together and at the rear of the column that laboriously made its way to the surface. Pasha appeared nervous and kept turning round making sure they weren't being followed. There was one guard at the front and another walking alongside some way ahead, not showing any particular interest.

"Stop at the next light," he murmured after awhile.

"Whatever for?"

"Do it!"

At the next light directly overhead in the tunnel ceiling Pasha suddenly stopped. "Look into my mouth," he said, sharply.

"What?"

"Quickly. Look. See." Opening his mouth he threw his head back.

Jan did as he was told, turning this way and that to get a better view.

"Wow!" He said when he'd seen enough. "What beautiful workmanship. It must have cost a fortune." They walked on, catching the column up.

"They're all yours my friend."

"Whatever do you mean?"

"My gold teeth. I give you my gold teeth. With them you can bribe the guards and get away from here."

"But....?"

"I told you. Today, tomorrow, I shall die. Pray I die in the tunnel and not the compound. Have some pliers ready. You'll need to act quickly."

"How could I possibly do that? I couldn't."

"Do you want to die here and be buried in an unmarked, communal grave with all the other poor sods? Your name blotted out for ever. Well? Do you?"

Jan had to admit he did not.

"Then have some..... " he broke off, coughing, and spat out a dark mass of phlegm. "Have some sort of tool ready." The anxiety in his voice softened suddenly. "They are all I have left in the world, but I give them to you Jan, my friend. Get hold of a boat and sail to England. It's your only hope."

Later that day they assembled once again in the early evening light in front of the tunnel complex's tall entrance ready to advance underground. Pasha stood along with the other men as the guards went through the ritual of counting heads. He had noticeably deteriorated during the day. Wide, dark rings encircled his eyes and his skin had adopted a sickly yellow pallor, and Jan couldn't help but wonder if the forecast of his demise would be proved true. The man looked dead already. He was coughing almost continually.

Yet, as he stood there, his breathing coming in short, shallow bursts, there was a peculiar presence about him. A peace. Considering all the commotion surrounding them, shouting soldiers; noisy engines; building work; he stood as if he was mentally separating himself from it all. He lifted his head, not with pride but in surrender. Watching a pair of magpies circling overhead; the way the weakening sun caught the spring shoots on the trees; a bank of cumulus cloud rapidly building in the west. He closed his eyes, and the ends of his moustache twitched with something like anticipation.

"You have the necessary?" He asked quietly. But Jan didn't respond. "Don't pretend you didn't hear."

"Yes," admitted Jan, eventually.

"Act quickly. It's your only hope. Stay close by." His body was swaying noticeably as he spoke as if it were using all his strength to remain standing. "Be brave my friend. Be brave."

Jan couldn't speak, his throat had shut tight. The thought of actually doing what the man suggested filled him with revulsion, and yet, wasn't it a great sacrifice? The chance of freedom bequeathed by someone who would never taste freedom again. A gift of hope from the hopeless.

He felt the cold metal pliers digging into his ribs. It hadn't been difficult to get them, but could he use them?

With a flourish of authority the guards announced the start of another twelve hours toil, and the column moved off.

All the way down neither man said a word. Pasha continued to cough, his whole body trembling, occasionally falling against the wall of the tunnel like a drunkard, only to receive a tongue lashing.

Eventually they arrived at the uncompleted section of bare rock face they had been working for weeks. Two thirds of a mile of tunnel in various stages of completion networked out behind them.

Even in the half light it was possible to see clouds of thick dust still hanging in the air after a recent controlled explosion. It went straight to the back of the throat and would lodge there for hours. It made visibility difficult and breathing almost impossible. The guards and overseers, cracking their leather whips, goading men into action, were not immune. Makeshift protection proved useless and within minutes everyone was coughing.

For Pasha it could not have been worse.

A halt was called, the men withdrew and the order was given to dampen everything down with water. After a while conditions improved and work resumed. But Pasha Ronofsky's fate was sealed. His exhausted lungs could not take any further punishment. His legs buckled beneath him and down he went. Collapsing to the floor like a pile of dirty, spent rags.

Jan was at his side in an instant, and cradled the old man's head in his arms, clearing dust from his mouth and eye lids.

"Don't give up! Please don't give up. You mustn't."

"I told you..... " gasped Pasha, fighting for oxygen, "my time has come. Promise you'll do..... . At least my death...... will bring you hope."

A sharp eyed guard, the one who had struck out at the Russian before, was soon on them.

"What's this!?" he snarled. "Laziness! Laziness!" His arm poised ready to bring down the lash.

Jan looked up at the man. The face, a picture of hatred and loathing, twisted by years of sadistic gratification. But for all that it was the face of a wretched, empty soul.

He held Jan's dark, penetrating eyes when, for an instant, something intangible passed between them. His arm lowered slowly and he nodded in the direction of a quieter section of the tunnel, turned his back without further word and walked away.

One or two of the other men were beginning to take notice. One, witnessing what had happened, offered to help and together they lifted the Russian to a less noisy place.

"Try and relax," offered Jan after they had propped him up against a wall of rock. But he knew he sounded as helpless as he felt.

The man left them alone and Jan looked around for some water to moisten the old Russian's lips, but by the time he had returned it was too late. Pasha Ronofsky was dead. His head had dropped forward dislodging the turban. The silver-grey hair was alive with lice.

Gently, almost reverently, Jan replaced the Count's coronet, deciding in his mind that it was now or never. Any moment the guard would return and order the body removed. Was he foolish to believe the plan could have any hope of success? But his fingers were already wrapped tightly around the handle of the pliers.

Taking the head firmly in an arm lock, doing his best to make it look as if he was caring for the sick man, he glanced around to see if anyone was watching and, pulling the mouth wide open inserted the 'Krupp' steel pliers, knowing that if he delayed for one second he would lose his nerve.

The tool's sharp, serrated jaws bit into the row of teeth, upper right. He took a deep breath, and with a sharp flick of the wrist felt them snap free with a loud crack. Dropping them into his free hand he repeated the manoeuvre, upper left.

The bottom teeth proved more difficult to hold onto, especially with so primitive an instrument, and each side required two or more attempts. Eventually he had completed almost a full clearance, thankful that no-one had overheard the sounds of shattering bone.

From habit he looked inside the mouth, which was dripping blood profusely, disgusted to see that he had been the cause of such butchery. He had, however, done what the old man had wanted him to do and removed all his gold teeth. Only the uncapped incisors and canines remained intact.

Jan knew he would have to move swiftly now, he had been absent from work long enough and the guards would be sure to come sniffing asking awkward questions. He dropped the teeth, some still supporting flesh and bone, into his pocket along with the pliers. Tearing a length of cloth from Pasha's chest he jammed it into his mouth in an attempt to stem the flow of blood, and readjusted the turban's chin strap to hold the jaw closed.

With the water he had brought only moments earlier he washed the blood from his hands and cleaned the Russian's beard, when something made him pause suddenly. He rested his hand on the man's shoulder and looked into the dusty, noble face. "Rest in peace my friend," he whispered. "Thank you for your sacrifice. I'll do my best to make sure it wasn't in vain."

He was interrupted by the familiar sound of leather advancing over broken rock, and he stood up. The guard had returned.

"Well!?"

"Dead." It was all Jan needed to say.

"Back to work. Schnell!" He shouted, anxious not to repeat his earlier display of weakness. "Now you will work twice as hard to make up wasted time". He punctuated his words with a crack of the whip. "My men will dispose of the body."

Hours later, when the other Polish workers were asleep, Jan crept into the toilet block and, using the pliers, began to chip away at Pasha's gold teeth. He removed any suggestion of bone, dentine and blood until he was left with a handful of bean size, 22 carat, finest Russian gold nuggets.

He flushed away the residue and wrapping the nuggets tightly in a cloth, placed them in an inside jacket pocket next to his heart, and returned to his bunk. Sleep, however, was impossible.

The following days turned quickly into weeks, and weeks passed by without even the suggestion of an escape plan. Positioned as the tunnels were, roughly in the centre of the island, meant that Jan never came close to the sea or had contact with anyone dealing with boats. He had been on the island so long, he could not remember when he had last seen the sea. He could smell the salinated air, and in the still of sleep his imagination allowed him to listen to waves pounding the shoreline miles away, only adding to his frustration on awakening with a start. As a consequence it wasn't long before the dream of escape and something better began to wither. Each day the routine was the same, especially difficult for those continually working the topsy-turvy world of the night shift. They worked twelve mind and body numbing hours, with only a short break for water based soup, cruelly called 'lunch', to emerge, like grubs, and stagger back to the compound and fall exhausted into hard bunks. Then rise and do the same again. Night after night and, all the while, guarded, counted and recounted.

Until one bright morning towards the end of May.

The day started out as all other days. The sound of the night shift dragging tired feet up the final slope before being spewed out of the huge, gaping mouth like entrance, as if unfit for the subterranean monster's distinct diet, to muster for roll call, thankful to breathe luxurious, fresh, clean air once more.

The count complete, the men were on the point of being led away, when an approaching Hauptmann and an authoritative sharp "Halt!", took them and their overseers by surprise. The command had come from a tall, thin officer, who couldn't have been more than twenty nine, perhaps thirty years of age. He wore a strong, confident expression and walked sharply across to the assembly, his heels tapping rhythmically on the concrete, and spoke confidentially with the Unteroffizier in charge, before turning to face the two parallel lines of Polish workers, everyone of them fearful of what this might mean.

In a strong, clear voice he called one of their numbers.

"942."

Jan's heart sank. Yet knowing hesitation would meet with a beating responded quickly. "Here, Sir."

"Step forward," ordered the Sergeant, pointing to a spot on the ground.

The Hauptmann walked over to him slowly, eyeing his scrawny frame up and down. His disgust at Jan's unearthly appearance unmistakable. "Are you 942?" he asked. Then took a sharp step backwards. "My God! You reek, man."

"942 is my number," Jan answered him slowly, careful to keep his eyes fixed firmly on the ground.

The man's pointed nose twitched as he read from a sheet of paper. "Kowalski, Jan, of Warsaw, Poland," but paused before continuing. "A dentist?"

"Yes, Herr Captain."

The Hauptmann eyed him over once again. "Are you truly a qualified dentist?"

"I am Sir. Berlin trained."

"You amaze me." He turned to the man in charge. "I want this pathetic creature cleaned up. Hair cut, shaved and showered, and find him some better clothes. Something that doesn't smell, - and some boots," he added, "that don't have protruding toes."

"Right away Herr Hauptmann."

"Maybe I should suggest to the High Command that we use these men as our latest weapon. We could stink the enemy into surrendering." The thought amused him.

The Unteroffizier laughed, as was expected.

"When he's ready bring him to me. Oh yes, you'd better give him something to eat. Something better than usual. Just a little better mind, we don't want to be accused of spoiling him."

"Herr Hauptmann. Heil Hitler."

Within a couple of hours Jan had been transformed. Even though he hadn't slept since his shift had ended, he felt revived and fresh, and smelt of carbolic. His clothes weren't new, nor were they a perfect fit, and he tried not to dwell on who they might have belonged to, but at least they weren't crawling and didn't smell. The boots even had laces.

The most difficult part of his metamorphic-like rebirth proved to be the shedding of clothes and taking a shower without the onlooker catching sight of the small packet of nuggets. Fortunately, the young Gefreiter assigned to the Pole hadn't paid close attention and Jan was able to keep the gold concealed in a tightly clenched fist.

Now, as he marched to the Hauptmann's office of administration, his only thoughts were, what was to become of him? Why all this special treatment?

The Captain made a joke about 942's transformation into a human being, and then told Jan he would be going to St. Helier, immediately.

"I shall meet you there directly," he said "and tell you what we have planned."

The thirty minute drive to Jersey's capital, being shaken around in the back of a canvas covered truck, would not have been most people's idea of fun, but after the tunnel it was exhilarating. Suddenly, his senses were overflowing with the sounds of life - traffic, the cry of sea gulls, the voices of English men and women, and once, when the truck made a stop, he was sure he heard a cow. Then, a gust of wind lifted a corner of canvas and he caught a glimpse of the promenade along St. Aubin's Bay bathed in sunshine, and something he hadn't seen in a long time - a young woman in a pretty dress. Suddenly, a wave of sadness swept over him. Would he ever see his sister, his family and home again? Was he to die like Pasha? Worked to death?

Then he smoothed his clothes and let his arm nudge the old Russian's gold. Surely not. Fate had another plan.

He glanced at the Corporal seated opposite. A spotty, stick of a youth, carelessly polishing the barrel of the rifle laid across his lap.

He thought of jumping him. A quick right hook and the lad would be out, but something held him back. This was not the time.

"Do you know where they are sending me?" he asked, tentatively.

But all he got was a kick in the shin and told to shut up.

Outside the noise of traffic began to increase and a German voice was shouting instructions. He could make out what appeared to be the clanking of chains, and in the distance a blast from a ship's claxon. Then, the churning of water by a big, powerful engine.

Not only the island's principal municipality, St. Helier was also the island's foremost harbour. But he couldn't understand why they were taking him down to the sea. Surely they weren't going to send him home? He quickly dismissed the idea as too ridiculous.

The truck pulled to a sharp halt and the back was thrown up abruptly, letting in a flood of bright light and view of the capital's bustling port. Sun glistening on the surface of a sea dotted with the sombre, grey coloured ships and boats of Hitler's powerful military arm.

The sudden appearance of the Hauptmann at the rear of the truck prompted the young conscript into life and he prodded Jan with his rifle and both of them jumped down.

The Captain was annoyed.

"The boat hasn't arrived?" He was questioning a bell bellied Unteroffizier Jan hadn't seen before, impatiently beating a fist in the palm of his hand.

"Nein, Herr Hauptmann."

"Well? Why not?"

"We don't know Herr Hauptmann. There has been no word."

"This is unacceptable. Couldn't they radio?"

"They don't have radio, Sir. It's only a small boat."

"They don't have radio? Maybe they don't have a compass, either! Maybe they're cruising around in the Atlantic, lost. Maybe I stand here all day waiting for a boat that will never arrive, when I have far better things to do, and maybe I don't! Well, the answer to that is I don't. Find an alternative."

The sergeant looked flummoxed. "Sir?"

"It's not that difficult, surely. You work here. Find another boat."

The Sergeant consulted a clipboard. "I..... I can't see..... I'm sorry Sir, but there is nothing else."

"Oh for goodness sake! The harbour's full of boats. Surely there must be one that's not in use. Anything."

The Sergeant's expression brightened. "We could always commandeer a fishing vessel."

"Excellent. Do it."

The man hurried away, only to return a short while later.

"About time."

"This way Sir."

A short walk brought the four men to a different and quieter area of the harbour where a number of fishing boats nestled redundantly against the quay. Only one was showing any sign of life, where a man and a teenage girl were sat on deck apparently mending nets.

(Legitimate fishing was strictly under supervision of the conquering power. What went on after dark was something else.)

"There is still the question of a crew Herr Hauptmann," began the Sergeant.

"Ah yes. A crew."

"But I have arranged a permit for," he checked his board, "'The Merry Gull' to deliver the Pole and Gefreiter. Captain Anders and his daughter will crew. It's not far. The couple are known to us. They are trustworthy."

"I see. Somewhat unorthodox but, well, that appears to be in order."

They had arrived at the boat in question; a fishing smack with brightly painted gunwales and wheelhouse. The putt, putt, putt of the diesel engine clearly discernable in the still, morning air.

The Captain and his daughter folded away their nets, without exchanging a word, and began to make ready for leaving the harbour as the soldier and foreign labourer boarded.

"Wait. Do you know where you're going, 942?"

"No Sir."

"You're going to Alderney. You'll find out why when you arrive."

"Alderney!"

"And you corporal. You have your orders, but be careful. Remember, the entire island is under the command of the SS. They have a reputation."

"Yes Sir. Danke, Herr Hauptmann. But my orders don't say what to do with him afterwards."

"I don't care what you do with him. You can throw him to the fishes if you like. But you look a little pale, man. Are you alright?"

"Yes Sir. I'll be fine. Heil Hitler."

Within less than an hour 'The Merry Gull' had taken on fuel, cleared harbour and was making good headway around Noirmont Point. Once they had passed the mouth to St Brelade's Bay and Corbiere lighthouse they made a sharp alteration of course to starboard, which put them along Jersey's western coastline following a northerly course for Alderney. The sea was slight with only a light swell running, and a gentle breeze from the south-west conducted the waves in an orchestration of dancing light, and it wasn't long before the voyage took on the feel of a pleasure cruise.

Captain Anders, a stern, thick set, heavily tanned islander, proved uncommunicative, speaking only when necessary, deeply suspicious of all Germans and those associated with them. He could only have been a fisherman. A stained roll-top jumper hung loosely from broad shoulders over navy blue trousers, and a cap that had moulded to the shape of his head was pulled forward at a defiant angle. When he spoke the pipe kept parked in the corner of his mouth bobbed up and down with the rise and fall of the sea, like a buoy cast adrift.

His daughter looked to be in her late teens. Quite a good looking girl in an outdoor, hardworking kind of way. With dark hair pulled back in a ponytail, and dressed in an oilskin jacket at least two sizes too large and smelling strongly of fish. She treated their passengers with interested suspicion, only occasionally allowing her strong blue eyes to drift in Jan's direction.

Jan had seated himself behind the wheelhouse, happy to feel the warmth of the sun and watch the girl go about her work. She was the first woman he had been close to in months and while she prepared some lines for fishing, their eyes met and she gave him a flicker of a smile, sending a bolt of joy surging through his weary frame.

The corporal had made himself as comfortable as possible near the boat's edge on the starboard side, with his rifle and helmet beside him. It was obvious he was no sailor, having turned an unpleasant shade somewhere in between yellow and green. It wouldn't be long before his breakfast reappeared.

The rocking and pitching of the little boat and the regular beat of the engine, with its heady fumes, soon began to have an effect on Jan. After a night in the tunnel his eyelids eventually became too heavy, and he curled up on deck and, using his arm as a pillow, was soon asleep.

The sun continued to move across a sky streaked with brush strokes of high, wispy cloud as the morning progressed.

Already the islands of Big and Little Sark were in view and Herm beyond, with the hills of Guernsey clearly discernable, to port, through the haze. Each island occupied and administered by the forces of the 'Third Reich'.

Suddenly Jan was awake. Wrenched from a deep sleep by a girl's hysterical screams. For a moment he didn't know where he was, conscious only of the absence of his familiar bunk, when a shower of spray swept over him and he realised the noise was coming from Anders' daughter. She was leaning over the side shouting and pointing at something in the water. Her father was at her side stopping her from falling in.

Jan jumped up and was immediately flung hard against the wheelhouse. The wind had increased and was now blowing out of the northwest. He staggered over to join the couple, but they were speaking so quickly he couldn't understand what they were saying, when suddenly he realised they were a member short. The Corporal !

Anders almost flung his daughter at Jan who instinctively wrapped his arms around her, before dashing back to the wheel to bring the boat about. But it was precious seconds before the rudder responded. Seconds that could mean the difference between life and death for them all.

In an instant, Jan understood why the girl was so hysterical. It wasn't that she cared for the enemy soldier particularly, but for her own safety and that of her father, and more than likely her entire family left behind on Jersey. If they were to arrive on Alderney, or return to St. Helier without the Gefreiter they would certainly be shot, regardless of what might have taken place. All fishing boat masters left the 'deposit' of a family remaining in the port. If they didn't return, the family would be executed. The Germans had thought of everything.

All the while the youth was thrashing about wildly. Being swept further and further away in the current. His cries becoming increasingly desperate.

Jan knew what he had to do.

He briefly tried to comfort the girl, yet whether she understood broken English, or not, was impossible to tell. But, she understood well enough when he began to pull off his boots and jacket, staring at him in amazement. He had his legs over the side just as Captain Anders brought 'The Merry Gull' round, when the wind hit the little boat broadside on and she leaned over at a precarious angle, tipping Jan unprepared into the water.

He surfaced quickly and getting his breath and bearings lunged out in the direction of the soldier, already fifty yards away, as Anders did his best to manoeuvre the boat closer.

When he eventually reached the corporal he came face to face with blind terror, and was in danger of being knocked unconscious by the man's wildly flailing arms. No amount of instruction or cajoling would calm him, and he grabbed hold of Jan with an iron-like grip and would not let go. Together they disappeared from view.

When they surfaced, gasping and spluttering, Jan immediately tried to knock him out, but only managed to catch him on the nose, which made the German panic all the more. Using his final reserve of strength, Jan threw a fist and at last the man was quiet, his head falling lazily back in the water.

Suddenly, the bow of the boat was upon them and the girl threw them a line and, together with her father, hauled the pair aboard. Jan collapsed onto the deck. Anders slapped the corporal around the face a few times, relieved when he started coughing and spewing up water. The girl stripped off her coat and kneeling beside Jan laid it round him.

"You are the bravest man in the world," she told him, gently wiping hair off his face. When suddenly she leaned forward and kissed him lightly on the cheek. But to Jan it was as powerful as the kick of a mule.

While the girl, Molly, was drying their clothes on the engine, Jan saw the opportunity he had been waiting for and went and sat next to the corporal in the stern. The experience had mellowed the man's attitude.

"I owe you my life 942," he said. "It was a brave thing you did."

"Yes, you owe me. Firstly you can tell me why I'm being sent to Alderney."

"I don't know."

"Oh?"

"Truly. My orders are to take you there for a special purpose. A job that needs to be done."

"Then what?"

"I don't know. You Poles are expendable. You know that."

"Tell me something else," said Jan. "What do

you think this is?" He dropped a single gold nugget into the soldier's palm.

"It's heavy," he said, "whatever it is." He held it up to the light, turning it around between his thumb and forefinger. "It's a gold filling," he said finally. "For teeth. Where did you get it from?"

"Where I got it from doesn't matter. But how would you like it and a lot more beside?"

"You've been pulling dead men's teeth, haven't you?"

"Perhaps."

"The junior officers usually do that. We don't get a look in. How many have you got?"

"Enough. Enough to make you rich."

"Rich!?"

"But you'll have to earn it."

"What do you mean?"

"I want a boat."

"A what?"

"You heard. A boat. A small boat."

"How am I going to get hold of a boat? The island's run by the SS, you know. They have eyes everywhere."

"That's the problem you must solve to win the prize."

"But I have to report the moment we dock, there'll be no time for boats."

"Of course. I understand that, but while I'm doing whatever the job is, you can be arranging a boat. With a sail."

"Ha! Anything else?"

"Some rations would be nice. See what you can do."

"How do I know you've even got more gold?"

"You don't. But if I don't come up with the gold, you can forget all about the boat. Think about it. Imagine what you could do with a pile of gold nuggets. A young man like yourself would have the world at his feet. Girls. Anything."

The corporal sat quiet for a while, thinking, toying with the nugget. "The job, whatever it is, may kill you," he said. Lots of workers die."

"Then you'll get to keep that nugget for doing precisely nothing."

"Why don't I kill you now? You've obviously got the gold on you."

"That you don't know for sure. But you don't strike me as a cold hearted killer who'll casually see off the man who's just saved you from a very watery grave. Think on it. You'll never get a better opportunity. Keep the nugget as a reminder."

The remainder of the journey proved uneventful except for a visit from a German patrol vessel. But when the Gefreiter gave them a wave they showed no further interest and, with a roar of their powerful engines, disappeared in a cloud of exhaust.

By mid afternoon the island of Alderney was clearly outlined against the northern horizon. Only 3½ miles by 1 mile, Alderney is one of the smallest of the Channel Islands, although its strategic position means it is one of the most important. Yet, as the 'Merry Gull' ploughed on towards its destination, the bright summer sun was unable to lift the island's dark and foreboding reputation.

The island's population of nearly 1,500 was almost completely evacuated before the invasion of July 1940, to be replaced with over 2,500 foreign slave workers and political prisoners, driven by force and brutality into turning Alderney into yet another island fortress. Life on Jersey was bad, but Alderney was the home of the walking dead.

Jan tried to console himself with the thought that the island was nearly half way to England, but try as he might, he was unable to sleep further.

Concerned for his deteriorating mood, Molly offered their passengers some tea and a cheese sandwich.

"No butter. Sorry," she said, when she returned and their fingers touched briefly around the chipped enamel mug.

"Still good," he told her as their eyes met. "You are very kind." It was the first cheese he had tasted in over four years.

She didn't say anything to the corporal, just passing him his tea and a sandwich which was less than half the size of Jan's.

As they neared the island, taking an easterly approach, there was a noticeable increase in activity both at sea and in the air.

Jan moved into the wheelhouse and focused a pair of binoculars on the coastline, knowing there were dozens of pairs of eyes watching the little boat's progress.

"You must be important," commented Anders, his pipe bobbing up and down as he spoke.

"Why do you say that?"

"I've never known them ferry one of your lot about like this. But whatever you are, you're brave. That took guts back there."

"How much further?" he asked, quickly pocketing something.

"Half an hour, maybe more, maybe less."

It wasn't long before they reached the far eastern extremity of the island, when Captain Anders brought the 'Merry Gull' over to port and around the rocks of Fort Les Homeaux Florains, and Cats Bay, following the northern coast for St. Anne's harbour. Suddenly, the wind picked up now they were out of the lee of the island. It appeared to send a message throughout the boat.

The corporal replaced his helmet and adjusted his crumpled uniform. The girl busied herself with ropes and the clearing away of fishing lines they had been dragging unsuccessfully all day. Jan began to feel sick. Not because of the sudden extra motion of the boat, but at the uncertainty of whatever it was that lay ahead. He went and stood alone at the bow, watching the churning white water streaming past, when suddenly there was

Pasha's hair, white and alive, reminding him that if he failed to escape from this prison island it would certainly become his grave.

He felt someone touch his sleeve and turned to find Molly standing there. It was a moment before she spoke. "It's almost time," she said softly.

"Yes, nearly there."

"I'll never forget you Jan, or what you did. It was the bravest thing I've ever seen."

"And I will never forget you. Always I will remember Molly Anders and her 'Merry Gull'."

She smiled, when for the first time he noticed her long lashes, and there was a moment's awkward hesitation between them. Then, with a flick of her pony-tail, she broke eye contact and went to join her father.

"942!" It was the corporal. "Get yourself ready."

The tip of St. Anne's long harbour wall, protruding out into the sea like a beckoning finger, was already in sight.

"Do your best," said Jan, giving him a wink, "and it's all yours, remember."

Chapter Two

"So you're the dentist, are you? Well we'll see what sort of a dentist you are. You'll start work first thing tomorrow morning."

The room in the single storey wooden building nestling on the quayside, hastily erected after the invasion, was only just large enough to take the three of them. An Obersturmführer of Hitler's elite SS, Jan and the corporal.

"May I speak Herr Obersturmführer?" asked Jan, mindful to keep his head down.

The lieutenant, a middle aged, sombre character with the bitterness of being passed over for promotion etched on his weasel-like features, sat drumming his fingers on the desk, scrutinising the latest arrival. Another poverty stricken, ailing individual, but, at least this one appeared educated.

"Speak," he said.

"May I ask what I shall be doing?"

"Don't you know? Didn't they tell you in Jersey?"

"No, Herr Obersturmführer. Nothing."

"Incompetent fools." He pushed back his chair, filling the room with the sound of wood scraping on wood, and went to stand by the window overlooking the harbour. Suddenly the brightness of the day had faded. The sky was full of thick, billowing cloud. "A number of workers have complained of toothache," he said, "too many in fact. It's beginning to have an effect on their work and hampering the building program. It'll be your job to get them sorted out."

"Yes Sir," said Jan, relieved.

"However," he continued, swinging sharply round. "There'll be no time for fillings and whatever else. Only extractions. We've no anaesthetic and only a few basic instruments. The only reason you're here is to pull teeth and you will do so as quickly and efficiently as possible. Do I make myself clear?"

"Yes, Herr Obersturmführer."

"0600 sharp." He nodded towards the door. "See to it Gefreiter."

"Yes Sir."

"What happened to your face?" he asked, referring to the angry looking bruise where Jan had hit him.

"I..... I er..... fell, Herr Obersturmführer."

"Clumsy oaf. You should be more careful. And smarten yourself up. You're a disgrace. Obviously standards on Jersey have become very lax. Well, it's different here you'll soon discover. Dismiss! My Scharführer will tell you where you're both to go."

47

The new day dawned chilly and dull. The sky low and threatening.

The corporal marched his charge directly to one of the island's four concentration camps and on to a compound that housed a large number of labourers, and was directed to a windowless, corrugated iron hut standing alone in the corner of a small field.

Both Jan and the corporal got a shock.

A queue, numbering between 150 and 200 men, was lined up outside under the watchful eye of armed guards with Alsation dogs. The line stretched left and right, snaking back on itself, made up of men of all ages and nationalities, but a more motley collection of humanity would be impossible to imagine.

Clothes were torn and ragged, many feet were bare, wet in the dew of the grass. Faces stared back, dirty, empty and gaunt. Older men supported themselves leaning on the man in front. Others had given up and were kneeling or sitting on the ground. Some had their mouths covered, moaning in pain. One teenage lad was in tears. The closer Jan got to them the more fearful he became at the thought of what was required. Most didn't look as if they had the strength to survive any further suffering.

"Is this the dentist?" asked one of the guards.

"He is." The corporal told him.

With a mocking gesture the man motioned

towards the hut. "Your surgery awaits, Herr dentist."

The dogs had been quiet up until now, but, anticipating change, started to bark and snap aggressively.

Inside, the hut smelt musty and damp. The size of a large garage, it was completely empty except for a table and single upright chair standing in the centre of the concrete floor. A bare bulb hung from the convex ceiling. Beside the table, on the floor, were two buckets. One full of water, the other empty.

"The Obersturmführer thought they'd come in useful." A guard had followed them in. "One's for washing, the other for teeth."

"How thoughtful of the Obersturmführer," said Jan, "but what of some instruments?"

"Here. You're to use these," and he gave Jan a cloth bag. But when he emptied the contents out onto the table he got another shock.

"But these aren't dental instruments!"

"That's all there is. You'll have to make do." At that, the man walked out leaving the door swinging wide. "I'll start sending them in."

Jan studied the collection of tools that had probably come directly from a mechanic's tool box, and his spirits fell. They even smelt of engine oil.

"You'd better get ready," the corporal told him, "here they come."

Jan quickly washed his hands in the bucket and shook them dry.

The line of peculiar patients had moved forward like a wriggling, squirming serpent, shuffling through the doorway; on command coming to a halt only inches from the table.

"Sit down." The guard ordered the first case. He was a middle aged man with dark, curly hair, who looked at Jan with wide, fearful eyes, as if he was about to be executed.

"Put your head back and open wide for me. Which one's causing you trouble?" asked Jan, immediately hit by the smell of a mouth that hadn't been cared for, in months.

He indicated an upper right molar, instantaneously letting out a terrible cry that bounced off the metallic walls when Jan touched it.

The next in line moaned in trepidation.

"It'll have to come out," said Jan, and, choosing a pair of long nose pliers, rinsed them in the bucket.

"Get a move on." The guard was tapping his leg with the handle of a lash, itching for an excuse to use it.

The offending tooth came out easily enough and dropped directly into the bucket.

"Rinse out with cold water. It'll help stop the bleeding."

"Next. Schnell!"

Even before the next man sat down it was obvious to a trained eye what was wrong. White stuff was oozing from between his lips and when he opened his mouth the diagnosis was immediately confirmed. Jan pulled back forcing himself not to throw up, gagging on the overpowering stench.

Eventually he forced himself to look. Filthy teeth encrusted with plaque, red and angry gums covered with ulcers, and the unmistakable signs of gum rot.

With a sigh he turned to the guard in charge. "There's nothing I can do here," he said. "This is trench mouth."

"Trench mouth? I've heard of trench foot, but never trench mouth."

"They're not that dissimilar."

Suddenly the guard jumped to attention at the arrival of the Obersturmführer, and saluted smartly.

"Everything under control?"

"Herr Obersturmführer. The dentist reports....."

"Trench mouth," finished Jan.

"And what is that exactly?"

"In a word. Gum rot. The result of poor diet, stress, lack of rest, excetera. I would imagine it's not the only case I'm going to see today. It's highly infectious."

"Treatment?"

"The exact opposite of the cause. Good food, rest, plenty of fluids and a course of medication."

"Examine the next man," ordered the officer, and with a wave of his hand dismissed the labourer, who scurried quickly away.

"Yes," said Jan after a moment. "Just as I suspected. Trench mouth again."

"And the next one."

The following four cases were all confirmed as having trench mouth.

"You'll notice, Sir," said Jan, "that all the men infected are from Poland. Are they housed together?"

"What if they are?"

"Only it'll sweep through a crowded compound like the wind, I know how dirty these places are. They're breeding grounds for all sorts of diseases. All their knives and forks, plates, cups, everything needs to be sterilised in boiling water. Daily."

"Right" said the lieutenant, after a moment. "To save time you will examine all the remaining men where they stand in line. They can't all have this trench mouth. They're not all from the same compound." He turned to the soldier in charge. "Those with trench mouth can be dismissed. Get them back to work. Those needing teeth pulling may remain and have them pulled."

"Herr Obersturmführer."

Flanked by a guard, Jan began to work his way slowly down the line of wretched humanity, conscious that a word from him would send the men back to slavery and a slow, exhausting death. Yet his suspicions were soon confirmed. Almost all the Poles were infected with trench mouth. But he also saw cases of gingivitis and gums leaking with puss. A sure sign of pyorrhoea. There was nothing he could do for them, either.

Some time later in the morning, he'd almost reached the end of the line. A light drizzle was not helping to lift his spirits. 182 men had been reduced to 27 in need of his attention.

Then, only two remained. The penultimate man, a Russian, needed an extraction, but the remaining man was holding back for some reason and very reluctant to remove the cloth tied over his mouth. He was French and started shouting and pushing Jan away, until he was given a couple of strokes of the lash. He then suddenly stood quite still and started to weep pitifully, tears streaming down his dirty face, his body sagging as if under a terrible burden.

Jan gently unwound the cloth. "Oh my God!" Horrified at what lay beneath.

The guard looked away in disgust.

"Help me Monsieur," pleaded the man, "I beg you."

His lips were swollen, angry and ulcerated, and, as he spoke white stuff dribbled down into his beard. His cheeks were red and inflamed where the soft tissue had been eaten away, leaving holes the size of sovereigns, open directly into the mouth. And, there was the smell of death about him. The lingering stench of rotting flesh.

"This is the worst case I've ever seen," said Jan. "He must have had it long before he arrived here."

"Whatever is it?" asked the German. "The plague?"

"Seriously advanced trench mouth. The mouth's soft tissue is literally being devoured. This man should be hospitalised."

Jan handed the man back his cloth. It was an acknowledgement of defeat. Of the hopelessness of their situation. Of the brutality of one nation over another. But for the Frenchman it was the last straw and he threw the cloth directly at the German, catching him in the face and following it with a flying mouthful of white phlegm.

With only seconds to live, he sharply pulled himself erect and in a voice both bold and passionate, proceeded to sing La Marsellaise. But, before he had completed even the first stanza, there was a loud crack of a gun. Jan Kowalski froze. His gaze fixed on the tiny hole in the centre of the man's forehead.

For a second the Frenchman didn't move. As if the moment of death was his decision and his alone. Then, slowly, like the felling of a redundant tree, he toppled back.

By mid afternoon there were dozens of teeth in the bucket. The last man had left, leaving Jan and the corporal alone. Jan sat down heavily on the chair, exhausted. "No matter how long I live I shall never forget this day," he said.

"I must admit you did well, 942."

"Thank you Gefreiter".

"And so did I".

"What do you mean?"

"A boat."

"You've got one!?"

"I haven't seen it, but I know where there is one. I met someone last night."

"But can they be trusted?"

"I don't know. It's a risk you'll have to take."

"So where is it? Does it have a sail?"

"Cats Bay. We passed it on the way here, and yes it has a sail. A few of the men use it when they're off duty, apparently. But."

"There's a catch?"

"The gold. You do have it. Don't you?"

"Of course. I told you."

"So, let's see it. I've taken great risks for you and I want to be sure it's not all for nothing."

Jan thought for a moment, forcing his weary brain to work. "Alright," he said eventually, removing the nuggets. "Half now. The rest when I see the boat." He then spilled the gold out onto the table, watching as the corporal's eyes grew wide.

"Why ever don't I shoot you now and be done with it? I could say you tried to escape."

"You could, but you won't."

They reported to the Obersturmführer that the work of the dentist was complete.

"Very well. See to it Gefreiter, that he returns to

Jersey. You'll have to arrange that yourself."

"Yes Sir. Danke, Herr Obersturmführer. Heil Hitler."

They were on the point of leaving when Jan hesitated. "May I ask a question, Herr Obersturmführer?"

"Well?"

"Was there any particular reason why your Medical Officer didn't deal with this situation?"

"You cretin! Do you seriously imagine that an officer of the glorious Third Reich has nothing better to do than pull the teeth of peasants? Get out of my sight!"

After something to eat Jan used the balance of daylight hours to rest, conscious that his greatest ordeal was yet to come. Too many things, however, were being left to chance and yet, he knew he had no choice.

Would the tide be right? Would there be patrols? Would the boat be too big to launch from the beach by himself, or dangerously small for the long voyage? Had the corporal tricked him after all?

He looked at the rustling trees through the dormitory hut window. At least there was a stiff breeze. Thank God it was from the south. But, the sky was grey and heavy. The earlier drizzle had dried up but more rain would be sure to follow.

The corporal arrived, as had been arranged, at 2030hrs. Not part of Alderney's regular work force it was relatively easy for Jan to move about, especially when accompanied by a guard, and together, in the rapidly approaching dusk, they set out to walk the one and a half, or so, miles to Cats Bay.

"Remember," said the corporal, "you're to walk in front of me at all times; and, if we're challenged for any reason, you're not to open your mouth. Leave all the talking to me."

"Oh I will. You have my word."

Once outside of St. Annes, Mount Hale Battery and the turn-off for Fort Albert, they were passed only twice. The first time by a troop carrier going in the same direction which almost forced them into a ditch, and a while later by an armoured car travelling west at breakneck speed. Considering the entire island was one huge garrison and labour camp, there were surprisingly few signs of life.

All the way, following a narrow road along the island's spine, the sky continued to darken and the wind built in intensity, until finally the last sight of day died on the western horizon cloaking them in darkness.

A narrow gauge railway line crossed the road twice before the road veered round to the right, skirting Mannez Quarry and a German munitions tunnel, where they branched left, off down a track towards a blacked out lighthouse that towered over them menacingly against the night sky, as they moved soundlessly around the low perimeter wall and outbuilding, from which, the sound of music over a radio told them was not deserted.

The darkness was intense. All across the island the Germans were careful not to show the Allies a single, guiding light.

The walk narrowed to nothing more than an overgrown path which dropped down, and suddenly they were standing on a narrow finger of sand with sea lapping to left and right, and the shadows of shapeless rocks ahead.

With spray in his face, the noise of the wind and waves filling his senses, Jan had to battle to hold his nerve. But, there could be no going back, not now.

"They told me it was hidden in the bushes well above the water line." The corporal had to shout to be heard above the wind.

Jan found the boat by accident, knocking his thigh against the bow. But, when he had cleared away some branches and saw what his life was to depend on, his heart sank.

It appeared to be a 14 foot dingy with a mast ready to fit into place, but on quick inspection it was obvious the boat had seen considerable service. He ran a hand under her hull which was rough with growth. Flakes of paint flew off into the wind. "I hope it's watertight." He did his best to sound optimistic - "at least the rigging appears to be in order."

"Have you sailed before?"

"No. Never."

"I didn't know you Poles could be so daring."

The boat leaned to one side as Jan climbed in and started to feel around. "There's oars at least. Ah! Here's the sail. And another. And a bucket".

"You'll need that."

"Why?"

"For baling."

"No provisions though. No food."

"I've brought you these," said the corporal handing him two apples. "It's all I could get hold of without arousing suspicion."

"Hardly worth a handful of nuggets!"

"Speaking of which."

"Yes, you'll get your gold. Help me down to the water first."

Together they dragged the boat down to the water's edge and, not without considerable difficulty, fitted the twin sails which flapped and snapped angrily in the wind.

"Here," said Jan, passing the corporal the bag of nuggets. "These are all yours now."

"So we're all square," he said, testing the weight. "You're sure you want to go ahead with this? It looks rough to me. At least you've got the wind behind you. But, how will you know the way? The right direction? I presume you don't want to end up in France."

"I pinched a pocket compass from Captain Anders. Better than nothing. But, how will you explain my sudden disappearance?"

"No-one's going to miss you 942. You're not important."

"No, you're right," said Jan, "I'm not important." But his words were lost in the wind as he pushed the boat out into the waves and lifted himself aboard, throwing a final backwards glance. But the German was already consumed by the night.

Safely back on the island of Jersey, Captain Anders stood at the door of his cottage, overlooking St. Helier's harbour, and sniffed the air.

"I'm glad we came back when we did," he called inside. "There's one hell of a storm brewing, believe you me. A real bad blow."

Chapter Three

The man carefully read the short paragraph of news for the second time.

'An unidentified body was unearthed yesterday by builders working in Newport on the Isle of Wight. Preliminary forensic reports estimate the body, which was minus part of a limb, may have lain undisturbed for between thirty five and forty years.'

Folding the Daily Telegraph deliberately, he placed it beside the silver plated toast rack on the breakfast table and, automatically taking a sip of tea, rested both elbows on the table and proceeded to cover his face with his hands, rocking his head gently from side to side in disbelief.

Through a window between his lean fingers he read aloud the date from the front page. "Monday, May 7th 1979. Almost forty years ago," he said, again aloud, but then continued silently almost as if he were afraid or ashamed, that someone would overhear, even though the house was quite empty and still.

'After all these years. 'Be sure your sins will find you out'.' He leaned back in the upright chair and gazed through the leaded-light bay window. The small, neat garden was already bathed in sunlight. It was going to be warm for the time of year. Inside, however, although he pulled his dressing gown closer he couldn't contain a sudden shiver and sucked sharply on his teeth. The spring sunshine was wasted. The day was seriously marred.

His gaze moved to the oak sideboard and a silver photograph frame surrounding a black and white picture of a woman playing in the snow with a young boy.

'Oh Ann. What am I going to do?' The uncertainty came like a lonely cry for help.

Although it was a happy laughing scene, the camera had still captured that deep intelligent face and the confidence he missed so much, and had depended on for so long.

'I can't just leave it. I must do something.' Even as the question formed in his mind he knew what he would have to do. For a person in his position it was the only thing he could do.

'If ever there was a day I needed your wise counsel, it's today. Today of all days.' He forced himself to look away. 'No, it's better you're not here. This is going to be painful and it wouldn't be fair on you.' With an unsteady hand he raised the cup of tea to his lips once again.

Breakfast had always been the most enjoyable meal of the day for as long as he could remember. Not for what it contained, mere porridge, on occasions a boiled egg, toast and tea, but for what it heralded. A new day of possibilities, of accomplishments, of consequences - who knows - but nevertheless a new day for getting things done. It was like walking down the long street of night and suddenly turning the corner to a new dawn, but, until breakfast was completed you couldn't possibly turn that corner and face whatever the day held with any confidence. Yet today the corner had led already into a street of uncertainties and pain. Old memories and events were awakening, wounds opening.

As if a great physical burden had suddenly been fastened around his shoulders he slowly eased himself from the chair and began to clear the breakfast things, having completely lost any appetite. Then he went upstairs to finish washing and dressing, knowing he couldn't possibly make a telephone call of such magnitude while still in pyjamas. There was a short delay before Directory Enquiry gave him the number, which he jotted down, and then hung up. With his hand still on the receiver he studied the row of figures for a moment, knowing once he'd been connected hurt would be sure to follow.

Eventually he dialled the number, hesitating momentarily over the final digit.

It was answered almost immediately.

"Newport Police. Can I help you?"

"Yes. Yes, I believe so."

"What can I do for you Sir?" It was a man's voice, friendly. Not at all what he expected.."The paper..... this morning's news." He was annoyed at himself at how uncertain he'd become.

"And which paper would that be Sir?"

"Yes, the Telegraph. The Daily Telegraph."

"So how can we help you Sir?"

"I read about the body. The one the builders found in Newport."

"And, Sir?"

"I have some information. Important information."

"I see. One moment and I'll transfer you to C.I.D. Hold the line".

He let out a sigh and ran the back of his hand across his brow. It had started.

After a pause, another male voice came on, younger than the first, introducing himself as Detective Constable Willard and within a few minutes, with the aid of some skilled questioning, he had quickly ascertained this wasn't a thrill chasing, crank call.

"So let's take some details then Sir. Your name if you please."

"Yes. It's Gray. Reverend Valentine Gray."

"And your address."

"High Park House, Hadley Green," he forced himself to speak slowly. "Barnet, Hertfordshire."

"Sounds nice. And the telephone number you're calling from."

Again the Reverend's voice was slow and distinct.

"Is that your home number?"

"It is."

"Right then."

"Tell me officer, do you know to whom the body belonged?" he asked, his confidence rising.

"Do you mean who the deceased is, or rather, was?"

"That is precisely what I mean."

"Not yet Sir. We're still making enquiries."

"Well, I am in a position to tell you exactly who it was."

"I see." The young man hesitated. This wasn't expected. "How can you be so sure?" he asked.

"A number of reasons, and, I assure you I wouldn't be wasting your time, nor mine, if I wasn't absolutely certain. The body is that of a man, and the missing limb the paper mentioned, was a hand." His voice was steady with restrained emotion. "Also, the location's correct. Was he found in a boarding house, by any chance?"

"Yes, he was as a matter of fact. The property was used as a boarding house some years ago."

"I thought so. And, the time scale, forty years is almost spot on."

There was a pause before D.C. Willard spoke again. "Could you hold on for a minute Sir, Reverend, only I'd like to have a word with my boss?"

There was a click as the line temporarily died, when the only sound was the regular tick from the grandfather clock in the hall of High Park House. The slow beat helped to calm his anxiety.

Shafts of sunlight caught an antique warming pan hanging on the wall between the lounge and kitchen. The barometer close to where he stood was set fine.

"Reverend Gray?" A new voice came on the line suddenly. "My name is Preston, Detective Inspector Preston." He sounded older than any of the previous speakers, seasoned, with a hint of fatigue. "I believe you think you know who the deceased was."

"Indeed I do. There's no doubt whatsoever. His name was..... "

"Just a moment, Sir." The inspector got in quickly. "This is not a secure line and these are delicate matters. Not for glibly discussing over the phone. I think it would be best if you and I were to meet some time. Don't you?"

"As you wish."

"I see you live in Hertfordshire. I'd really like to come and visit you and have a chat, but glancing at the pile of paperwork on my desk here, that's not possible today."

"I see." There was a pause. "Do you know, I've just had a thought Inspector, whyever don't I come to see you?"

"That would be very accommodating of you Sir."

"Not at all. I'm retired and widowed, so my time's my own." He had planned a full day but it was a question of priorities and this took precedence over everything. "I haven't been back to the island for one reason or another since the war, you know."

"Good heavens!"

"Quite. That's how I know about the body, you understand. A visit would be...... well, a visit is long overdue, anyway. I have quite a story to tell, inspector."

"I look forward to hearing it Sir."

"Now let me see. It's," and he glanced at the grandfather clock, "a little after nine. I should be with you at the latest mid afternoon, I would have thought."

"Will you be coming to Portsmouth?"

"I think so, yes. The Waterloo line."

"Then we'll meet you at the ferry."

"The ferry, yes. I remember. I hope I'm not putting you to any trouble. But how will you know what I look like?"

The inspector smiled to himself having already built a mental picture of the clergyman. "Give me a brief description of yourself then Sir."

"Certainly. Now let me see," he began, and checked himself in the mirror hanging at the end of the hall. Is it possible for someone to age in less than an hour? The stoop was definitely getting worse and he quickly pulled himself upright, squaring his shoulders as if someone was watching, reading his thoughts, knowing everything. He quickly dismissed the idea, annoyed at the power of his own imagination. "Well, I'm five feet ten inches in my stockinged feet, of what you might call wiry frame, with thinning grey hair, a ruddy, clean shaven complexion and brown eyes. And," he mused, stretching the word. "I'll be wearing a Harris tweed jacket with grey flannels. Oh yes, and I think I'd better bring an overnight bag, so I'll be carrying a small brown case with the initials V.A.G. on the front. A gift from my late wife. The A stands for Arthur by the way."

"I had you to a tee," mumbled the policeman.

"I beg your pardon?"

"I was just saying, anyone who can give a detailed description like that should be working for me. Perhaps you had better stay over, Reverend."

"Mmmm. Forty years ago I nearly did stay, Inspector."

"You didn't mention a dog collar, or don't you wear one now that you're retired?"

"On occasions certainly. But, today it's strictly civvies."

"Shall I arrange overnight accommodation?"

"If you would. Nothing too grand or expensive, though. I am on a pension."

"Leave it to me. Just telephone this number when you arrive at Portsmouth, and I'll have a car there waiting for you when you dock at Ryde Pier Head."

Valentine cradled the receiver, and regarded himself once again in the mirror. "Not as bad as you imagined", he said. "Ah, but this is only the beginning remember."

He turned back to the telephone and stared at it for a moment. Then, with a sudden burst of resolution lifted the receiver and dialled a number from memory.

It was answered quickly. "Good morning, Reinbeck Pharmaceuticals. May I help you?"

"Extension 1732 please."

"One moment. Putting you through."

It rang three or four times before a young man spoke. "Hello?"

"May I speak with Dr Gray please."

"Sure. Just a mo. I saw him around here somewhere a second ago. Hold on."

He listened patiently to distant voices and movement before another man's voice came on. "Gray speaking."

"Martin. It's Dad."

"Dad. This is a surprise. Everything alright?"

"Er, yes. Yes fine. I'm sorry to call you at work I know you're very busy. I won't keep you."

"What's up?"

"Well, yes something's come up and I have to go away for a couple of days."

"Is everything O.K? Only you sound a bit agitated."

"Yes, yes really I'm perfectly well only something unexpected has happened and I'm going down to the Isle of Wight for a day or so. I thought you should know, that's all."

"The Isle of Wight. Bit sudden isn't it?"

"I suppose so. Only I thought you should know where I am if you need to contact me for any reason. You can get me through Inspector Preston at Newport Police Station."

"The Police!" Whatever have you been doing?"

"Nothing, really. But I suppose you could say I'm helping the police with their enquiries."

"I'm not sure I like the sound of that. Are you quite sure you're O.K.?"

"Yes, truly. There's nothing to worry about. Nothing at all," he said, wishing he could believe what he was saying.

"Well, if you're sure..... ."

"Oh dear, now there's someone at the door. That's all I need right now. I'm sorry, I'll have to go. I'll call you as soon as I get back. Susan alright?"

"Yes fine."

"And the twins?"

"Yes, not too bad. Ben's got a bit of a cold, but Alex is O.K."

"I must go. God bless you son."

"Enjoy yourself."

"I'll try."

"Oh, it's you Mrs Hemmings." The disappointment was transparent. "I quite forgot it was your day." He stood back as the stout woman negotiated the step.

"Vicar." She said, never one for conversational pleasantries.

"I'm all sixes and sevens this morning Mrs. H.," he told her, watching as the woman removed her anorak, hanging it on one of the iron hooks behind the door.

"Well you needn't worry about me, I won't get in your way. Never have. Never will." She announced, at the same time smoothing the folds of a pale green nylon house coat. "I thought I'd start in the kitchen this morning, then seeing how the time goes I might start spring cleaning the lounge. Lots to do, as always."

"I'm going to have to leave you to it today, Mrs. H.," he got in quickly, anxious to move on. This was a distraction he could well have done without. "Only I've been called away unexpectedly so I'll have to ask you to lock up when you've finished, if you don't mind."

"Mind? Whyever should I mind? I've done it all before, you know I have."

"Indeed you have," he said.

"So where you shooting off to so sudden like?" she asked, running a finger along the edge of a shelf and turning her nose up at what it revealed.

"The Isle of Wight as a matter of fact."

"Hmmm. Alright for some gallivanting off to the seaside at the drop of a hat, while the rest of us ordinary folk have to carry on working."

"It's no holiday, believe me," he told her, as she moved into the kitchen.

"No-one's ever asked me to go to the Isle of Wight."

"You must forgive me Mrs. H.," said the Reverend Gray, holding up his hands in sham surrender. "But I have a train to catch."

The initialled suitcase, together with its handler began their unexpected journey south at a little after ten, eventually arriving at High Barnet Underground, where the Reverend Gray caught a Northern Line train directly to Waterloo, affording himself a coffee and an apricot danish pastry, as a late addition to breakfast, while waiting for the fast train to Portsmouth.

Train journeys held a curious charm for Valentine, as they did for most men of his generation. Gone were the sights, sounds, smells and hypnotic rhythms of steam, yet there remained, still, that indefinable wonder planted in every small boy on the day of his first train journey, which, in his case, the years and no amount of travel had ever diminished.

Today, however, as he sat in the corner seat facing the engine, his mind was not so much on the stimulant of the journey as on the consequences of his arrival.

A number of times he attempted to read the paper, but his eye continually returned to the paragraph that had so dramatically altered the course of his day. In the end he folded it away and gazed, instead, at his reflection in the grimy window, and when tired of looking at the worried man staring back, tried to focus instead on the delights and distractions of the Hampshire countryside as it flashed by in a hundred different shades of grey and brown. Even this failed to hold his attention, however, as with each fleeting mile he found his mind travelling not forward, but withdrawing back to the turbulent years of a world at war and, by the time the train juddered to a halt shortly before two o'clock at Portsmouth Harbour Station, the Revered Gray found he had unearthed all the ensuing years had buried.

As he stepped down onto the platform he knew that for the next few hours, at least, those years would have to be awakened and lived again. How, he asked himself, would he handle the consequences a second time?

A glimpse of the old iron hulled Warrior, through the glass partition, failed to attract his attention as he made his way along the platform and down towards the Island ferry terminal where he telephoned Newport Police Station.

There was a brief delay while a mixture of day trippers, returning Island residents and holiday makers, suitably laden with baggage and small children, boarded the motor vessel 'Shanklin' before the gangway was raised and the ferry made her way out of Portsmouth's ever busy harbour and into the open waters of the Solent against a stiff south-westerly.

The air was thick with the tang of salt and the lonely cries of seagulls overhead were just audible against the regular throb of diesel engines, as the Captain increased revolutions, sending a dense black smoke trail off to port from her single stack, ploughing the bow on into the cold, rushing waters.

The sun, first glimpsed from the garden of High Park House, was now high in the sky, catching the tops of waves, like aquamarine crystals as they fired off into the wind. Yet the breeze, so applauded by yachtsmen lifting the spinnakers high, was pushing a bank of dark cloud forward in from the Atlantic. There would be rain before very long.

As Valentine gazed through the spray soaked window he saw not the ships, trading boats and pleasure yachts bobbing about in the choppy, dark waters, but the Solent he remembered before 'Operation Overlord' and the D Day landings. At that moment the past began to close in on him like the night. Then became now. The past ,the present.

Standing proud from the sea like great leviathans were the old, round, stone fortresses built originally to repel invaders during Napoleonic times. Now refitted, rearmed and ready to stand guard over the Empire's rear, in waterways suddenly thick with landing craft, troop carriers, all types of boats. It was said to be possible to walk from Portsmouth across to Ryde, Yarmouth to Lymington without getting wet. For him the sea was abruptly alive with every known machine of war - guns, ammunition and men. Thousands upon thousands of free men ready to face the evils of Nazi Europe and their own private hell on earth.

He glanced up at the watery blue sky where the horizon was pock-marked with glistening, silver coloured barrage balloons, like giant Christmas baubles reflecting the spring sunshine. Over Portsmouth, over Ryde and Cowes. Anything to stop the relentless bombers which regularly fell victim to the guns of the Royal Navy or one of the many anti-aircraft batteries that littered the Solent - Spithead stronghold. And, over all, the young men in blue, many still in their early twenties, continued a never ending flight of defence. Weaving their way across the skies, like acrobatic spiders forever repairing their damaged, yet deadly, webs. Yet the enemy and their lethal loads all too frequently made it through, keeping you guessing if they were carrying one with your name on.

The nights were the worst. In the blackout you couldn't see the enemy. You listened, straining, hearing them flying ever and ever closer, knowing they were about to drop their whistling cargoes which, in an instant, would destroy life, hope, a past, a future.

The fires, the smoke, the cries for help. The cold sweats of pure terror. So many friends plucked from this life, as quickly as apples fall in a summer storm.

'Was it really forty years ago?'

He lifted a hand and ran it along his shoulder feeling for his officer's pips.

Gone, of course, but not forgotten. Never forgotten.

Ryde Pierhead had hardly changed at all. As he handed the man his ticket the official could easily have been a Military Policemen checking his landing pass, or a Constable of the Hampshire Constabulary scrutinizing the passes of civilians, asking them the reason for their visit. The island was closed to just anyone, you had to have a genuine reason for being there and carry a valid pass with you at all times, or be prepared to suffer the consequences.

Forty years on, however, and crowds were arriving on the island in their droves and he was quickly caught up in the throng as travellers hurried to greet waiting family or friends, or jumped into taxis, anxious to be off the pier as quickly as possible to get on with their holiday, business, or day to day routine.

Those who were foolish enough to dress as if it were high summer were now rubbing goose-bumped arms and legs as the breeze increased. Valentine watched as a man dashed past, chasing a rolling hat before it disappeared over the edge of the pier and into the Solent, thankful he had chosen not to wear his own.

Familiar words were brought to mind, 'For your tomorrows these gave their today.'

"Reverend Gray?" The question brought him back with a jolt.

"Er, yes. Yes, I am."

"How do you do Sir," said the man, holding out his hand. "My name's Willard. Detective Constable John Willard."

"Oh yes, of course. We spoke on the telephone."

Valentine looked at the young man who was roughly the same age as he had been forty years ago. He was tall and smartly dressed in a double breasted, grey suit. His dark hair was brushed almost flat, emphasising a high, intelligent forehead above blue, deep set eyes.

"How clever of you to spot me so quickly in the crowd."

"Must be all that police training." He smiled, when for a second time his lips parted revealing a line of uneven and badly stained teeth. It detracted from the clean cut image.

"May I take your case for you? My car's just over there."

"Thank you."

The sun had just begun to lose its strength where advanced ridges of grey cloud had moved from the direction of the Needles. Those who'd chosen to walk the length of the pier would need to get a move on if they wanted to reach land before the rain arrived.

Valentine had been concerned at the thought of being met by a police car and was relieved to see an unmarked, navy blue Ford waiting for them. Gradually they weaved their way out into the line of traffic which was slowly making its way down the Victorian pier, past ornate cast-iron railings where a group of young men were leaning, patiently watching their fishing lines. He became increasingly conscious suddenly of a peculiar thunder-like noise, which was growing louder with every second, and turned to see what it was. "Of course. The train."

"Well, if you can call it that. It's ex-London Underground."

"But whatever happened to the beautiful steam train?"

"Don't ask me Reverend. That puffed its last, years ago."

"That's a great shame," he said, watching the brightly painted carriages as they passed by on the tracks parallel to the concourse. "A great shame". He sounded genuinely disappointed. "We spent many a happy hour riding the trains around the island."

"You can't do that any longer. It's a greatly reduced line now."

"Oh dear, really. A legacy from the good Dr.

Beeching no doubt. Or, perhaps, the not so good Dr. Beeching."

"Things change Reverend. Not always for the better, but they change nonetheless."

"Ah, do I detect a philosopher?"

The young man gave the vicar a sideways grin. "Hardly," he said, "just an observer."

"Important enough in your profession I would have thought."

"I hear you haven't been back to the Island since the war," he remarked. "Is that correct"

"That's right. Forty years ago. A lifetime really. I was stationed here."

"You'll notice a lot of changes."

"I'm sure I shall," he said, looking after the train, remembering. "I'm sure I shall."

"Inspector Preston had hoped to be here to meet you himself, but he was called away. We'll go directly on to Newport and wait for him in the office. I'm sure he won't be too long. He knows you're on the Island."

They had reached the end of the pier and were making their way along the Ryde seafront, already on the way to Newport when it started to rain.

"We greatly appreciate your taking the time to come and help us out like this Reverend."

"That's alright. At this precise moment it's just nice for me to reminisce, seeing old familiar places." As he spoke he turned and looked at the young man behind the wheel just as they drove over Wootton Bridge, past lines of boats moored along the banks of the creek. "I'm in no doubt as to whom the deceased is, officer. Tell me, it was his left hand that was missing, wasn't it? Do you know?"

"Yes that's correct. The left one."

"I thought so. Not bad a memory for an old man."

Willard didn't respond.

"I know who this poor unfortunate fellow is," he continued, adding more as an afterthought, "and I also know who killed him."

Chapter Four

In the centre of the Island sits the ancient and historic town of Newport, known as the Island's capital.

The rain hadn't eased but deteriorated into a cold, penetrating drizzle much to the annoyance of the constable on duty outside a double fronted, wooden clad residence in Pyle Street, near the town centre.

It wasn't a particularly long or important street and could certainly boast nothing to distinguish it from other similar streets nearby. Merely terraced houses interrupted in places with newer buildings and retail outlets. Yet what was taking place inside made this, one of the oldest buildings in the street, unique.

Inspector Roy Preston stood on the bare boards of the compact hall, taking a moment to brush the rain from his coat, but unable to shake off the prevailing air of gloom quite so easily. Since the body had been discovered he'd been to the house a number of times, but on every visit as soon as he entered a sense of sadness surrounded him, invading his spirit. Today was no exception.

With the power off, the antiquated dwelling was depressingly dark, the only light coming from the open door, and an unpleasant, almost nauseous, musty smell had permeated the whole building.

Faded green, flower patterned wallpaper, had lifted in numerous places and dangled - like the curled edges of rotten, putrid lettuce - adorned with the build up of many years worth of cobwebs, on top of cobwebs, helping to hide peeling chocolate - brown paintwork. The gloom was contagious.

He turned to the copper on the doorstep. "Why ever don't you stand inside man?" he called, catching sight of paint flaking off the door like dead skin. "You'll catch your death out there."

"Thank you Sir, don't mind if I do."

"Don't let anyone in, mind. Especially the press."

Directly in front of the entrance stood a steep, short flight of stairs. Preston carefully held on to the banisters negotiating the worn, stained, wooden steps, imagining what it must have been like for anyone living there.

The house had only just changed hands, having stood empty for a long while after the owner, a gent in his late nineties, had died intestate. The new owners, a family from Surrey who wanted it as a holiday home, had only just begun modernisation when the body was discovered, under the floor, by the builders working in one of the bedrooms. The contractors had downed tools and walked out, refusing to have anything further to do with the project.

At the top of the staircase, to the left, was a single door, while on the right a short passageway ran for a few feet, from where muffled voices, accompanied by the sound of a small motor, were coming from behind another door at the end. His footsteps echoed in the emptiness as he passed two further doors to the left and a small window facing out onto the street. He pushed open the door, which squealed in protest on hinges thick with years of paint and disuse, leading into an oblong shaped room where two men in white, full-body boiler suits were working around a hole in the floor in one corner, next to a small window. Beside them was a pile of sawn-off floorboards. A powerful arc lamp had been installed, powered by a small generator that droned on in the background, the bright light casting shadows all around the walls, making the occupants appear bigger than they were, and highlighting a fine dust that hung in the stale air like petrified powder. The musty, damp odour that filled the house invaded here too, made worse by the close proximity of death.

It was clear one of the men had just completed taking photographs with a modern and sophisticated looking camera. He looked up as the door opened.

"Hello Inspector", he said cheerfully, yet unable to stop his voice sounding hollow in the crude surroundings. "Come to lend a hand? We were just about to lift him."

"Oh no. Far be it from me to interfere with the workings of forensic science. I'll leave that to you boys."

"We've cleared a lot away," put in the other man, removing his face mask. "See for yourself."

Preston moved across to where a recess, a little larger than an average man's body, had been cut into the floorboards right up to the back wall which was pitted and black with damp. Tentatively he peered in and was immediately greeted by a stained and discoloured skeletal frame resting ten or so inches lower than the level of the floor. The vacant skull stared back at him with unseeing eyes; the redundant jaw hung limp, eternally waiting to tell its tragic story, with an intimidating smirk over yellowed and missing teeth. The whole skeleton appeared to have been buried in something akin to concrete randomly embellished with strips of fabric laid over the old wooden rafters of the ceiling below, which were now exposed beneath the body which had lain peacefully undisturbed in its semi-mummified state for nearly forty years.

"What is that grey-green substance?" asked the Inspector.

"It's cement," one of the men told him. "Cement that's reacted to the damp in the wall. He'd been covered with dry powder cement and then sewn into a type of canvas body bag with more cement on top. Over the years, of course, most of his clothes disintegrated and the cement set hard."

"How did you determine how long it had been there?"

"That was easy. We got the approximate time slot from a trace of the canvas's manufacturer."

"But rotting bodies smell, don't they? Surely someone would have smelled it?"

"Yes perhaps," the forensic archaeologist continued, as his partner carried on working on the body with a fine dusting brush. "But this was well covered over and under the boards, and some sort of floor covering too, remember. We've chipped away about fifty percent of the cement casing, but we want to lift it before we remove any more, otherwise any evidence could be lost should the skeleton disintegrate."

"I see."

"And the hand. It's definitely missing. It's not here." He said, pointing to the remains of the stunted left arm. "It hasn't just fallen off either. I'd say it was surgically removed."

"So why did you call me over?" asked Preston, beginning to feel he'd been in the tomb-like room long enough.

"I thought you should see something before we take him away." At which point his colleague stopped work and moved away. "I'm as sure as I can be, without further detailed examination," continued the man, "but there's possible scarring between the fourth and fifth ribs conducive with a knife entry."

The policeman knelt down beside the body and examined the scarred bone. "So it's murder then," he continued, "just as we always suspected."

"Yes, I think that's a safe bet, Roy. Not many people purposely stab themselves in the chest."

"You do surprise me," he said, standing up. This was neither the time nor place for sarcasm.

"You'll have your work cut out though. Forty years ago. Wartime. Difficult."

"It might have lain there for another forty years if not for the builders."

"Indeed it might," agreed the scientist.

"You checked the rest of the house?"

"Yes, we lifted the floors, up and downstairs. Nothing."

"So all I've got to do is find out who he was and who murdered him."

"Good luck. You'll need it."

"Let me have your full report a.s.a.p."

Inspector Roy Preston lifted his collar and took the short walk back to the Police Station deep in thought. Yes, this was going to be difficult, but perhaps the vicar from Hertfordshire had been heaven sent.

The policeman and the clergyman met in the interview room in Newport Police Station where Valentine had been plied with tea and digestive biscuits.

"I'm very pleased to meet you, Inspector," declared Valentine as they shook hands. Then as if reading the man's thoughts, added, "it's always nice to put a face to a voice, isn't it?"

"Certainly it is. And I must say how much we appreciate your coming all the way down here to see us. It's very good of you." The Inspector smiled, which was strangely out of place given the surroundings, when suddenly furrows appeared across his forehead which were too deep for a man who was obviously still in his mid forties. Well established 'crows feet' sat at the corners of brown eyes, the whites of which were not white at all, but a watery, insipid pink. The top of his head was caught in the light of the ceiling lamp, presenting him with a peculiar halo effect, but even this divine-like distraction couldn't hide the pepper and salt streaks which within a few years, or less, would turn a distinct shade of grey.

As the two men sat on opposite sides of the table D.C. Willard entered the room, carrying a note pad and sat down next to his boss.

"I trust my Constable's been looking after you alright?"

"I think the visit's already awakened some old memories for the Reverend," put in Willard.

"Yes and yes, is my answer to that Inspector."

"Good. Now what I propose is that we have a preliminary chat and learn a little of what you can tell us. Then as it's getting late and I'm sure you must be tired, if you're O.K. to stay the night..... ."

"I'm quite prepared."

"Excellent. Then we can talk some more tomorrow and get down to making a statement. We've got you booked into an hotel in Bembridge."

"Bembridge!?" he started.

"Yes. Is there a problem? If so I'm sure..... ."

"No, no. It's just that I haven't heard the word for some time. It made me jump. That's all."

"It's a pleasant enough hotel," Willard reassured him. "I think you'll be quite comfortable."

"I'm sure I shall."

"I live in St. Helens which is only a stone's throw away. I thought I could pick you up in the morning and we could drive into town together." Preston looked at the stranger trying to imagine what was going on behind his eyes. Surely there had to be something more than a simple willingness to help at the bottom of it all. Something with roots that went back a long way. "So you believe you know who this man is then Sir?" he asked directly.

"There is absolutely no doubt about it. And, I'm sure you realise it was murder."

It wasn't news, but in the confines of the closed room his words still came like a detonation.

"We've just had that confirmed as a matter of fact," Preston told him. "So who was he?"

"His name Inspector, is Thomas. Ethan Thomas."

"We know a Mr and Mrs Thomas lived there, we got that much from the Town Hall," said Willard.

"That's right, they did."

"So this is the poor husband."

"Classic case of the Missus topping her old man then?" Willard again.

"No! Not at all," said Valentine quickly, annoyed by the interruption. "This isn't, wasn't her husband. This was her son."

"Her son!"

"Yes Inspector. There was no husband as far as I know. The mother and son used to let rooms during the war years. I was acquainted, shall we say, with one of her tenants."

"A lady friend?"

"Yes, Constable, a lady friend, naturally." Events were beginning to take their toll, the strain was telling.

"You said in the car, Sir, that you know who killed him," said Willard, enjoying the rare occasion of knowing more than his superior. The remark brought the Inspector's eyebrows up sharply.

"That's quite correct. I do. Ethan Thomas was murdered by my lady friend, as your Constable called her. Of that I am perfectly certain."

"Well!" exclaimed Preston, unable to contain his surprise. If the Vicar's story was genuine this was a very unexpected bonus. "How can you be so sure?" he asked.

"I've known for years. I've always known, but I remained silent. Then, when I read the piece in the paper that the body had been discovered I knew it would have been wrong of me to remain silent any longer. Very wrong."

"You're quite sure you're not mistaken? Forty years can play strange tricks on a memory."

"Oh no, Inspector. There's no mistake I assure you. Besides, there's the question of the hand."

"Mr Gray knew which hand was missing Sir," Willard told his boss, unconsciously dropping the vicar's title.

"Do you know what happened to his hand?"

"If my memory serves me correctly, it was an accident at work. He was a printer by trade."

"So tell me about this lady friend of yours, Sir."

"Inspector," he paused, unsure of how to proceed. "I have a very long and involved story, which I shall be only too pleased to share with you. It is, after all, the reason I've come all this way. But not here, not now, if you don't mind. I feel I need a rest. It has been a most..... unusual day."

Preston glanced at the wall mounted clock. It was almost six. The Vicar did have a point. He looked all in, too. "I can agree to that," he said, "but tell me. Whoever was this woman?"

"Who was she?" he repeated quietly. "She was someone she never meant to be. That's who."

"What became of her?"

"I know what happened immediately after the

war, but where she is now, if still alive at all, only the Almighty knows."

"Are you going to tell us her name?" asked Willard.

"Yes. Tomorrow. As I say, it's long story."

Willard didn't pursue the point. The man was right. There'd be another day tomorrow.

"But tell me, Sir, before we go, were there any other people involved in this murder, do you know?" asked Preston.

"No. No-one," came back Valentine, quickly.

"You sound very confident."

"I am Inspector."

"Did you know any of the other lodgers, apart from your lady friend?"

"No. I had no dealings with anyone else in the house at all. I'd met Mrs Thomas and Ethan, of course. But, no-one else. It was wartime as you know, people were on the move constantly."

"Alright," he said decisively, gently lowering the palms of his hands onto the table. "Let's call it a day. I'll run you over to Bembridge, Reverend, on the way home. Then pick you up at eight thirty in the morning, when we'll hear some more. Especially of your friend, I think"

On the way out Inspector Preston spoke with D.C. Willard.

"Telephone Barnet nick and see if they've ever heard of our Reverend gentleman. The town's not that big, surely, and vicars are usually well known pillars of the community."

"You don't doubt his story do you Sir? It sounds O.K. to me."

"Just making sure Willy. Just making sure. Then telephone me at home when you get an answer. I've a funny feeling I've heard his name before somewhere."

In less than an hour Reverend Valentine Gray was established in The Birdham Hotel in the village of Bembridge, on the far eastern extremities of the Island; and, shortly after arriving at his home nearby, Inspector Preston received a telephone call.

"He's one hundred per cent kosher, Sir. Everybody knows him. He even married one of the sergeants there."

"I think that perhaps you mean he officiated at the wedding. There's a subtle difference."

"You know what I mean."

"Thanks for the call. See you in the morning."

Following a restless night, Valentine was revived by a full English breakfast and found he was looking forward to finally unburdening his tale, so made sure he was ready on time. The morning had dawned bright and clear. The air fresh with a bite of salt and, at a little before eight-thirty Inspector Preston's Ford Cortina pulled up outside the Birdham, to find the vicar ready and waiting on the hotel steps.

The conversation during the drive to Newport in the spring sunshine was strained, yet as they left the Downs road and made their way into town Valentine suddenly spoke out.

"Inspector, I have a special request," he began, looking directly at the man. "It's unusual I know, but I have my reasons. Believe me."

"What is it?"

"I would like to visit the old house where Ethan's body was discovered. I know it's unorthodox procedure to take someone involved to the scene of the crime, but I feel, or rather I know, that being there again will stimulate my memory to the all important details."

The detective thought for a moment before responding. The forensic work was complete; the house empty. Why shouldn't he go there? "Yes, it is unusual," he answered. "But very well. In fact, we're almost there."

A short detour and the car came to a halt. A different bobby to the previous day was standing outside the now infamous old house.

'Ah yes,' muttered Valentine to himself. "What is the name of this street Inspector?"

"Pyle Street, Sir."

"Ah yes, Pyle Street," said Valentine, taking in what the street had to offer. "I remember now. The famous Pyle Street."

"Why famous?"

But the clergyman didn't reply.

The uniformed policeman respectfully touched his helmet as, Preston leading the way, the two visitors entered the house.

Nothing had changed from the day before, except, that now with the absence of a generator the building was silent and still. The Inspector closed the door, shutting out the last hope of any sunlight and warmth, and it took a few seconds for the men to become accustomed to the darkness. Light could only enter now via a grimy, cracked fan-light above the front door.

For a moment neither of them spoke, the dank, dark surroundings invading their senses.

"Pretty grim isn't it," said Preston eventually. But Valentine said nothing, simply looking around nodding his agreement.

"There's nothing to see downstairs, all the rooms have been stripped bare. Do you want to go upstairs?"

"Yes," he responded, his voice thick. Surely he'd done the right thing in coming. Surely.

"I'm sorry it's so dark. The power's off." Preston told him. "Mind how you go. These stairs are very iffy."

"I presume no-one's living here at the moment."

"No, no-one. The new owners were beginning to do it up when the body was discovered."

Preston paused at the top of the stairs and was

about to move down the passage when Valentine stopped him.

"No!" he said. "In here. I want to go in here," (pointing to the door on the left), when he noticed his hand was trembling, he quickly withdrew it.

"But the...... "

"I know. The body was found in the room at the end of the passage. I know that. But I want to go in here first. Please Inspector."

"There's nothing in there," Preston told him. "But, alright, if you want to, do. But there's nothing there. Nothing at all."

Valentine put his hand on the dented, brass door knob, steadying himself, hoping the policeman hadn't noticed his sudden uneasiness, and turned it slowly. His mouth was dry suddenly and he ran a hand across his damp face. Had he done right in coming?

Deliberately unhurried, he pushed open the door that juddered defiantly and, with ill disguised trepidation, stepped cautiously into the small, square room.

It was exactly as Inspector Preston had told him. Empty. A plain, bare room of approximately twelve feet square, with a single sash window facing a brick wall belonging to the property next door, just a few feet away. As the two men moved further in, Preston looked at the gentleman beside him and was about to say something to the effect that this was a waste of time, but gasped instead at the sudden change in him. Something major had taken place. Even in the poor light it was obvious to see his countenance had altered completely.

Gone was the elderly vicar, replaced instead by the self assured expression of a much younger man. His back was straight suddenly, his shoulders square, and when he spoke it was as if the intervening years had been peeled away.

"A table," he said. "There used to be a small square table there in the corner and a chest of drawers here. Next to the window, opposite a mirrored wardrobe which stood right here." He strode across the room, his footsteps echoing. "The bed was here," he added "right here." Then turning and looking at the window, his eyes distant, seeing things others could not. "She liked this room, dark though it was, because she couldn't be overlooked she said," then added, "we couldn't be overlooked."

But suddenly his shoulders fell and the stoop returned once again, and a great sadness came over him.

The sight of it made Preston shudder. "I think..... I think," he began, uncertain if he should disturb the moment or not. "I think we should move on. Don't you?"

Reverend Gray didn't answer at once, but moved across to where the table would have stood and ran a hand along the top of an imaginary chair. A chair he'd sat in often enough. He turned, when even in the impoverished light, Preston just caught his expression. It was an illustration of absolute grief.

He reached out, afraid the man was on the point of collapse. " Can I ..... ?"

"It's alright Inspector," and he let out a long sigh, forcing his head erect. "But how true it is," he spoke slowly, emphasising every syllable, "when it says that 'we are fearfully and wonderfully made.' The mind is like a book. In an instant, a flash, the years are plucked from obscurity and relived all over again. Every detail, just as sharp as if it were yesterday." He nodded at his own observations. "I knew this would happen, I just knew it." But then he looked directly at Inspector Preston as if sight of the man suddenly realigned his thoughts. "But yes. Enough," he said. "Enough of this depressing graveyard of memories. Let's move on."

Relieved, Preston lead the way out, back into the passage and to the door at the end.

The forensic team had done a good job and cleared the room completely, leaving only a pile of broken floorboards and the crude, open grave. Without the addition of an arc-lamp the room, slightly larger than the one just vacated, was illuminated only by weak light forcing its way through a window overgrown with ivy, casting shafts of broken, pale sunlight onto the bare floor. But a peculiar smell still hung in the air. It made Preston sniff in disgust.

"Are you familiar with this room too?" he asked, stepping aside.

"Unfortunately so," said Valentine, walking directly over to where the body had lain for nearly forty years, staring down into the now empty hole, to the exposed rafters of the room below. "What was it like when you found it?"

"Completely decayed. Just bone."

"Just as one would expect I suppose," he said, suddenly turning on his heel. "I've really seen all I want to see Inspector. May we leave now?"

"Of course Sir."

"Thank you for agreeing to my visit," he said, as they stood together on the pavement. Both were relieved to breathe fresh air once again. "I just had to see it again. Painful though it has been. But now," he began as they walked to the car. "But now I think it's time I relayed the full account of exactly what happened to Ethan Thomas. I'm sure you must be anxious to hear it?"

"Indeed I am. I'll listen to what you have to say first of all, then I'll get you to make a full statement."

"Whatever you say, Inspector. I'm just pleased to be able to tell someone the truth after so many years."

"You've never told anyone?"

"Never. Anyone. Not even my wife. I am the only person who knows what exactly took place."

"Except the murderer, Sir."

"Quite. Except the murderer. As you say."

The two men were seated opposite each other in the same Interview Room where they had met the day before.

"So," opened Inspector Preston, draining his coffee cup expectantly. "Tell me about yourself and this lady friend. Why were you on the Island during the war? Where would you like to begin?" As he spoke he removed a note book and pen and laid them neatly on the table between them.

"That's something I toyed with all the way down on the train. As my story goes back so many years, I thought it would be helpful if I were to begin by telling you something of my background."

"Sounds good." He smiled and withdrew a packet of cigarettes. "Do you mind?"

"Not at all. I used them myself when I was younger. Which rather neatly brings me to my story." The Clergyman paused, drawing in a deep breath before resuming. "I'm a widower, as I believe I've told you already. My wife, Ann, died eight years ago of cancer." He spoke slowly, all the while keeping his eyes on his folded hands resting on the table. "We only ever had the one child, Martin. He's a Doctor in the pharmaceutical industry; married with a family of his own. For my own part, up until quite recently I was Vicar of Christ Church, Barnet, - where I still live - as you know. But I haven't always been a man of the cloth, that came much later in life. When I left university I qualified as an engineer, almost immediately war was declared and I went into the Royal Engineers. And, that's where my story begins." He looked up, enquiring, "Is that alright?"

"Excellent." It was obvious the man wanted to get a lot off his chest.

"You know Inspector. I've always thought it peculiar how people have an inherent need to blame someone, or something, when things go wrong. The allocation of blame syndrome, I call it. Have you ever noticed that?"

"You're not alone in thinking like that, I'd agree with you. But the apportion of blame is the very foundation of our criminal justice system."

"That's right of course. But I didn't mean from a criminal point of view. More, everyday life. I've seen it rear its ugly head so often in my work with the Church. An unwillingness to accept responsibility. 'It wasn't my fault.' And I'm just as guilty of thinking like that too, I'm ashamed to say. But, whenever something goes awry it nearly always helps to blame someone. You feel better if you can point the finger of condemnation at someone other than yourself, and alleviate a sense of guilt arising from one's own involvement in a particular matter.

Yet wherever does one apportion guilt in this instance, I ask myself? With Churchill? I think not. Lord Mountbatten? Hardly, and I'll explain why I include him. Then Hitler, surely? Yes. He's much nearer the mark. You see Inspector, even talking things through with you now, I find it helps if I can point the finger of blame at someone other than myself. It's the only way I've been able to live with myself all these years and know God's forgiveness for my actions."

Inspector Preston did his best to maintain a steadfast expression disturbed though he was by a sudden thought. 'Is he going back on what he said yesterday about the lady friend and confess to the murder himself? Is that why he's come forward?'

"If only," Valentine continued. "If only Hitler hadn't..... But he did! And because Hitler did what he did at virtually the same time I became an engineer in 1943, I found myself on the Isle of Wight through no fault of my own.

Tell me Inspector, have you ever heard of Operation Pluto? It's the foundation of my entire story."

"Remind me."

"It's got nothing to do with cartoon characters or planets. It stands for 'Pipe Line Under The Ocean' P.L.U.T.O. It all started with a message Mr Churchill sent to Lord Mountbatten in October of 1941. Two years into the war. Mountbatten you'll remember, was the King's cousin and at the time commander of the aircraft carrier H.M.S. Illustrious. It was a famous message. It read simply 'we want you home at once for something you will find of the highest interest.'

Mountbatten had only just turned forty one and had been promoted to Admiral of the Fleet and

Chief of Combined Operations, so the job could only mean one thing, preparation for the invasion of Nazi Europe. I know you weren't around at the time, of course, but it's extraordinary when you consider that as far back as 1941 Churchill was already thinking of the invasion of Europe. Yet, one of the many millions of problems that had to be solved before that could take place, was how to satisfy thousands of landing craft, tanks, all types of motorised war machines, with a constant supply of fuel. So, as I say, onto the scene comes Mountbatten who characteristically threw himself at the problem.

Now, without delving too deeply into events which are naturally important to me; it was decided to try and lay a fuel pipeline from the U.K. to the invasion beaches of Normandy. And what's the nearest landfall to Normandy?"

"The Isle of Wight."

"Exactly. A prototype line had already been tested between Swansea and Ilfracombe. And it worked! So we got the green light and it was all systems go. Miles and miles of three inch steel pipe under the ocean. PLUTO. The operation here on the Isle of Wight was called BAMBI......"

"BAMBI?! You're pulling my leg."

Valentine had to admit it did sound foolish. "Sadly Inspector this was no sophisticated acronym like PLUTO. I seem to remember it was named after a stag's head discovered in a bombed out property in Shanklin. But anyway," he continued, "by the time I arrived PLUTO had already reached the northern shore of the Island. Tankers would arrive in the Mersey and Bristol Channel and unload their cargoes into a network of overland pipes that ran across country down to Lepe, south of Fawley, from where they crossed the Solent to Thorness Bay."

Roy nodded in recognition. "You're very knowledgeable."

"We were fighting for our very survival, Inspector. To be honest, in my early twenties as I was then, it was all a bit of an adventure; but you never forget. Never. It was my life."

'We owe your generation much more than we realise'. The policeman reflected soberly.

Valentine took up the story, anxious now that he'd started, to reach the conclusion as quickly as possible. "So, from Thorness Bay the line ran through Parkhurst Forest, boosted by a secret pumping station, to a massive reservoir west of Shanklin, from where the fuel ran by gravity to further pumping stations on Shanklin and Sandown seafronts. And that's where I come into the story. I was involved in the building of those pumping stations, particularly the one at Shanklin. Sandown station was a back-up if Shanklin was ever destroyed by enemy action.

I want you to appreciate Inspector, how vitally secret this whole fuel line was. If what we were up to had ever leaked out..... well..... the consequences would have been nothing short of catastrophic."

"Hitler would have known our plans."

"Exactly! Yes! The outcome of that doesn't bear thinking about. Keep that secrecy in mind as it has great significance to my story. With twenty eight pumps shared between the two towns it was our top secret task to be absolutely sure that precious, vital fuel reached its destination. Security was everything, and it was tight. Very tight.

In Sandown the operation was based in the Grand Hotel, from where the line ran into the old Victorian fortress. While in Shanklin our H.Q. was the Royal Spa Hotel, right on the sea front. Both areas were sealed off from the general public. But, oh dear," he reminisced. "You should have seen the mess. The place was reduced to a shell. There was a huge concrete mixer in there for a start."

"Were there many people involved?"

"I should say so. The Royal Engineers, of course. Then there were around a hundred or so from the Pioneer Corps, and then on top of that we also employed a lot of local labour. Bricklayers who were too old for the armed services, apprentices from various building firms. They were all drafted in. But what made life so difficult was the constant threat of discovery. The local labourers weren't even told what the project was in the early days. The Nazis may have been an evil bunch, but they were far from stupid and our biggest worry was the threat of discovery by reconnaissance aircraft. Aerial photography.

I remember when lorries drove in and out, doors had to be opened and closed P.D.Q. and then details of men would quickly brush away the tyre tracks. We even told the local workers to take different routes to and from work each day. Lines of men all walking in the same direction every day? You understand?"

"Of course."

"A great deal of work had to be done under the cover of darkness. I did feel sorry for the hoteliers though."

"Oh, why?" asked Preston, stubbing out the first of a number of cigarettes.

"We stripped their premises bare. We had to. We needed the wood and such like to strengthen and shore-up the pump houses. By the time we finished you could look up from the ground floor and see the tiles on the roof. They were completely gutted. And, yet, at the end of the day we somehow overcame a myriad of difficulties and the pipeline fell by gravity down the cliff via the empty elevator, along the gutter of the Esplanade to the pier, where it eventually joined the underwater section already laid by ships towing thousands of yards of steel piping wound around gigantic floating steel drums.

By June 6th, D Day, both PLUTO and BAMBI were ready. But unfortunately, because of German mines, the pipeline was delayed and the precious oil had to go ashore to the beaches directly from tankers via mini pipelines."

"After all that!?"

"True," concurred the clergyman with a flicker of annoyance, "but when the line did go into action in mid September it was delivering some 100,000 gallons of fuel a day."

"So it was successful after all."

"Without a doubt. Without that line, hundreds of thousands of jerricans would have been needed every single day, which would have been quite impossible. Without a doubt PLUTO hastened the demise of Hitler and the end of the war. It was a fantastic piece of ground breaking technology and brilliantly engineered, even if I say so myself. I'm proud to have played a part in it all - however small."

"Obviously. So now tell me Reverend," said the Inspector, looking at the clock. This all taking much longer than expected. "Intriguing, fascinating even though this history lesson has been, where does the body come into it all?"

"Yes. You've been very patient Inspector. But I just wanted you to understand the legitimate circumstances for my being on the Island at the time and what I was doing here."

The officer jotted something down as Valentine resettled himself ready for another and more serious recollection.

"It all started one day in the winter of 44. I had a twelve hour pass and I took the bus into Newport. It was a cloudy day and I remember feeling somewhat miserable. I may have been on a wartime adventure but the work was still hard and very demanding. We were all under great pressure; serious deadlines had to be met.

I had a walk around town. I'd been there before of course but it was still nice just to see what was going on and, if I'm honest," he smiled to himself at the memory, "check out the local talent."

The Inspector smiled too.

"The Island was crawling with troops by then of course, so there wasn't a lot of spare talent about. I remember I came across a small park. Don't ask me what it was called, just a pleasant green area to walk through, when I got the shock of my life."

Preston's back straightened anticipating the long awaited breakthrough.

"I must have been in a bit of a day dream for I walked straight past a small stone obelisk, only half reading what it said. Then I distinctly remember stopping dead in my tracks. I had just read my own name."

"Your own name?"

"And it's all still engraved on my heart today, just as surely as on the stone itself. 'To the memory of Valentine Gray', it read, 'the Little Sweep'."

"I knew I'd heard your name before!" exclaimed D.I. Preston. "I'm ashamed of myself. Of course, the Little Sweep. Didn't he die stuck up a chimney or something?"

"Something like that. But I was amazed. What are the chances of seeing your own name on a memorial stone?"

"It's an unusual Christian name as well."

"I've my mother to thank for that, bless her."

"Let me guess. You were born on the fourteenth of February?"

"Exactly. I had a terrible time at school. But think how you would have felt reading, 'To the memory of..... .' I'm sorry I don't know your name."

"Roy."

" 'To the memory of Roy Preston'."

"Surprised to say the least."

"And, you'd want to know more. Which is exactly what I did. Suddenly I wanted to know who this other Valentine Gray was."

"So, what did you do?"

"What did I do? I went to the library. As good a place as any, or so I thought. Surely they'd know. And that's where I..... ." He stopped himself suddenly and a look of deep distress passed across his features. His voice had dropped a tone when he resumed the story. "If only I hadn't gone there. That's where I first set eyes on her." He paused, "Do you believe in love at first sight, Inspector?"

"It's..... It's not something I've experienced personally." He answered, surprised but truthfully.

"It happens. From my own experience I can tell

you that it happens. Yes, I was young and away from home, and, up to my neck in the great event of a world at war and like all men in uniform I wore my heart on my sleeve. But I tell you now, when I walked into that library and saw this girl behind the desk wearing a sort of red and white frock, that was it. I was in love. Madly, deeply, passionately in love for the first time."

There followed a natural rest in the narrative for a minute or so. The only sound a car manoeuvring outside in the adjacent car park.

Eventually he took up the story.

"Are you married Inspector?" he asked.

"Yes I am."

"And I'm sure your wife is very lovely. But this girl. Well..... ," and he rocked his head slowly from side to side. "I can only say the good Lord must have been on top form the day he created her. She was absolutely stunning. Stunning. So much so I didn't have the pluck to go up and talk to her. Instead, I can remember studying her from over the tops of books or round the corners of shelves. It was like watching a magnificent work of art in motion. How long I remained in that state I couldn't tell you, but, eventually I plucked up the courage and stammered my way through a request for information on Valentine Gray, the Little Sweep boy.

Close to she was even more beautiful. Her eyes were the biggest, brownest, darkest eyes I had ever seen, with sweeping long lashes, and the whites were as white as the pages of one of her books. Her hair harmonised perfectly. It was black, cut short. Now I sound like a love sick poet but it really was as black as raven's wings. And, she had high cheek bones; a narrow little nose and the most perfectly formed pair of lips. I should have guessed then it wasn't the face of an English girl."

"She wasn't English?"

"No, she wasn't. For all intents and purposes she was German."

"German!? In 1944?"

"Yes. But please let me talk this through Inspector. I have to for my own sake."

"Please," he encouraged, "I'm intrigued."

"There were so many signs, little signs, but I failed to spot them at the time. I guess my eyes must have been blinded by love.

She was lovely, and yet she was peculiarly unaware of it. Almost as if she was preoccupied. I didn't notice at the time, I was too overcome. I didn't notice it until it was too late, but she also possessed the face of a deeply troubled girl. And that deeply troubled young girl, Inspector, was the murderer of Ethan Thomas."

D.I. Preston had waited patiently listening to copious amounts of totally irrelevant personal recollections, all the while straining for this very information but now that he had received it, it proved something of an anticlimax. "So, what happened?" he asked.

"What happened? A young soldier lost his heart to a girl who didn't know he existed. That's what happened. And perhaps it would have been better if I hadn't. Which rather brings us back to where we started. If only. If only I hadn't walked through the park and seen the memorial stone to the Little Sweep I would never have got involved."

"So she didn't feel the same way about you then, I take it?"

"No. Not at first, or so I believed. But I tell you, I became the Isle of Wight libraries best customer - ever! Over the months I must have borrowed almost every book they had and I would always wait until she was free so that she could stamp my books. And, every stamp became a kiss."

"You did have it bad."

"I came away with armfuls of books. None of them ever got read needless to say. Who had time for reading books? Certainly not me. But every spare moment I had, I spent in the library and eventually she noticed me. First it was a smile, then a comment about the huge number of books. I've never been much of a ladies man, Inspector; I know I blushed every shade of red. But then one day I remember I somehow managed to borrow a car. It was raining, and who should I see waiting at a bus stop? The poor girl looked like a drowned cat. I pulled up beside her, delighted when she immediately recognised me, and in she jumped, without hesitation. Her hair was so wet it stuck like a swimming cap.

We talked as we drove and I offered to buy her a coffee. I learned her name was Charlotte Ross. I still think it strange that my namesake, the Little Sweep boy, should have brought us together. She thought it funny too. We talked about it during the afternoon. I even walked her round to see the stone."

The clergyman stopped abruptly, interrupted by a knock at the door.

"Yes?!" D.I. Preston was clearly annoyed.

It was D.C. Willard. "Excuse me Sir, but there's been a development in the Simpson case."

"Oh dear," he complained, getting up, collecting his notebook. "I've been expecting this. Excuse me a moment."

It was some time before he reappeared and when he did he looked irritated. "I'm sorry Reverend, but something's come up which demands my attention and I'm going to have to leave you. It's almost 1 o'clock, time for a break though, anyway."

"But there's so much more." Protested the Vicar, disappointed at the thought of it dragging on.

"I'm sure there is, but this is unavoidable and I'm afraid it'll mean you staying another night."

"Oh no! Really?"

"Sorry, but there we are. What can I say? I'll get Willard to run you back to Bembridge."

"Dear, dear, dear. I ought to telephone my son, he'll wonder where I am otherwise."

"I was just going to say Doctor Gray telephoned enquiring after you. D.C. Willard told him you were quite well and would probably be staying another night."

"That was very foresighted of him."

"He has his moments." The two men shook hands. "Thank you for what you've told me so far and I look forward to the next instalment. I'll collect you at eight-thirty again. But tell me," he said, standing near the door. "You implied a guilty conscience in something you said earlier. What exactly were you referring to? Were you involved in the murder? Even though I've heard a lot I'm still none the wiser."

"I would tell you if you weren't leaving."

"Hmmm. Alright. I suppose I asked for that," he commented drily. "But what a coincidence you should have exactly the same name as the sweep boy. He was very young when he died, wasn't he?"

"I've not forgotten the poor lad's story even after all these years. Yes, he was ten. Back in the dark days when they used to use little boys, usually orphans, to crawl up the inside of chimneys and sweep them clean."

"How awful is that? I remember it now from school."

"His death eventually lead to the 'Climbing Boys Act' of Eighteen something or other." Then added, "his abandoned, beaten and emaciated body was found in Pyle Street."

"Pyle Street!" repeated the detective. "Not another body in Pyle Street. One's more than enough. Until tomorrow then, Reverend."

"Until tomorrow, Inspector."

Before Willard drove Reverend Gray back to the hotel, Inspector Preston instructed him to run a check with the Royal Engineers and Newport Library Service.

"Is that really necessary, Sir?"

"If a thing's worth doing it's worth doing properly, Willy. I don't know why but I'm developing a gut feeling about this one and I want it to be played by the book. It may not be quite as clear cut as we imagine. I should learn a lot more tomorrow though."

After a light lunch the Reverend spent an hour or so with a newspaper in the hotel's Edwardian lounge, then later took a stroll down to the lifeboat station where he sat in the afternoon sunlight, for some time, gazing out to sea, thinking deeply. But there was nothing to be seen, except the occasional passing ship.

Taking a different route back along a shady lane he made his way up to the village, pausing to window shop, and then down the hill to the front, disappointed by the way things had altered since his war days. 'What was it Constable Willard said? 'Things change. Not always for the better but they change nonetheless.' How true.' After a mug of tea in the café he made his way back to the hotel and supper, and, tired by events combined with fresh air, an early night.

At the end of his day, Inspector Roy Preston motored out of Newport taking the route for Ryde and home, but at the last minute he pulled off the main road shortly after crossing Wootton Bridge to call on his stepfather in the nursing home nearby.

Preston's blood father had also been with the police, in their traffic division, but when Roy was only six the man he'd loved and idolized had been killed by a hit and run driver one night, during an incident on the motorway around Southampton. When his mother broke the news, the little boy vowed there and then that one day he would bring the killer to justice. A vow that with the years he knew he would never be able to realize. Almost three years after her husband's death Roy's mother married George Stretch, a policeman with the Isle of Wight C.I.D.

It took time for man and boy to bond, but they did and now George was slowly dying of emphysema.

"I had a word with the nurse. She said you'd seen the doctor today, what did he say?"

"What could he say? - We both know I'm not going to get better." George Stretch spoke between short, gasping breaths, his worn out lungs battling

115

to bring precious oxygen to a body desperate for air. Numerous pillows propped his feeble frame almost upright, but even this did little to alleviate his suffering, while in the background the unmistakable sound of a breathing aid machine hissed continually, like the warning of a deadly serpent anxious to claim another victim. The room was dimly lit, the only light a clinical looking bedside lamp, and was heady with the mixed scents of old age and human waste. Roy knew the visit would be painful, they always were.

"I'm glad you've come, there's something I want - to talk about."

"What's that?" Roy sat on the bed knowing he wouldn't be staying long. He never did. Long visits taxed the poor chap too much.

"The body - the one they found in Newport."

"How do you know about that?"

"The paper and - it made the local T.V."

"What would you like to know?" His step father's body may have been failing but there was nothing wrong with his brain. He liked to be kept abreast of what was going on.

"It's your case - isn't it?"

"Yes it is."

"I thought so. Tell me - what you know. - If I'm right, it's the - same case I was on."

"You were on?"

"Yes. - Tell me, Roy."

"Well the body was discovered by builders

working in Pyle Street......"

"Pyle Street. - I thought so. - Go on."

"You were on the same case, you say?" Surely the sick old man was mistaken.

"Yes. Go on. - Go on. - A one handed man I bet."

"Yes!" exclaimed Roy, any tiredness suddenly fading. "He was buried under the floorboards in a very unusual fashion. Possibly since the war. And a gentleman from the mainland has come forward, in response to a newspaper report, who obviously knows all about it. I'm in the middle of listening to his story and taking a statement."

"Gray?"

"Yes! But however did you remember that? It was years ago?"

"I've been lying here racking my - brain trying to remember his name. - It was wartime. I was on the case in 19 - 44 with Chief Superintendent Cartwright. - Gray was involved with the oil pipeline."

"PLUTO. I've just been hearing about it."

"Ah, but he was also involved - with a girl who disappeared at the same - time as the one handed man. - And there was a shooting in Shanklin. - A spy. - Caused a terrible stink at the time."

"A shooting? Spy? I don't know anything about all this. Are you sure you're not mistaken?"

"Give me some credit. - I'm not dead yet. - We always suspected the two things were connected - but couldn't prove it. - Question him. - I bet you find Gray murdered the girl - and the one handed man. - It's too much of a coincidence that - his name should appear twice."

"Valentine Gray."

"That's the fella'. - Get him Roy." The old policeman caught the scent of the chase over again.

"Fancy you being on the same case. What an amazing fluke. But I ask myself whyever should he come down here and volunteer information at the risk of implicating himself in any way. Especially after all these years? It doesn't make sense."

"A dog will always return - to its vomit. You should know that by now. - They all do it."

'Is that why he wanted to see the house,' thought Roy, 'returning to the scene of the crime?' "But he's a retired vicar now," he said, "a holy man of the cloth".

"So he's got a guilty conscience suddenly."

"He's already told me a foreign girl was the murderer."

"What foreign girl? I don't remember anything about a foreign - girl. He's trying to pass the buck. - I tell you the man's a low - life murderer. Hang him.!"

"You know perfectly well they don't hang them anymore."

"More's the shame. - Get him Roy. - Do it for me before - it's too late. - I hate to see the guilty walk - free."

"Yet, listening to him he certainly doesn't give the impression he's guilty. Far from it. I should learn a lot more tomorrow though. I'll see if the original files on the case are still available."

"Watch out son, he's clever. I remember. - But you be more clever. - Nab him Roy. - Lock him up and throw away the key!" The old man's eagerness for justice got the better of him and he broke into a painful bout of coughing. Painful too for his stepson, who could only stand by helplessly and watch.

Chapter Five

"Do you have time for a cup of coffee?"

"That would be nice. Warm me up a bit." As the girl spoke she nervously toyed with her wet hair twisting it around delicate, sensitive fingers. "I've been standing here for ages. You can drown and grow old at the same time waiting for a bus here."

"Well you know what they say," Valentine encouraged her, his heart racing.

"Tell me."

"There is a war on you know."

Charlotte laughed. "It's the excuse they use for everything these days."

"Well let's just hope they haven't run out of coffee."

"If they have I shall personally write to Berlin and complain. This war has to stop! I can't even get even get a decent cup of coffee on the Isle of Wight." They laughed, as only young people on the edge of a love affair can.

Valentine parked the car, and together they made a dash through the rain for 'God's Providence' in St. Thomas' Square. It hadn't run out of coffee, nor did the new couple run out of conversation. Before the waitress had even taken their order they found that they could talk as freely as if time and space had never separated their former years, and they chatted and laughed, attracting disapproving glances from other customers.

After the rain had stopped they walked in the watery afternoon light and he showed her the park with the Little Sweep's memorial. But all too quickly the satisfying time passed. Her free afternoon was over and Lieutenant Gray had to return to the task in hand. He was a man under orders.

"I've really enjoyed this afternoon." He told her with a whisper of sadness as they walked to the car.

"So have I." She gave him a heart stopping smile which lightened up her deep brown eyes.

"May I walk you home?"

"That's nice of you, but I only live a minute away."

"I'd very much like to see you again." His heart was thumping so loud he couldn't hear himself speak and prayed he hadn't said something stupid.

"But you see me regularly in the library. You're our most frequent borrower," she teased.

"I meant..... ."

"I know what you meant, Valentine. Yes, I'd like to see you again too. Talk to me when next you're in town."

"Oh yes I will. I promise you I will," he told her, knowing there was a pile of books ready in the car waiting to be returned. "Just as soon as I can."

"Wear your uniform," she said, "you look very handsome in it." Charlotte stretched out her hand to say goodbye, which immediately he grasped, surprised to feel it ice cold. Yet, just the touch of her skin and an excited thrill vaulted through his body and, uncharacteristically, without thinking, he lifted it up, brushing the delicate flesh across his lips, catching a subtle hint of perfume before letting go. Watching as it slowly fell away and out of reach.

Valentine looked up, noticing her eyes had moistened. As she turned to hurry away he only just caught her parting words.

"I mustn't. I mustn't. How can I?"

As the giant satanic wheels of war continued to grind on towards their ultimate and dreadful conclusion, so two small insignificant cogs within that terrible machine moved closer and closer until, within a matter of months, they were running with an exact precision that was, for them both, beautiful and joyous.

The sun had started its timeless descent on the broad blue canvas of the heavens, punctuated only by feather edged wisps of haze that had stubbornly refused to disperse during the day.

Seagulls rose lazily on spiralling updraughts like puppets on giant unseen springs, content to cry their mocking lament at lesser earthbound beings. As, over all, an expectancy hung in the clear coastal atmosphere, anxious to announce the approaching summer of 1944.

"How beautiful it is here."

He studied her silhouetted outline against the sapphire sky. Her shiny, charcoal black hair moving lazily in the breath-like breeze, that gently stirred wild flowers growing all around them, like drops of paint dotted amongst the meadow grass. Charlotte had removed her jacket and folded it as a pillow, exposing smooth satin-like arms from a sleeveless blouse, which rose and fell with an enchanting regular evenness as she lay there stretched out, enjoying the warmth of the sun against her body.

"It certainly is," he spoke approvingly, "gorgeous."

She smiled secretly, knowing he was looking at her. It was the type of remark she had come to expect from him; affectionate, warm and with a tenderness she'd never experienced previously.

"But, surely you've been here before?" he sounded surprised.

"No, I told you. I haven't been on the Island very long." She sat up, suddenly disturbed, and gazed around at the broad panoramic view from their position near the top of Culver Down.

To the right the wide sweeping crescent of Sandown Bay, fronting Shanklin and Sandown itself, sat vulnerable yet defiant behind rows of tank traps and barbed wire, hastily erected when an invasion first seemed imminent. The guns of the battery mounted high over the neighbourhood were pointing eastward to the open sea with, it seemed, even deeper resolve now that the Channel Islands had collapsed under the all crushing Jack Boot.

It is common knowledge that if the Isle of Wight ever fell, the Germans would use it as a stepping stone to the mainland, where it would simply be a matter of bloody hand to hand combat all the way to the capital. And, the ignominy of defeat.

On the left, the wide open stretches from the mouth of the Solent extended as far as the eye could see, dotted with countless ships and boats of every shape and tonnage from the Royal Navy, Merchant and Allied fleets, preparing for D Day and doing their bit to maintain the defences and liberty of the Motherland and the life and times they knew and valued. This was an Island, the nation in miniature, at war.

It didn't occur to her but from the same hillside position almost 350 years earlier, she would have witnessed another attempted invasion. The Spanish Armada.

"What are you thinking about?" he asked, as she smiled down at him spread out on the grass beside her.

"Just taking it all in."

"We're very lucky to be allowed up here. This is all W.D. land."

"War Department. Yes. You have friends you say."

"It's not what you know but who you know that counts these days."

"Can we walk up to the very top later?"

"Even I can't arrange that. There are hordes of very sensitive installations up there. Strictly not for the likes of you and me, I'm afraid."

"I like to see what's going on, that's all."

"Bit different to Norfolk isn't it?"

"Norfolk? Oh yes, Norfolk. No down-land where young, innocent damsels can be taken by handsome Lieutenants and kissed in the grass."

"So Norfolk's out for a holiday then?"

"Yes, it's a no for Norfolk," she said, tickling his nose with a blade of grass.

"Come to think of it, you haven't got the usual Norfolk accent, have you? How come?"

"And how would you know what a Norfolk girl should sound like, I wonder? Perhaps you'd like me to hear your confession?"

"There's nothing to confess I'm afraid old girl, but I would have thought I'd hear the occasional Oooh and Ahh surely."

"It's all to do with a distinctive stress on the aspirates," she told him, "but then according to you I'd sound like a cross between a farmer and a pirate. Is that what you'd want?"

He laughed. "So what made you leave and move down here?"

"I've told you before. There were too many boys in blue who wouldn't leave me alone. East Anglia's littered with R.A.F. bases."

"Do you think a handlebar moustache would suit me?" he asked, twirling its imaginary ends.

"No, I definitely don't. I think you'd look silly."

"So now tell me the truth."

"I've told you already, Valentine. My mother died and I wanted to get away and have a fresh start. We were very close."

"Yes you did tell me, I'm terribly sorry. Rotten bad luck. What of your father?"

"My dear Papa died a long time ago." A sadness appeared in her voice.

"What did he do?"

"So many questions today. He was a teacher. A very well respected teacher."

"In Norfolk I take it?"

"Norwich. And I'm not answering any more questions." She tried to sound as if she wasn't annoyed and gave him a smile. "Why don't you take me for a drive in your nice little car?"

"Alright then. We may as well make good use of it while we've got it," he agreed, sitting up. "It was jolly decent of Roger to lend it to me. I'm surprised he can fit in it."

"Who's Roger?"

"Another engineer. We're billeted together. Big

chap he is too. I believe his father's very wealthy."

"You haven't told me yet what it is you do in the Royal Engineers."

"Who's asking the questions now?"

"Well, what do you do?"

"I can't tell you that darling. Sorry. Classified."

"Oooh, how exciting," she feigned. "Top secret is it? Hush, hush."

"I can't tell you Charlotte, that's all. Please don't ask. It's just something going on over there." And he gave an all encompassing sweep of his arm.

"So, what is it? Something in Sandown?" A suspicion of impatience had risen to the surface.

"I told you, I can't tell you."

"Well that's not very friendly. You expect me to answer all your questions but you won't answer one of mine."

"Charlotte really! There is a difference."

The mood between them changed suddenly, disappointing them both.

"Come on," he said, standing up and giving her a hand. "Let's drive round to Bembridge and have a cup of tea."

"Ah! Your English elixir. The solution to all problems."

"What do you mean 'your English'!?" he questioned. It sounded such a strange thing to say.

"I meant 'our' English elixir of life." And she gave him a smile and swiftly compensated by following it with a kiss. Pleased when he hugged her close. "I saw Bembridge on a map in the library."

"You want to be careful reading maps these days. Many an innocent's been arrested for less."

To the northern edge of Culver Down sits the village of Bembridge. Following a short, but pleasant, country drive they parked the M.G. Midget at the bottom of a hill down by the harbour railway station, then stood alongside the low fence watching in fascination, as rail men strained to move a small locomotive around on the turntable, ready to push the handful of carriages back along the line to Ryde.

After a time they crossed the road and took afternoon tea and a piece of altogether disappointing shortbread, in the elegant and once grand surroundings of the Spithead Hotel where, for a few moments at least, had it not been for the men and women in armed services uniforms the war could have been another world away.

An elderly gentleman, sporting a winged collar and a rather tired looking banker's pinstripe, which looked as if it had once belonged to someone else, was performing on the violin, weaving his way between tables and potted palms, bringing a moment or two of light relief with a medley of tunes. When he arrived at Charlotte and Valentine's table he noticed the young woman's face was tearful.

The violinist stayed until the tune was completed, then he spoke. He was like a grandfather sharing a confidential moment with a child.

"I trust my playing did not upset you Mademoiselle?"

"On the contrary," she answered him, swiftly wiping her eyes. "That part of Tchaikovsky's violin concerto always affects me."

"Ah! You recognise the master."

She nodded. "Yes I..... You play very beautifully."

"You are most kind."

"Do I detect a Polish accent?"

The man bowed courteously. "Not only is Mademoiselle very beautiful and with an ear for music, but also very clever." Then he said something in Polish which Valentine didn't understand, but which made the girl smile.

"I'm sorry, I don't speak Polish." She told him quickly, her cheeks suddenly reddening.

"Of course. I quite understand." He stared at her. "Then I give you a blessing Mademoiselle," he said. "May God go with you. May he watch over you and bless you and keep you from all harm, and grant you long life." With that he bowed once again and, with a sweeping gesture of his bow, moved on, striking up another air.

"Whatever was that all about?" asked Valentine.

"Music from my youth. Happy memories. My parents were very fond of it," she told him. "What a nice man."

Valentine reached across the table and took hold of her hand, which to his surprise she squeezed very tightly.

"It would be good to get a walk in, old thing, before I have to get back," he suggested, breaking the moment.

"Good idea. Yes, it doesn't do to dwell on the past. I've done enough of that. Let's go for a walk." With that she stood up, doing her best to hide her damp eyes.

They walked hand in hand up the hill flanked by fields, taking a turning down an unmade road, past expensive looking houses, which eventually led them to a stony beach. With the tide out it was pleasant enough to stroll along the unmined section of shore line, weaving their way in and out of the defences and concrete anchor blocks of anti-submarine nets, until they arrived at the lifeboat station perched precariously at the end of a walkway built above the level of the waves.

"Someone told me a great many of our boys landed here after Dunkirk. Right on this spot," he told her, trying to imagine what those awful dark days must have been like. "Apparently some of them were so weak they could hardly walk. Not to mention the sick and wounded."

"How terribly ghastly."

"They had nothing. No food, no weapons. The locals came out of their houses and just gave them whatever they could."

"It was a miracle they survived at all."

"Lots more landed in Ryde." He sounded thankful and yet at the same time ashamed not to have been counted amongst them. "Lots of boats from the Island were involved in the rescue mission you know."

"And each one has a unique tale of deliverance to tell."

"Yes, each and every one."

There were very few other people about as they walked up from the beach and, with arms entwined they turned down a track which eventually led to a quiet lane overhanging with mature trees where sparrows and bluetits, unaffected by the brutalities of war, sang of the joys of living.

"Did you notice what this way is called?" she asked.

"No?"

"It's called 'Love Lane'," and she stopped suddenly and stood quite still, allowing herself time to absorb the natural serenity. "Oh, kiss me Valentine," she told him, oblivious to whoever may have been watching. "I always want to remember this day and this place, no matter what."

Walking up to the village they paused briefly at the cluster of various small businesses.

"Let me buy you something," he offered, when they reached the interesting display of the village jeweller and watchmaker. "I'm afraid it can't be anything too grand though. I'm 'boracic lint' as per usual."

"You're what?"

"Boracic lint. Skint."

"You're short of money you mean?"

"Yes, of course. Didn't they teach you anything in Norfolk?"

But Charlotte seemed surprised by the suggestion. "No-one's ever bought me jewellery before."

"There's a first time for everything you know," he told her.

They stepped inside, a tinkling door bell announcing their arrival, and a tall elderly man emerged from behind a curtain greeting then with an expectant smile.

The Lieutenant's embarrassed funds rather reduced the available selection, but Charlotte eventually settled on a marcasite and silver brooch, allowing the man to pin it to the lapel of her white jacket.

"Charming," he said, stepping back.

"Yes," echoed Charlotte, with a broad grin. "It's charming." She kissed Valentine as if the assistant hadn't been there at all. "Thank you darling."

With Charlotte on his arm and the sun already low in the sky, they strolled back down the hill to collect the car, knowing their snatched afternoon was coming to a close.

When they arrived back at the terminus a small group of children appeared to be playing around their vehicle and along the white picket fence of the railway station's compact, little car park.

"What on earth are you doing?" queried Valentine, when he noticed they were all wearing gloves and clutching bunches of weeds.

"We're collecting nettles to sell to the chemist, Sir." one boy told him.

"But whatever for?"

"He makes medicine from them, Sir."

"He doesn't give us much though," added a little girl with pigtails, "only a few coppers, and my brother keeps chasing me and stinging me, miss."

"Well," began Charlotte, trying to treat the girl's protests seriously. "If you were all to work hard the more you'd collect, the more you'd get paid and then you could buy yourself something nice."

"See," said the girl looking at her brother, "that's just what I said." And she turned away to resume her picking with new found enthusiasm.

"Evacuees," said Valentine, as they climbed into the car.

"The poor dears."

With little time to spare before he had to get back to his duties in Shanklin, Valentine dropped Charlotte outside her lodgings in Pyle Street and they parted with a swift kiss.

"Next time you must come in and I'll introduce you to my landlady and her son. They're an odd couple."

As Valentine pulled out into the line of traffic and accelerated away he failed to notice a man watching them from a doorway nearby.

Because of the pressure of work on the PLUTO line it was over a week before he was free to visit the grand, almost gothic building that served as Newport library once again. As always he planned to wait until Charlotte's desk was free to be sure of having the chance of a quick word and arrange a date without attracting the attention of the supervisor. Sometimes if the library wasn't busy she would come over to wherever he was amongst the tall shelves, and ask if he was able to find what he was looking for, and they would steal a quick kiss.

However this particular morning, a Saturday, the library was much busier than usual and, in the crowd Charlotte hadn't noticed that Valentine had arrived, anxious as always to see her.

He made his usual customary, casual selection of books he had no intention of reading and glanced across to see if she was free. But every desk was fronted with long lines of borrowers, all clutching various publications, anxious for any reasonable distraction from the terrible realities of war. He was on the point of leaving, determined to return later, but at the last minute decided to join the back of Charlotte's line and just wait his turn. There were five people in front of him, but the time passed quickly enough, satisfied as he was to be entertained by her every move.

She looked particularly lovely in a mauve dress trimmed with lace around the collar, and he was delighted to see the marcasite brooch pinned at her breast. She was smiling and pleasant to customers, greeting some by name, and he thought how lucky he was to have met her and, how extraordinary that the Little Sweep boy should have been the one to have brought them together. How jealous his pals would be when they met her. Could this be the future Mrs Gray? Could he be looking at the mother of his children? The thought warmed him and, in his imagination, he pushed the queue aside and went down on one knee in front of the desk, thrusting a huge bouquet of flowers in front of her face.

It was then that something odd happened.

Charlotte had just finished looking after a very prim lady in a wide brimmed hat, chatting freely and answering questions about her chosen reading matter, when the next person but-one in line in front of Valentine, a man in his mid-forties, or so, and wearing a dark raincoat, stepped up to the desk. Immediately Charlotte's whole countenance altered.

Standing there watching her it was as if he were witnessing a threatening black cloud pass directly across her face.

The man didn't speak, but gave a short nervous high pitched cough and simply placed a single volume on the desk which Charlotte quickly snatched up. Valentine watched, transfixed when, with the speed of lightning, her hand went to her breast pocket, removing a small slip of paper which she randomly slipped between the pages. She dealt with the card, stamped the inside cover and rudely thrust the book back at the man, without uttering a solitary word.

As the man left, walking towards the exit, he turned slightly and Valentine caught a fleeting glimpse of grey spiky hair, glasses and a moustache. The episode had taken only a matter of seconds, but the effect on Charlotte was obvious, although she did her best to conceal it by attending cordially to the woman directly in front of Valentine. Yet, when it was his turn and she looked up and saw his face, she couldn't mask her surprise at seeing him standing there.

"Oh! It's you! Well. How nice. I didn't see you come in."

"Is everything alright?"

"Of course it is. Why shouldn't it be?"

Valentine desperately wanted to talk, but knew it would be impossible and he could already feel the building impatience of the woman behind him.

"I've got the day free tomorrow. I thought about a picnic."

"Lovely."

"I thought we could go to the beach."

"Oh yes, that'll be nice." She sounded sincere

enough. "I'll do the picnic," she offered. "Pick me up at ten."

"Bring your cossie."

"My what?"

"Your swimsuit."

"Oh yes, of course I will."

"Please!" Protested the woman. "This isn't a social club!"

Charlotte flashed him a smile, once again she was her old self, and leaving the confines of the library building, he looked around to see if the man was still in the vicinity. But there was no sign or trace of him at all.

'Whatever was it I've just witnessed' he asked himself. 'That wasn't normal behaviour.' But whatever it was he was determined to have an answer.

Sunday dawned bright and clear with the promise of a fine, warm day. Thanks to Roger's generosity and the promise of drinks in the local, Valentine had managed to scrounge the use of the M.G. once again. As he drove along, with the roof down, following a quiet road into Newport, his mind should have been full of delightful anticipation at the thought of spending the day with so lovely a girl, but it wasn't.

Over and over again he kept seeing the look on Charlotte's face as she dealt with the man in the library. It was a look of intimidation, fear even. And, what was it she slipped from her pocket?

Newport was quiet, there not having been an air raid the night before, with little traffic on the narrow streets and only a few people milling about, mostly early church goers. He parked directly outside her lodgings in Pyle Street and was about to switch off the engine when Charlotte suddenly emerged, looking gorgeous in a strapless pink sun dress, giving him a wave, as her face broke into a joyous smile.

"Hello darling! I saw you from the upstairs window," she said cheerily, climbing into the car and resting the wicker basket on the back seat, then leaning over to give him a long, lingering kiss. "Isn't it a beautiful day? I've got the picnic. Not too wonderful I'm afraid on four ounces of butter and three of cheese a week, but we won't go hungry. Gosh, I've never seen you out of uniform. How nice you look in your shirt and slacks."

"You look lovely too, darling."

"Why, thank you. Wait until you see the swimsuit I borrowed from a girl at work. It's really quite daring. You'll love it. So where are you taking me darling, somewhere nice?"

"I thought we'd motor over to West Wight. Find a quiet beach over there."

"Lovely." She kissed him again. "Are you feeling alright, only you seem..... thoughtful?"

"I was thinking what a lucky man I am."

"How sweet you are." She kissed her finger and held it up to his lips. "I'm lucky too," she told him, "very lucky".

Tracing the road out of Newport past Carisbrooke Castle, moving unhindered through one of the island's many check points, they drove along quiet country lanes, through the somnolent village of Shorwell, passing the old watermill at Yafford, and a column of Italian prisoners of war, and on in the direction of Chale.

The sun was climbing higher as the M.G. purred away happily eating up the miles. Charlotte chatted continually as if she hadn't a care in the world, watching the diverse landscape slip by and letting the fresh breeze blow through her silky, raven hair.

"It was kind of Roger to lend you his sweet little car again, but however do you manage the petrol?"

"I pull a few strings in the right direction," he told her, trying to sound important. "Oh! I almost forgot."

"What?"

"I've been promoted."

"Have you! Well done. Congratulations General."

"Well, hardly. First Lieutenant."

"Well done, I'm very proud of you. Does this mean you get a different uniform?"

"Gosh no. Only an extra pip, and a bigger head."

"Whatever did you do to earn promotion?"

"Hard work, efficiency and enterprise," he grinned.

"You still haven't told me what it is you're involved with."

"Who was the man in the library, yesterday, Charlotte?"

"Man!? What man?" Her expression changed abruptly.

"The man in front of me. You seemed quite put out by him."

"Oh, you mean him," she said indifferently. "Yes I know who you mean. He's been in before. Nasty little chap. Why do you ask?"

"You gave him something."

"Only his book."

"No. You gave him something, something you took from your pocket. I saw you, Charlotte."

"It's....." and she let her head drop. "It's not something we should really do, you understand. I'm ashamed of myself as a matter of fact."

"No. I don't understand. Whatever do you mean?" Just what was this girl up to?

"He..... Well, he keeps pestering me for information on, you know, dirty books. You know the sort of thing I mean."

"Dirty books!" Valentine couldn't have sounded more relieved. "I don't believe it! Dirty books." And suddenly his spirits lifted. "The filthy swine. Couldn't you report him or something?"

"I could, but I don't want to get into trouble myself. I just give him what he wants and he leaves me alone."

"The dirty old man. I didn't know the library kept..... ."

"Please Valentine, let's not let him spoil our precious day together," a pitiful, pleading note had risen in her voice and she gently laid her hand on top of his as he changed gear. "Today is for you and me. Let's put the war and the library and everything else aside for a few hours. Please."

He glanced across and could see at once that he'd upset her. "Of course my love. I'm sorry to have mentioned it. I think that sounds like a jolly decent proposal. Today'll be exclusively for you and me."

They enjoyed the drive through forest and open farmland, where even on a Sunday morning girls of the Women's Land Army were clearly visible in their distinctive green uniforms and jodhpurs, herding cows, and working in the fields doing their bit to help fill the stomachs of a nation fighting for survival, when suddenly they came face to face with yet another reminder that the war wouldn't leave them alone even for a single day.

Rounding a blind bend in the road just before the village of Chale Green, they had to swerve sharply and pull in to avoid colliding with a Mark V tank, a relic from the first world war, slowly, noisily, trundling along the road, followed in snake formation by a column of open topped trucks, full of men from the Home Guard.

"Not many tanks like that on the Island I would

have thought. Except in a museum. If that's all there is defending this island - God help us."

Once the tank had passed and the reeking cloud of thick, grey exhaust fumes cleared, the men of the part time army got an uninterrupted view of the beautiful girl in the sports car, and right away a chorus of cheering and wolf whistles filled the summer air. Charlotte responded with a smile and a wave, but couldn't stop her cheeks from flushing pink.

"Must be nice to be popular," he said, feeling proud to be seen with such a cracking girl. "Looks like a combined operation," he told her. "The volunteer chaps of the Home Guard and some regular lot."

"Does that often happen, combined operations?"

"I've no idea. Why?"

"No reason."

They arrived at the far western side of the Island, rich with tales of wicked ship-wreckers and smugglers exploits. They were parking the car at the top of the cliff, in sight of the Needles, when a flight of Spitfires and Hurricanes flew in from out of the sun, passing low overhead, punctuating the stillness with the instantly recognizable roar of their powerful Rolls-Royce Merlin engines. Neither Charlotte nor Valentine said anything and, avoiding massed coils of lethal looking barbed wire and metal stakes, they made their way carefully down the precariously steep path leading to the long, stony and secluded beach.

"What's the name of this place?" she asked, taking his hand, jumping down on to the shingle.

"A friend recommended it. Providing we're in the right place this should be Whale Chine."

"Isn't this near where they're building a so called Military Road?"

"Don't ask me, that's not my department at all. You seem to know all about it."

The beach was almost deserted. Just a handful of other couples snatching a few moments solitude. After a while they found a secluded spot, changed into swimsuits, and lay together wrapped in each others arms. Except for a quick dip they remained like that for the rest of the day. It was the sort of day memories are made of.

"Surely such blissful moments like these always remain with you, precious, gem like," Charlotte said, enjoying everything about the day; the sounds, the velvety breeze, the warmth, his nearness. "I'm so happy. I never thought such happiness would ever be mine."

"Even if Hitler ever does invade and turns our lives upside down, I'll never forget today either. If I knew I only had a few hours left to live, I can think of nowhere I'd rather spend them than in your arms. I'm the luckiest man in the world."

"No," she said, "this isn't luck. That I should meet you is something far more powerful than luck."

"If I hadn't walked past the sweep's memorial......"

143

"You would never have come into the library....."

"And I would never have seen you behind the desk."

"That's not luck darling, it's..... destiny. Our destiny. Listen to me, Valentine," she said, "whatever happens, whatever the future holds for you and me, remember I love you. Something has brought us together but something far greater than both of us may well try to force us apart."

"Never! I won't let it."

"Brave talk. But we don't know. These are dangerous times. A bullet, a bomb, a treachery. Who knows. Those aeroplanes earlier could easily have been enemy planes and killed us both. I couldn't bear it if anything ever happened to you. But, whatever happens, good or bad, I know I will always love you, Valentine. Always, no matter what. Will you remember that?"

"How could I ever forget anything you say? I thought I knew what being in love was, Charlotte. There's been others of course, but I know now they were nothing more than dress rehearsals for the real thing. You've awakened emotions and passions in me I didn't even know I owned. No, I won't forget".

He studied her face closely; the curve of her nose, the elegant jaw line, and she closed her eyes allowing him to trace his finger across each eyebrow. Slowly, tenderly, first the right arch, then the left. The long sweeping lashes lifted and her black-brown eyes contemplated the man who had aroused a tenderness she thought had been buried forever. Was it the glow of the sun or could she feel herself colouring under the intensity of his gaze.

"So, do you like what you see?" she asked him softly.

"Tell me first what it is I see in your eyes, Charlotte Ross. Because there's something there I can't quite penetrate. A mist, a haze like a veil across your heart. I see you, but only in part."

She didn't respond right away, but when she did her answer surprised him.

"You see a soul searching for inner peace," she said, her voice sounding suddenly nervous. "I had it once, but I lost it. It was cruelly taken from me, slipping through my fingers like water. I thought it had gone forever."

"Perhaps you'll let me help you find it again?"

"Yes I will. I believe you will, too."

He brushed his lips across her cheek and softly kissed the tip of her nose. "I am so..... "

"Don't say lucky!"

"I wasn't going to. I was going to say blessed."

"Yes that's better. Blessed, highly favoured as we are. In the midst of all this terrible painful war God has somehow chosen to smile down on us..... if only....."

"If only what?"

"It doesn't matter."

"No, tell me what you were going to say. If only what?"

She hesitated. "If only the sun would stand still and today would last forever. That's what I was going to say."

The sun did not vary its endless celestial voyage and at four o'clock they climbed the path up and out of the Chine to begin their journey home, deciding to take a different route, stopping off at 'Gillings' in Totland for beans on toast, with Victor Sylvester playing harmoniously over the wireless in the background. Then it was back to Pyle Street, catching a glimpse of the steam train as they drove into Newport, its smoke trailing pennant-like in the still evening air.

By the time they arrived the sun had lost any strength and had already gone into hiding behind rooftops and chimneys, casting long dark shadows across the old thoroughfare.

Valentine walked Charlotte to her door, knowing their parting would be brief as he had to be back in Shanklin well before dark. They were on the point of kissing their farewells when the door opened unexpectedly and a peculiar looking couple spilled out onto the street.

"Oh, it's you!" The voice belonged to a short, plump woman in her early sixties. She was as wide as she was high, with a spherical shaped face supporting two bulging fish-like eyes, only just

146

visible under the wide brim of a straw hat weighed down with imitation fruit attached by a broad red ribbon.

"Hello Mrs. Thomas," said Charlotte trying to hide her disappointment. "Valentine, this is the couple I mentioned to you. Mrs. Thomas and her son Ethan."

"How do you do?" said Valentine. But Mrs. Thomas only made a strange noise in the back of her throat in acknowledgement. Her son, by comparison, was quite profuse in his greetings.

"Hello," he said, and gave Charlotte a grin which all too closely resembled a leer, revealing a nasty and broad gap between yellowed and uneven teeth. "Any friend of Charlotte's is a friend of mine." With a palm that looked and felt clammy to the touch he pumped Valentine's hand enthusiastically.

Ethan Thomas was as unlike his mother as it's physically possible to be. He was of average height, but a thin, wiry, bean-pole of a man with grey wispy hair, and many days stubble protruding from emaciated sunken cheek bones, under deep set, shadowy grey-green eyes. He was fiddling with the strap of his gasmask case when Valentine noticed that the man's entire left hand was missing, right up to the remains of a wrist, and to force himself to look away.

"We're just walking up to the 'Castle' for a drink. Would you like to join us?" Ethan's offer prompted another guttural response from his mother, but whether in approval or not it was impossible to determine.

"That's very kind of you, Mr Thomas," Valentine assured him, feeling sorry for the man, "but I'm afraid I have to get back. Duty calls and all that."

"What is it you do exactly?" he asked.

"Army."

"Oh, I see. Perhaps you then Charlotte my dear, would like to join mother and me?"

"That's very kind of you, Ethan, but we've had a very tiring day and I promised myself a night in and I'm washing my hair, too."

Ethan gave their lodger another strange look which Charlotte had obviously become accustomed to, along with his halitosis.

"Never mind. Another time then."

"Yes," agreed Charlotte. Another time."

The two couples parted and the lovers watched as Ethan and his mother set off in the direction of the pub.

"Good Lord!" exclaimed Valentine just as soon as they were out of earshot. "When you said they were an odd couple you weren't joking, were you? However do you put up with them? Especially him. He gives me the creeps."

"They're harmless really and the rent's cheap, and besides I'll be moving soon."

"Oh?" This was news.

"Only round here, local, I meant," she added as reassuringly as she could. "Somewhere nicer."

"How did he lose his hand?"

"An accident at work, apparently. He used to be a printer and it somehow got caught in the printing press."

"Poor blighter, what rotten luck. But now," pulling her closer, he softly kissed her on the cheek. Her skin already freckled and pink from the sun. "It's poor me - I've got to get back."

"Then it's poor me, too. Thank you for a wonderful day darling."

"You could always round it off nicely by joining the Thomas's at the Castle."

They laughed, kissed again and parted. As he drove away, she stood by the front door and waved until the little car was out of sight.

She was on the point of entering the house when a sudden voice made her jump and she spun round in alarm, almost dropping the picnic basket.

"A very touching scene."

"You!"

"Why so surprised? I told you, I am everywhere."

"I thought you said we weren't to meet in public. You were noticed in the library yesterday you know."

"What do you mean?!"

"Someone noticed me slipping you a note."

"And?!"

"It's alright, I covered for you. You've nothing to fear."

"Good. I hope not. You must be more careful in future. Now," and the man coughed nervously, anxious to say what he had to say and be away. He spoke quietly. "Berlin has told me to tell you that they're not at all happy with the quality of intelligence you've been returning. They need much more local information and of a higher calibre."

"Well, you can report back that I'm doing the best I can. They can hardly expect me to put an advertisement in the newspaper."

"I don't like your attitude, Miss Ross."

"Well bad luck! I'm not here by choice remember."

"We all have our part to play. You must try harder. Berlin has spent a lot of time and effort in training you and they feel they're not getting a justifiable return. You know what will happen if you don't demonstrate your loyalty. Do you need me to remind you?"

"No! No."

"If it isn't too late already."

"What do you mean?! What do you mean, too late!? Tell me!"

"Keep your voice down. I have no news at the moment. You must learn to trust me. Things are happening very swiftly in Germany now."

"Trust you?"

"We're watching your soldier friend and we know that he's involved with something important, but, we don't know what exactly. You must find out."

"I..... ."

"No excuses. You must."

"I'm doing my best, damn you."

"Come, come Miss Ross," he mocked, "that doesn't sound like a well bred English rose."

She took a deep breath, ready to respond, but it was too late. The man was already walking away and other people were moving busily to and fro. Clutching the basket handle so tightly her knuckles turned pale, she stepped inside the old house, slamming the door shut. Falling back against it, emotionally drained, unable to stop a sudden rush of tears. 'Oh Valentine! What am I going to do?!' Her legs gave way and she slid slowly down, collapsing on to the mat. "Help me" she sobbed. "God help me!"

Less than twenty four hours later the South Coast of England was hit by a severe storm. Originating in the Atlantic, it continued to build in intensity, moving steadily northeast, passing over the Bay of Biscay, buffeting Brittany and the Channel Islands, with storm force winds and torrential rain. Eventually crossing the English Channel, unleashing its full ferocity on the South Coast at a little after one thirty a.m. Coinciding with a high tide.

Fleets of every type of battle craft assembled ready for the invasion of Europe, were tossed around like toys in a bath, many dragged their anchors or were wrenched from their moorings, to be blown onto beaches or smashed against pontoons at the mercy of the wind and waves.

Huge seas pounded the Isle of Wight for over two hours, drawing shingle from the seabed, slamming it against sea defences in a hail of bullets, as gales and monsoon-like rain continued to uproot trees and destroy everything that wasn't secure.

The PLUTO line was no exception. In Shanklin, officers and men were roused from their beds and immediately set about installing pumps in the pump houses themselves, ensuring the precious machines weren't contaminated with water. Outside, equipment, tools, and machinery were quickly covered with tarpaulins and doubly secured. Nothing would be allowed to destroy months of hard work and the hopes of so many.

The steel line itself was safe, but with such mountainous seas no chances were taken and patrols were maintained along its exposed length throughout the night, until the storm had passed and the first sight of dawn lifted the eastern horizon.

That was when the discovery was made.

Like everyone else, Valentine was exhausted and soaked through. He had been put in charge of the detail responsible for the line. It had been a bad night, but PLUTO remained intact. On his word the watch was called off, and the men began to head back, encouraged by thoughts of hot tea and dry clothes. When suddenly a cry went out.

"Look! Over there. A body!"

Everyone turned, looking at the Corporal, following his gaze down the beach to the anti-tank defences that ran right across Sandown Bay. Box-like scaffolding constructions, on which a motionless body was stuck fast.

"Good Lord! Come on you lot." But Lieutenant Gray needn't have spoken. To a man they had already started running across the sands, and with the tide ebbing, were soon wading, chest high, in the freezing water and clambering over the high frame.

"It's a man alright."

"Watch out, he may be German."

"He's no soldier. Look at his clothes."

"The state of him! Poor bugger."

"Is he alive?"

"Not after last night he ain't."

But he was, just.

"Careful there," said Valentine, "he might have broken bones".

"Who is he?"

"What on earth's he doing here?"

"Maybe fell off a ship."

How long the man had been hanging there no-one knew, but his fingers had locked tightly around the metal work and had to be prised free. Matted hair stuck to his salt encrusted, ashen face, and dark, blood-shot eyes stared at them as they worked. Swollen, cracked, blue lips tried to move and made a sound as if to speak.

"It's alright mate, you just relax. We'll soon have you sorted out."

In the strengthening light the soldiers carefully lifted his body free, and carrying him above the level of the waves, transferred him up the beach.

"Where to Sir?"

"The first building you come to, and someone fetch the M.O. quickly. And some blankets. And get over to the N.A.A.F.I. and arrange some hot, sweet tea. For all of us."

Within a few hours the man was showing some signs of recovery. Enough to tell them his name was Kowalski. A dentist, by profession, from Warsaw. Miraculously escaped from the slave labour camps of German occupied Jersey. He was transferred to hospital and, as soon as possible, questioned by a representative from Army Intelligence.

The shattered remains of a small wooden boat were washed up on the next incoming tide.

The following Wednesday evening after a particularly hectic day supervising work on the fuel pumps for the PLUTO line, Valentine and Roger Merryfield adjourned to the pub. The two young men had become acquainted when the army brought together a number of qualified engineers to manage the vital fuel line project and, being of a similar age and sociable disposition, they hit it off almost at once. It was just as well Roger had joined the privileged ranks of the Royal Engineers, because at over six feet and built like a rugby player, in the infantry he might very possibly have had his head blown off.

A public school education and a wealthy advantaged background had left Merryfield with a devil-may-care attitude; live for today and let tomorrow worry about itself. In some respects a commendable attitude especially during wartime, but with the D Day invasion on the horizon and the lives of men and their machines depending on you knowing precisely what your plans and procedures for the future are, it was an attitude that had delayed any suggestion of promotion. Not that he cared; on the contrary it supplied him with an unlimited quantity of ammunition to fire off at First Lieutenant Gray.

"Is Sir buying tonight?"

"No, Sir isn't," returned Valentine. "Sir's broke. You are, and that's an order."

"Yes Sir!" he saluted. "You heard the officer, innkeeper," he said, addressing the man behind the bar. "Two imperial pints of your very best for two of His Majesty's most loyal and most knackered subjects."

The barman couldn't resist a smile. It cheered his heart to see young soldiers unwind and relax. With his hand on the pump waiting for the froth to subside, his thoughts turned to his own son in North Africa. There'd been no news now for over a month. But, it didn't do to dwell on such things, at least not in public. "Coming right up gentlemen," he said jovially, as the officers settled themselves on a pair of bar stools.

"What more can a man ask for," declared Roger. "Good surroundings, good company and good beer. All I need now is a pretty young filly to bounce on my knee and tell me how much she loves me." As he spoke, Merryfield looked around, his tired eyes taking in what little of interest the antiquated pub had to offer.

It was a typical old country hostelry, boasting a low beamed ceiling he'd more than once come into contact with. A large, open, brick fireplace decorated on three sides with rows of dull, tired looking horse brasses, stood just as it had for generations at one end of the room where returning veterans of the Great War, Boar War, perhaps even Waterloo, had stood and warmed themselves on winter evenings entertaining their peers with many a soldier's tale. Thick blackout curtains were drawn tightly across the windows that usually looked out over the wide reaches of the Solent, tonight at least, shutting the world out, creating the look and feel of a safe environment where, for a while, a man with a drink could forget; until his money ran out or the subsequent morning's hangover had worn off. A mixed blue-grey cloud of cigarette and pipe smoke hung low in the thick atmosphere, haze like, lessening the already dim light, but the handful of patrons seemed unconcerned, engrossed as they were in their own private little worlds. It was all so English. It was what they were fighting for.

It was an extra quiet night, a social in the village hall had seen to that. A handful of locals sat in one corner playing cards, watched over by an elderly man, his wife perched nearby; three farmers, their voices rich with the local accent, were located in another corner discussing the exorbitant price of grain, leaving Roger and Valentine as the only representatives of the military. But it was already late and they had no intention of staying.

"But alas," concluded Roger, "there wasn't a pretty filly to be had." He took a long draught from his glass in compensation. "So where's this gem of a woman you keep on about, old boy? You've talked of nothing else for months now. She'll be a grandmother at this rate if you don't bring her out soon. Oh dear!"

"What's the matter?" said Valentine, falling into the trap.

"What's the matter? Look into this officer's eyes innkeeper and tell me, in your educated opinion, is this or is this not the face of a man whose heart has been pierced by loves lethal arrow? Yes, it's official. Look, just the mention of her and you turn to jelly. She's got you Val' old boy. Hook, line and sinker. It's written all over your face."

"Shhh," said the barman, enjoying stringing the boys along. "What's that noise?"

"I don't hear anything," said Valentine, trapped again.

"Do you know, I could have sworn I heard wedding bells."

It felt good to laugh and they continued to talk and rib one another in a similar vein, when the door was pushed open abruptly by two men, strangers, brushing aside the blackout curtain.

Immediately all conversation ceased. Every eye turned in their direction, following them as they crossed to the bar and ordered their drinks. Yet as soon as they had made themselves comfortable at a secluded table against the wall, the distraction was over, and the card playing and chat resumed. Neither of the young officers paid them any attention, deciding to get in another drink before closing time.

That was when the air-raid warning sounded.

"Oh dear, here we go." The man behind the bar sounded weary but followed quickly with a more authoritative tone. "Alright ladies and gents! Your attention please! Those of you who would like to take cover can go below into the cellar, which has been converted into a proper shelter. Nice and comfortable like. Alternatively, you can stick two fingers in the air to mister Adolf and stay where you are." His suggestions met with a mixture of laughter, the choicest of crude comments, and someone blew a raspberry. Only the elderly couple chose to go below.

"If anything happens," explained the gent as

they passed the bar, "my wife wouldn't be able to move fast enough."

"We quite understand," Valentine answered them. "You'll be fine down there. We'll look after your drinks." The old man smiled, trying not to show how nervous he was.

The barman led the couple out of the public area and down into a cellar deep under the building, making sure they were comfortable and supplying them with a light should the electric fail, as it so often did. By the time he returned, the drone of enemy bombers was clearly audible.

"Thank God it's not one of those flying bombs like they had over London. Hundreds killed," he told them as he poured himself a brandy. "We don't get too many raids compared with other towns on the Island. Not like Cowes or the radar installations down at Ventnor. We get more tip and run raids. Low level, quick fire attacks. Make you blood run cold all the same, they do."

"You're telling me," retorted Roger.

"Seen them yourself have you?"

"Oh yes," put in Valentine, "we've seen them alright. Rum show. And, you're right what you say. Your blood runs cold. Ice cold."

"You're forgetting February last," one of the farmers reminded them.

"Yes, I heard about that," joined Roger. "Bad lot, was it?"

"Six dropped on Shanklin hereabouts," continued the farmer. "Saint Paul's was hit, and the vicarage. That was when Bob Irons, the vicar, bought it. And his missus. And her old mother, too."

"Aye that's right," added his companion, nodding gravely.

"Twelve in all died that day, they did."

The barman took up the story. "Eight Focke Wulf 190's it was. They swooped in from the southwest late one morning, strafing buildings with machine gun fire over Wroxall way and then closed in on Shanklin. Nasty. Very nasty business," he said, and drained his glass.

"And, what good did it do?" It was one of the locals who had been playing cards. "Just made us hate them all the more."

At that moment one of the men who had recently arrived gave a peculiar little cough. It was the cough that gave him away. Valentine had heard it before.

"What's the matter old boy?" asked Roger. "Not worried are you? We can always go below if you want to, I don't mind. They do sound jolly close I must admit. Let's hope they pass us by."

"No, no, I was thinking about something."

"The delectable Charlotte no doubt."

"No. Well sort of..... . That's it! Charlotte. The..... ." and he continued confidently. "The man with the funny cough."

"The what?"

"Those two, over there, who've just come in."

"What about them?"

"I've seen one of them before. The one with the very distinctive cough."

"So what do you want me to do? Rub his chest with Vick?"

Valentine continued quietly, getting a swift glimpse of the man. "He doesn't know I was standing behind him in the library."

"Well fancy that," said Roger, "the island's full of intrigue, isn't it? One thrill after another. Whatever next?"

"Listen you clot," and Valentine told him of the man's secret.

"Are you quite sure?"

"That's what she told me."

"I didn't know libraries did that sort of thing."

"It was information or something he wanted."

"Well there's obviously another side to your Charlotte you hadn't realised old boy." Roger turned and looked at the two men who were leaning across the narrow table, talking quietly. He turned back. "Which one?"

"The one with the moustache and glasses."

He glanced over again. "You can never tell, can you? Come to think of it the blighter does look a bit shifty. You can see his sharp little eyes darting around all over this place."

Valentine turned and looked at the pair. "Maybe they're discussing the latest book now."

The remark made Roger laugh. "Maybe they've got one under the table." Now Valentine was laughing too. "Maybe it's due back tomorrow and they're having a last minute peep."

"It's the Shanklin peep show!"

"Roll up! Members only!" announced Roger, looking across at the pair again. "Entry only on production of a valid library ticket."

Neither of them had noticed the men's conversation had developed into a heated exchange when one of them, the one Valentine had not seen before, left his seat suddenly and crossed over to the bar. He was short and dark with a Mediterranean complexion and built like a bulldog. He squared up boldly to the two officers.

"My companion and I appear to be the source of some amusement. Perhaps you would like to share the joke?" He spoke slowly, menacingly, the pronunciation of every syllable perfect. Too perfect perhaps.

"Clear off you little pervert!" Roger told him sternly, unmindful of any consequences.

"What are you talking about?!"

"We know all about your filthy little hobby."

"I demand to know what you are talking about!"

"I saw your pal in the library," joined in Valentine. At which the man with the glasses left his table. "I think it best if we leave." He told his friend, clearly agitated. "Quickly now. Come!"

"No! This man called me a pervert and I demand

162

he explain himself. They've been looking at us and laughing ever since we arrived."

All eyes were on the four. All thoughts of the imminent air raid forgotten.

"I really think we should leave!" His friend physically tried to pull him away.

"No!" he exclaimed, brushing him off. I am not leaving until I receive a full explanation."

"What are you going to do old boy?" Roger had stepped down from the bar stool, standing head and shoulders above the man. "Hit me with one of your dirty books?"

"Are you quite mad?!" He'd had enough, and undeterred by the size of his opponent a switch-blade appeared from his coat pocket, the poor light just managing to emphasize the polished blade as it sprang into place with a deadly click.

"No!!" shouted his companion. "For God's sake let's get out of here!"

"That's good advice chum." Valentine told him, standing alongside Roger ready for the inevitable.

"How dare you call me a pervert you..... ." "He didn't complete his sentence.

Roger landed a powerful right hook square on the man's generous nose, while the whole pub watched aghast as the punch sent him reeling backwards. But he was still on his feet and with only a second's hesitation lunged forward, unconcerned by the torrent of blood flowing from the middle of his face. Roger was prepared for him and had already grabbed a bar stool ready to bring it crashing down on the man's head.

To everyone's surprise the man suddenly fell and landed face first in a heap at Roger's feet.

"What the..... ?!?"

"I'm sorry." It was his friend again. He had purposely stuck his foot out and tripped him up. "This is very wrong. We should never have got involved."

Roger, meanwhile, was taking no chances and stamping down on his attacker's hand he worked the knife free, ignoring the groans and shouts of revenge. Then, with a vice-like grip, he twisted the hand right over and behind the man's back to the very furthest point. "I think you need to calm down old boy."

Valentine was watching the man's friend who was sweating profusely. His instincts told him there was something seriously wrong here. This was much more than a simple brawl.

"Who exactly are you?" He questioned the stranger, stepping closer.

"It's not important. I'm just sorry all this has happened. We'll be leaving directly."

"Oh no you won't. Not until I've had a look at your identity papers."

"Ha!" He gave Valentine a derisory glance up and down. "There's no need. We're leaving right now anyway. Right away."

"You heard the officer mate!" It was the barman, who spoke with the confidence that comes when you're holding a double barrelled shotgun. "Show the gentleman your I.D. or suffer the consequences!"

"And, wherever did that demon spring from?" asked Roger, still holding the other man in an arm lock on the floor.

"I keeps it under the counter for unwelcome visitors. So come on!" he repeated, his face flushed. "Show us your papers."

For the blink of an eye Roger's attention was diverted. His prisoner saw the opportunity and took it. With one mighty heave of adrenaline charged energy, he pulled himself upright, knocking Roger completely off balance and sending him sprawling across the floor, so that the arm hold slipped free. Instead of pursuing the fight the man made a dash for the exit and, before anyone had a chance to move, the door was flung open and he was through it and gone. Lost in the thick black-out of night.

"Ugh" spat Merryfield. "Let him go."

With every eye on his companion and the still wide open door the man with Valentine suddenly saw his chance and turned, prepared to make a dash. However, the barman was too quick and the normally quiet public house reverberated to the sound of both barrels of a shot gun exploding at once, as the man let out a blood curdling cry, staggered towards the door in one final bid to escape, then collapsed on the floor writhing in agony.

"My God!! You've shot him!!" Valentine couldn't believe what he was witnessing.

The barman went to speak but no words came. He just stood there behind the bar, frozen in disbelief, still holding the gun before him like a contestant in a side show waiting to be told he'd won a prize.

Roger got to his feet and went and relieved him of the weapon, placing it carefully on the counter top before anything else could happen. Then he turned his attention to the injured man who was already being seen to by Valentine.

"He's alright!" declared Valentine, looking directly at the barman. "You shot him in the legs. But about a hundred times I shouldn't be surprised. God knows what that gun was loaded with."

The news went directly home and the landlord collapsed with relief. Almost everyone else in the pub had been glued to their seats watching in astonishment, (they'd seen enough to keep their bar room tales going for the next twenty years), but now as the power of mobility returned, to a man they came and stood around helplessly watching the stranger still spread out on the floor obviously in very great pain. It was then he signed his fate for the second time that night, for suddenly his cries and protests switched from English to a language everyone immediately recognised, with a gasp, as German.

It was Roger who confirmed what everyone was thinking. "Why I do believe you've bagged yourself a spy, innkeeper!" Adding, "they'll probably give you a medal. You'll be famous old boy. Famous."

A little later just as people were beginning to relax and Valentine had secured a necktie around one of the man's thighs and his own service tie around the other in a bid to stem the bleeding, which had already soaked through his trousers, a man in uniform and a tin hat suddenly stormed in.

"What the hell's going on here!!? Don't you know there's an air raid warning on? Put those lights..... ." It was the A.R.P. "Good God!" he cried, almost tripping over the body. "What's happened here?!"

"I think you'd better call the police," Valentine told him, sounding far more controlled than he really felt, "and an ambulance. And, kindly shut the door on the way out."

The man stood rigid for a moment unable to assimilate what his eyes were telling him.

"Well?" It was Roger. "Don't just stand there Warden. Jump to it!"

"Yes..... right..... Police." He was ushered out of the door by one of the farmers, who unintentionally stepped on the injured man's glasses, which had fallen free during the excitement, snapping the frames in half.

"Drinks on the house! Drinks all round, except for the Kraut of course."

As the landlord was setting up a row of glasses along the polished wooden bar Roger called Valentine aside. "Listen old boy," he said quietly.

"What a night, what?"

"It certainly makes a change from pumping oil, but listen. I think you should get over to Charlotte's right away."

"At this time of night? Whatever for?"

"Come on, wake up! Put two and two together Lieutenant. Or has love completely fogged your brain? If the lovely Charlotte knows this bloke who's obviously a Kraut, what more does she know that she's not told you?"

"Oh my Lord! You don't think .....?

"I don't think anything. But take the car and tell her what's happened and see how she reacts. That's all I'm saying. Nothing more. Just see her reaction."

"I can't believe ..... ."

"Go, will you! Before the police get here, otherwise you'll never get away."

"What will you say about my involvement?"

"I won't tell them anything. I'll just say you were called away and you'll be back later when you can tell them whatever you like. I'll get the landlord to say there was a phone call for you. The euphoric state he's in at the moment he'll agree to anything."

"You're a good pal, Roger."

"Go on, clear out while you can. And Valentine," he added, clasping his friend's arm. "Be careful."

As Valentine moved over towards the door he turned and gave the scene one final look. How quickly things could change. What had started out as a quiet evening's drink had been turned upside down in a matter of moments and would now undoubtedly end in a complicated, lengthy and awkward investigation, whether the man was a spy or not. He looked down at the foreigner still lying where he'd fallen. From his painful, defeated expression he'd clearly resigned himself to whatever fate had in store, yet now that it was all over no-one appeared to be paying the man much attention. Valentine realised he hadn't checked to see if he was armed in any way and he bent down, running his hands professionally over the man's body. A small pistol in his back pocket. Funny he'd made no attempt to use it. Things could have got a whole lot nastier. The man didn't speak, but just lay there looking and feeling both vulnerable and helpless.

"Roger!" he called, catching his friend's eye and after checking the pistol's safety catch was engaged, threw him the weapon. They held one another's look for a second, and then he was gone.

A moment longer and he would have seen the elderly couple emerge from the cellar. The 'all clear' had sounded.

"Is it safe to come up now?"

"Safer than ever." Shouted someone.

Chapter Six

A waning moon occasionally pierced thick cloud cover hanging over Newport which was otherwise dark, silent, lifeless. Every building and home faceless and uninviting, void of any identity hiding behind thick layers of regulation black-out fabric, even where a handful of people were still awake, no-one wanting to be the one to give the bombers the guiding light they so needed. He turned into Pyle Street and pulled to a halt outside the house. The silence was oppressive, heavy. Even the click as he gently shut the car door echoing in the stillness like a minor explosion. He hesitated to knock the front door. Much to his surprise the handle turned and he went straight in uninterrupted. Presumably it was left open for tenants to come and go as they pleased.

There was a light, a single dim light, showing from the end of the hall, coming from the Thomas's quarters, and he shut the door quickly, quietly. Should he announce his arrival? He decided against it. Following Charlotte's description of where her room was he climbed the awkward, unfamiliar stairs, as noiselessly as he could, in the semi darkness.

Before he reached the top he wondered what he would say to her once she'd overcome the shock of his walking into her room, in the middle of the night. Then, he heard the unmistakable sound of a woman, a young woman, crying. But crying, like he'd never heard before. So awful, so pitiful and painful to listen to, he had to fight against an urge to run out of the house and hide from it.

When he reached the top of the staircase he felt the hairs on the back of his neck stand proud. This was Charlotte's room, there was no mistaking the faded label pinned to the door, announcing 'Miss Ross', and the sound was coming from the other side of it. Whatever was wrong? A light was showing under the door and he tapped gently two or three times before turning the brass knob. The crying stopped abruptly. The door squeaked, but he pushed it open unsure of what lay behind. What met his eyes, however, was to stay with him for the rest of his life.

It was a small square room, sparsely furnished and Charlotte was lying face down across the single, narrow bed. She lifted her head, startled by his sudden appearance. Even in the poor light of the naked bulb that hung from the ceiling, it was possible to see, at once, that her whole face was red and swollen from crying.

"Valentine!" she cried, with a mixture of relief

and shock, yet made no attempt to move but buried her head in the sheets, collapsing into a fresh bout of tears.

Valentine shut the door, and was about to move over to cradle her lovingly in his arms, when he noticed something lying on the floor blocking his way. He glanced down, taking an involuntary gasp of breath for, staring back up at him, with a fixed look of absolute terror, was the scrawny face of Ethan Thomas. What had happened?

He was dressed simply, in a plain dark shirt and flannels, and appeared to be lying in the position in which he landed. His body twisted at an unnatural angle. His limbs splayed out like those of a discarded marionette. A slight movement caught the glint of something protruding from Ethan's chest and Valentine fell back against the wall in horror.

Something happened to him then. Had there been someone there to ask what it was he would not have been able to describe it, but it was a feeling of desperation and fear he was never to experience again. At that moment standing over the body of Ethan Thomas beside the woman he loved, his world collapsed. He was looking at the handle of a small knife.

He tried to speak but his mouth was dry suddenly and no sounds would come. He forced himself to kneel down and touch the man's only remaining hand. It was warm, but there was no pulse. Nothing. Valentine slowly stood up, his mind a turmoil of questions and doubts, and just when he thought his already weary brain could handle nothing further, he saw something on a table against the wall which, in a single glance, answered too many nasty, nagging fears.

It was a simple, cheap, oak dining table, but, resting on it was a brown leather suitcase. The lid was open, leaning back against the wall, clearly revealing the contents - a battery transmitter with a set of headphones dangling redundantly to one side. He allowed his eyes to follow the solitary wire emanating from the case, across the room and up to the ceiling light, around which it was wound a number of times.

Part of him said that what he was seeing wasn't, couldn't be, real. But as he glanced around the complicated room at the vase of dried flowers, the Constable print and Charlotte's dark dress, which seemed so macabrely apt under the circumstances, he caught a glimpse of himself in the mirror fronted wardrobe and one look at his face told him instantly the nightmare he'd walked into was no sham.

He remained standing supported by the wall, forcing himself to focus and act, to do something, when Charlotte's unrestrained weeping stopped suddenly and she slowly raised her head, sitting up and wiping swollen eyes. He noticed her make-up. Her voice sounded weak and trembled with emotion.

"I didn't mean to....." she was still fighting back the tears. "He did me no harm...... but he would have ruined everything, everything."

"But why Charlotte? Why for goodness sake?"

"He saw me..... at the radio. I forgot to lock the door."

"But what were you doing on the radio in the first place?!!" Anger was beginning to rise above the initial shock.

"Please don't be cross with me," her eyes begged, "I couldn't bear it."

"Don't be cross? For heaven's sake girl, what do you expect me to be when I walk in and see..... see all this?"

"It's not what you think."

"And how do you know what I'm thinking? You're a German spy, aren't you?"

"No, no, no I'm not! I had no choice, they made me. They've got my parents and if I don't work for them they'll kill them."

"What?"

"It's true Valentine. You must believe me. You must!"

"I don't know what to believe."

"My parents, my adoptive parents in Germany are Jewish, but I'm not and they promised me that if I worked for them they wouldn't harm them."

He went to speak but she carried on, the words tumbling and falling from her.

"My father was a professor of languages at the

university and he'd taught me ever since I was a little girl."

"So?"

"I speak Polish and French as well, but the Germans were particularly interested in my English because I speak it without an accent. Father taught me too well."

"And I thought ..... ."

"We were all snatched one night with dozens of other Jewish families. September 1941 it was. But, as soon as they discovered that I wasn't Jewish and could speak as I do, they took me aside and forced me to train as a spy. I was in France for a while before coming over here last summer."

"And I thought you loved me." He pushed himself away from the wall in an unconscious act of rejection.

"But I do!" she wailed. "Don't you believe me?" She tried to stand but collapsed back onto the bed. "I do, oh Valentine I do. You are everything to me. I thought my life was over before I met you. You're my life now. My everything. My all."

He wanted to believe her, to hold her in his arms and love her and kiss away her pain, but how could he? At her feet lay the body of the poor defenceless man she'd just killed.

"Is he the first?"

"The first? Of course he's the first! What do you think I am?" The fight was returning and she ran a hand through her hair.

"I don't know, that's just it. So everything you told me about Norfolk was a lie?"

"Yes, I'm sorry but I had no choice," she was twisting her little gold signet ring round and round. "That was all part of my cover story. It's true what I told you about my parents though. They were both killed in a car accident when I was little, and a dear couple, Malkah and Aniol, friends of the family, adopted my brother and me. They couldn't have children themselves, but they loved us as their own. This is Malkah's ring," she said, extending her hand. "My handler, a man called Bracher, said she passed it to me as a sign that she was well. But you can't believe a word they say, but then I had no choice."

"So now tell me the truth about the man in the library."

"Oh." Her head fell in reproach, just as it had once before at the mention of him. "The man in the library," she repeated. "Yes, I'm sorry." But then her head lifted, defiantly, and she continued with revulsion in her voice. "That disgusting, evil, vile excuse for a man is my contact. His name is Aiden Urquhart. Whether or not that's his real name I've no idea. His code name is 'Mercury'."

"The winged messenger."

"Yes. I have to slip him weekly reports."

"So why the radio transmitter?"

"I only use that once a month in case his reports don't get through."

"Well, he won't be winging any more messages for a while."

"What do you mean?"

"He's just been shot."

"Really!"

"But he's not dead."

"Oh! That's a shame." But her reasoning raced on. "But he's been arrested? Tell me!"

"Probably as we speak."

"But don't you see what that means?! If he talks they'll come after me!" This time her legs didn't fail her and she jumped up, terrified by what she'd just realised. "What with that, and this," indicating her landlord's corpse, "they'll shoot me for sure. I'm a spy and a murderer!"

It couldn't look much worse.

"What sort of things have you been spying on? Perhaps they might, under the circumstances..... if you gave yourself up..... ." Even as he spoke he knew it was hopeless.

"It's a nice thought, but we both know I haven't a chance," and she shook her head despairingly. "Berlin was getting annoyed as a matter of fact. They know something's going on, on the island, but can't decide what exactly. That's why I was brought in."

"How do you mean?"

"Apparently there are far too many oil pipelines coming on to an island of this size."

"And?!" he demanded.

"And that's all I know. Mercury and another man were following you ...."

"Following me?!" Could this get any worse?

"I'm afraid so," she could feel his anxiety. "But don't worry. Whatever it is you're working on, as far as I know, your security's good. Not that it makes much difference now anyway. I'm finished."

"Do you know who the other man is?" he asked, remembering the man with the broken nose dashing off into the night.

"No, I never met him. We kept contact to an absolute minimum."

"So there's just the three of you?"

"As far as I know, yes."

With two agents accounted for, that left only the one at large, and, with the description every person in the pub would be sure to give the police, he'd be behind bars soon enough. PLUTO had to be kept a secret. He didn't know whether to hit her, kiss her, cry out or laugh. So he did nothing but surrender his head to the rule of his heart.

"And were you instructed to..... befriend me?" He had to know.

For her answer she carefully stepped over the body of Ethan Thomas and stood next to Valentine, the bare light casting a serene, shadowy glow around the outside of her face. But she remained quite still making no attempt to touch him.

"Valentine Gray," she said looking directly into

his eyes, her voice steady once again. "I fell in love with you the very moment you walked through the library door, that day when you wanted information on the Little Sweep boy."

"You saw me?" he couldn't conceal his surprise.

"I saw you watching me for ages before you came up to the desk. It's what spies are trained to do."

"I thought..... ."

"But I had to put thoughts of love out of my head. I didn't know how long I had here. Anything could have happened. And then, one rainy day, you stopped at the bus stop and my life began again. No-one could make that happen and certainly not the Nazi's, it just did."

She stood there before him like a beautiful child captive to the whims of wicked, faceless adults controlling her every thought and action, and he stretched out a hand, not surprised to see it trembling, and gently rested it on her shoulder. It was all the signal she needed and she almost collapsed into his arms.

"Oh my love, what am I going to do with you?" He kissed her again and again - her lips, her hair, her neck, her cheeks, their passion mounting with every reckless touch.

"Just hold me Valentine," she pleaded, her lips quivering. "For God's sake hold me."

They stood there in front of the mirror, each action, each movement, each fierce act of affection, duplicated on a screen no audience would ever see. And they remained there, minds, bodies and spirits entwined, drawing on one another's final reserves of strength.

It was Valentine who let reality prise them apart. "But what about Ethan? What are we going to do with him?"

"The poor helpless man..... he didn't even put up a fight." She knelt down over the body forcing back fresh tears of self-recrimination. "If only I had locked the door."

"What was he doing in here, anyway?"

"His mother's away visiting her sister in Bournemouth and he was pleased to tell me we had the house to ourselves tonight. I know he likes me and, well it wouldn't be the first time he'd tried something. The other lodgers are out, don't ask me where."

"So the house is empty then? You're sure?"

"Yes."

"Well, that's something in our favour."

"What do you mean?" She was forcing herself to look at the dead man's face.

"I can't just let you give yourself up, can I? How could I lose you now? I'd never forgive myself. We've got to do something."

"But you'll be endangering yourself, as an accessory."

"I'll worry about that some other time. The first thing we've got to do now is dispose of the body, somehow."

Charlotte stood up confronting the truth. "We could bury him in the garden," she said.

"No, that's the first place the police will look."

"So you think they'll come looking then?"

"Eventually, of course they will. Be realistic."

"And they'll find him and if 'Mercury' talks they'll shoot me or hang me. I don't know which is worse."

Valentine didn't want to agree but this wasn't the time for fantasy. "You've hit the nail on the head. So we've got to be very clever and very quick, my girl."

"I know he was doing some work in the room at the end of the passage. Something about damp, he told me. Perhaps there's something we can use there."

"I wouldn't have thought he'd have the strength for work, poor man. Is anyone living in the room at the moment?"

"No, the last tenant left a few weeks ago."

"First of all, go down and lock the front door. An intrusion now is the last thing we need."

"Right", she said, thankful for his leadership and went to open the door, but hesitated looking back. "You do know I love you Valentine, don't you?"

He'd started to straighten out Ethan's limp body when the knife appeared to protrude even more than he'd first realised. A dark patch of blood had already congealed around the wound, shockingly stark against the plain shirt.

"But however could you murder him in cold blood?"

"He would have betrayed me...... ruined everything."

"But cold blood!" The thought sickened him.

"If you had been through what I have and seen what I have, you would have done anything to protect yourself too. Anything. Believe me. They even forced me to practice stabbing, on the swollen corpses of executed Jews."

He nodded in revulsion. News of what the Nazis were doing to the Jews had already filtered back across the Channel.

"But can you be sure your parents......?"

"My adoptive parents."

"..... your adoptive parents are still alive?"

"No, I can't be, that's just it. In fact something Mercury said the other day already makes me fear the worst. I know the Nazis can't be trusted, but I had no choice. It's that fear they play on."

He nodded again in acknowledgement. "The front door," he repeated, but she could tell by his tone that they were now working together.

The room at the end of the passage was similar to Charlotte's except that it was larger, but the basic contents of low grade furniture and fittings were almost identical. A quick inspection told Valentine that Ethan had indeed been carrying out some repairs, for in one corner the furniture had been moved aside, the lino floor-covering rolled back and a section of floor boards removed where, it was obvious, damp had seeped into the brickwork. Yet the smell of new paint told him the work must have been nearing completion. The moon light coming through the bare window was sufficient to see that the gap, between the level of the floor and where the ceiling below ended, was unusually deep. A box of tools sat nearby, and within a few minutes he'd prised a further number of boards free until he had opened up a man sized aperture. It was clear what he had in mind, and, having locked the door to the street Charlotte joined him.

"But won't it be discovered when it starts to decompose and smell?"

"Yes is the answer to that. But I don't know what else to do."

"The people in the house next door but one had builders in recently, bomb damage. They left their things in the side alley. Worth a look."

He glanced up at her from his position on the floor. "You're very observant."

"It's what spies are supposed to be, I'm afraid."

He left the house, making sure the street was deserted, and found the alley-way without difficulty. Sure enough an assortment of builders materials were randomly stacked at the end of the narrow walkway. But most of what he saw was useless; scaffolding, ladders, a pick axe and the like. Then, just as he was about to turn back, through the darkness he made out an unopened sack of cement sitting under a roll of canvas tarpaulin and an idea began to develop. Better than nothing. Snatching up the tarpaulin he returned to the house. Charlotte was ready with the door.

"I've found this," he whispered as they stood together in the darkness of the small hall. "We can wrap the body in it and there's a big bag of cement back there which we can cover it in. Sprinkle it all over. That should do the trick when it sets hard." He handed her his uniform jacket and rolled up his sleeves.

"I don't know what I would have done if you hadn't turned up."

He said nothing, but moved out into the darkness of Pyle Street once again.

Not wanting to risk making a noise and disturb the neighbours by dragging the cement, there was no alternative but to carry it, and he crouched down in front of the large sack and attacked it with a bear hug, pulling it tight to his chest, yet with his breathing so restricted, by the time he'd dumped it down heavily in the hall he was so exhausted he almost collapsed on top of it. He was surprised to see how much he was perspiring. Was it exertion or nerves? If they were caught!?......

Charlotte fetched him a glass of water. "I'm sorry I haven't anything stronger. Perhaps you'd like a cup of tea?"

"Our English elixir you mean?"

"Oh yes. I rather let that slip, didn't I?"

"No, not now. Let's get on with what we've got to do." He hauled the bag of cement up the stairs one at a time and along the passage to the room at the end. Charlotte had the tarpaulin.

"Right," he said, taking a breather, "now the worst part. The body."

Pulling Ethan Thomas's corpse, shoulders first, into the room that was to be his final resting place, proved much easier than moving the bag of cement. Ethan was a light weight, but even so this was the worst part of the operation and Valentine kept himself busy knowing that if he stopped, even for a second, he'd be sick at the thought of what he was doing. The knife still protruded from the chest like a flag of condemnation.

Laying the body down, he spread out the tarpaulin sheet and dragged Ethan into the centre of it. "Now's the time to remove the knife," he told the girl, "any earlier would have left a trail of blood everywhere." He was about to reach out and grab hold of the handle when Charlotte stopped him.

"No! I was the one who put it there, it's only right I should be the one to take it out." Valentine didn't object, only asking where the knife originated from.

"Standard issue," was all she said, as she bent down over the body, wrapping her fingers around the handle, which felt cold and brutal to the touch; she took a deep breath, glanced at Valentine, and pulled.

The knife slipped free with a nauseating sucking sound and she slowly straightened up, holding it at arms length as if it was about to bite her back for what she'd done, watching as thick drops of blood dripped down onto the tarpaulin like heavy drops of rain before an angry thunderstorm.

It was too much. It was the last straw and it slid from her grasp and fell point first to the floor, landing with a hollow thud, piercing the cover, rocking gently backwards and forwards, before standing to attention as if somehow knowing all eyes were riveted on its every move.

Charlotte staggered back with a cry, a mixture of delayed shock and realisation suddenly hitting home. A fresh wave of revulsion swept over her and she gasped, fighting to find the next breath.

Valentine was quickly at her side and had her in his arms, but nothing he could say or do would still her anguish and, eventually he sat her on the edge of the bare bed. The springs as naked as her emotions. She sat there, staring at Ethan Thomas with a look of regret and bewilderment. Eventually she quietened, sitting with her hands clasped around her knees, rocking gently to and fro.

Moving over and picking up the knife, Valentine determinedly slit the top of the cement sack open, careful not to spill any on the floor, then returning to the corpse lying on the sheet, he dragged the whole thing over to the recess he'd made, and slowly, though not without some difficulty, lowered it in, working it around and under the floor beams as best he could.

When it was all finally in place he pulled the sack of cement across and poured in about half of it, covering the entire body. When that was completed and the dust settled, he bent over the hole once again and pulled the tarpaulin over and around, wrapping the corpse as tightly as possible.

Nearing the point of complete exhaustion, he managed to pour in the remaining cement, which completely covered the tarpaulin in a fine powder that in time would, he hoped, set solid. He then collapsed back, landing down hard on the bare boards, hoping the ceiling below would bear the sudden extra weight of Ethan's body.

Running a dirty hand across an equally dirty face he looked at Charlotte still seated on the edge of the bed. "O.K.?" he asked.

She nodded. "Yes, I'm O.K. Thanks to you. As O.K. as I'll ever be, I suppose."

Something told him it would be better if she had something to do and he thought for a moment. "I want you to go and dismantle the aerial to your transmitter and bring it all in here, along with anything else from your.....your spying business."

She nodded and left him alone without question.

When he'd got his breath back and the second cloud of dust had eventually settled, he started to replace the floor boards, using a hammer with an old rag wrapped around the head to deaden the noise, until all were neatly back in place and the body completely hidden from view. No-one would ever know.

The final task was to roll back the floor covering and rearrange the furniture. Just as he'd finished Charlotte returned with the suitcase containing the German battery powered radio transmitter.

"Open it up," he told her.

Into the case, on top of the radio, he arranged the empty cement sack wrapped around the knife still showing signs of Ethan's blood. "Anything else to go in before I shut the lid?"

"Yes, this." When in the moonlight Valentine suddenly caught sight of the butt of a Liberator handgun, as she passed it over, holding the barrel in an unthreatening fashion.

"Good Lord!" For a moment there was an awkward silence between them before he reached out and snatched the gun away. This girl really was an enemy agent. "Anything else?" he snapped.

"Just this," she said, handing over a small note-type book.

"What's this?"

"My code book."

"Your code book?" he repeated, fingering the leather binding. Surely this could be extremely useful in the right hands. But, however would he explain it?

Enough said, and he almost threw the things in,

slamming the lid down in disgust and snapping the locks shut.

"And that, my dear girl, is the end of your spying career."

"What are you going to do with it all?"

"Dump it. Probably in the sea."

"Thank God it's all over. I just hope ... ."

"Your parents again I suppose?"

"Yes."

"Frankly I think you need to be realistic."

"I know you're right. I've felt the same way for some time myself. I just hope I'm not letting them down after all they did for me."

"I'm afraid you don't have a choice, and there's another thing. You can't stay here. And, with your agents cover blown and a Jew sympathizer, you can't go home either, they'll eliminate you without a moment's thought."

"So what's going to become of me?" A note of panic had crept in.

"As yet I don't know. But, I'll sleep on it. Trust me."

"I do, Valentine. I do. Believe me I do."

"But for now," he said, "I want you to get a damp cloth and wipe over every surface, removing all traces of dust. The floor, furniture, everything, really well. And open the windows, get rid of the smell, but be careful not to show a light. We don't want a blasted warden knocking on the door."

"Yes darling."

"And, when you've finished rinse the cloth out thoroughly. You understand… thoroughly! The police mustn't find a trace of cement powder."

"Right. What are you going to do now?"

"Wash myself. I'm filthy."

"There's a small bathroom downstairs. Where's your tie by the way?"

"Don't ask." And he looked around checking that all was correct and in place before finally leaving the room for good. "I'd better take the tool box downstairs, then I think that's just about everything. I don't want to draw attention to this room in any way if I can help it. All I've got to do is wipe the tools and door handles, and so on, free of finger prints. Your prints don't matter. A missing person's search shouldn't involve finger prints, but better be safe than sorry."

"You've done wonderfully well. Thank you." But her thanks sounded quite inappropriate under the circumstances and he let it go.

"What's the time?" he asked instead, checking his watch. "Crikey, it's nearly four a.m., it'll be getting light soon. A few minutes shut eye would have been just the ticket, I'm whacked out."

"I know how you feel, and I haven't worked anywhere near as hard as you. We could catch a few minutes in my room."

"Alright then. But I must be out of here by seven o'clock. I've got to face the music at the other end."

"What do you mean?"

"It doesn't matter, I'm too tired to explain."

Charlotte went off in search of a cloth.

Six thirty found them both awake, but the new day brought with it new and bigger problems.

"I've been thinking," Valentine told her as he dressed, "I'm sure it would be for the best, if we made it look as if you and Ethan had run off together. As lovers."

"Tell me you are joking!"

"That's what the police must believe anyway. How long before Mrs. Thomas returns?"

"Another day at least, maybe two. But everyone knows I'm your girl not his."

"But don't you see? All I've to do is play the part of the heart broken lover. It's the best plan, believe me. Just as soon as she gets back and finds he's not here, and no note, she'll inform the police and then they'll discover you've gone too. Mrs. Thomas can't be so dim that she doesn't know her son fancies you."

"I don't know what she thinks. She's got no son at all now, poor woman."

Valentine quickly moved on before Charlotte sank into despair. "It's not a perfect plan but it's the best we've got in the time." He became pensive for a moment, sitting on the end of the bed buttoning his shirt. "I don't know how but one way or another I'll get you out of here tonight. It would be better if you disappeared completely of course, because if 'Mercury' does talk and the police learn there are enemy agents on the loose they'll hound you day and night until they catch you. Your life would become a living hell. Guaranteed."

"Oh Valentine ..... ."

"Does, or rather did, Ethan have a job?"

"Not as far as I know, he wasn't up to one."

"Good, so he won't be missed. But you must go to the library today as usual. Don't let them suspect anything. Oh, before you leave here tonight I want you to go downstairs wherever the Thomas's live, and make it look as if he didn't," he emphasised, "didn't leave in a hurry. Make it look as if he planned everything. Use your common sense, tidy up, shut all the windows and so on. Then pack everything of yours and be ready to leave. And," he paused, "sorry, but now we're in the cold light of day make sure there's no sign of blood anywhere."

"What can I say?"

"I don't know." He twisted round and looked at her sitting up, leaning back, half dressed, against the iron bed-head and gave her a pensive smile. "I don't know, so you'd better not say anything. Just be ready tonight. I've no idea what time I'll be here or what's going to happen, but I won't let you down. I love you too much for that."

"I know you do my darling, which makes me love you even more."

He leaned over and kissed her, cupping her chin in his hand, drawing her closer. "But now I must go," he said, eventually pulling away.

"God go with you, my love."

"After what we got up to last night that's highly unlikely".

With the transmitter suitcase in one hand, Valentine opened the boot of the M.G. and tossed the case inside. During the few hours he'd been there his whole life had been turned upside down; surely things couldn't get any worse. It was still early and very few people were about in Pyle Street, except for the milk-girl with her horse drawn cart, whistling and rattling bottles and far too busy to pay him any attention. It was cloudy and overcast, and there was a nip in the air. Or, was it through lack of sleep he felt chilled? But, what could be more natural than a young man placing a suitcase in a car, he told himself. Then, with his mind still buzzing with the night's events, he set off for Shanklin, watched anxiously by Charlotte from an upstairs window.

Unaware of what had been happening during the hours of darkness in his absence, Valentine took the downs road back, passing through an early morning mist that clung to the fields and pasture lands, like a damp curtain waiting to part and reveal the next scene of the drama he'd been sucked into. Rounding a bend in the road, within a few miles of his destination, the unscripted production suddenly opened.

A policeman was standing in the middle of the road, in front of a makeshift barrier, with a hand held high in warning. Another man was standing to one side as the little M.G. screeched to a halt.

"What's this all about?" asked Valentine, as the policeman approached the car.

"Haven't you heard?"

"Heard what?"

"There's a manhunt on. There's an enemy agent on the loose," answered the bobby, then, noticing the uniform politely touched his helmet. "Spot of bother in Shanklin last night, Sir. One was captured, but another managed to escape."

"I see." A few syllables and he was right back in the thick of it.

"There's road blocks on all routes in and out of the town. We're stopping everyone. Can't have a Nazi spy roaming around free, now can we?"

"I would have thought it more likely the fugitive fled across country under the cover of darkness," he said, praying the man wouldn't ask to check inside the boot.

"Ah well, there we are Sir. But then I don't give the orders, do I? I only obey them."

"I know what you mean. So who's in charge of all this?" With Charlotte and Ethan occupying his mind completely, he hadn't given a moments thought to the run-away agent on the loose. Of course he had to be captured. PLUTO had to be protected at all costs.

"That'll be Detective Chief Superintendent Cartwright, Sir. They've set up shop in the parish church hall. Big operation. There's the regular army boys, plus the Home Guard's been called out and more police have been drafted in from the mainland. Dogs, the lot. They're systematically combing the countryside, searching everywhere." He was obviously enjoying every minute of it all. "It's amazing when you think about the trouble just one person can cause."

"Yes it certainly is, Constable. Amazing."

The barrier was pulled aside and with a sigh of relief he shifted the engine into gear.

"Mind how you go Sir. He's armed and dangerous."

The young Lieutenant said nothing, just nodding his agreement. 'If they were going to all this trouble looking for one spy whatever would they do if they knew there were two on the loose?'

Valentine didn't know what to expect on his return, conscious only that his sudden absence must have aroused some suspicion in the eyes of the law. But, thanks to Roger's resourcefulness and a very quick word between them, back at the digs they shared, before Roger disappeared for duty, told him he needn't have worried. He'd failed to mention that Valentine had previously seen the man in the library and there'd been no reference to Charlotte at all. There had been so many statements from eye witnesses, all duplicating the same course of events for the evening, that surely one more wouldn't make that much difference. Yet, after a wash and shave before reporting for work, Valentine purposely made himself available for questioning by a very eager Detective Inspector George Stretch.

"Ah yes, Lieutenant Gray. You're the gentleman who disappeared suddenly."

The village hall was humming with activity. The authorities were taking the presence of a spy in their midst extremely seriously. A large scale map of the Island had been pinned on a board in front of the stage, and was being closely examined by three uniformed officers, speaking together in hushed, confidential tones. A young W.P.C. was busy tapping at a typewriter, taking instructions from a man in plain clothes, when the shrill ring of a telephone suddenly filled the building, answered by another uniformed officer at a desk near the far end. Everywhere people were moving about quickly, nervously. Their actions adding to the air of urgency that hung over everything like a menacing cloud. What did the enemy agent know that might endanger them all? The war? The victory?

Valentine was seated behind a desk in one corner of the large hall facing the detective, who was drawing heavily on a pipe as he spoke. "Good of you to come in Sir, and help us with our enquiries," he said slowly.

"I came as quickly as I could, Inspector."

"Certainly saves us the trouble of having to find you." He gave the soldier a grin. However, Valentine could feel that here was a tough and intelligent man, not a great deal older than himself, who would stop at nothing to get the job over and done with as quickly as possible. He was right, for behind the man's deceptively gentle, blue eyes lurked a sharp intellect.

"We know what happened," began the detective, "so no need to go through all that again. The barman, however, tells me you received a telephone call."

"That's right."

"What time was that?"

"Shortly before closing time. Before the trouble started."

"And who was it that called you, Sir?"

"My girl friend, Charlotte Ross."

"I see you've put her name and address in your statement."

"My ex-girl friend she is now."

But the man wouldn't be side tracked. "Tell me, how did Miss Ross know exactly where to find you so late in the evening?"

"I'm a creature of habit, Inspector. We usually pop in at the end of the day for a swift half, given the chance."

"And, why did she call you?"

"She said we had to talk. We were having problems, you understand."

"I think I do Lieutenant. But let me see if I've got this correct. A man's been shot, a spy has escaped, and you just pop off and spend the rest of the night with your girl just because you're having problems? Is that correct, Sir?" He drew on his pipe, sending up a fresh spiral of blue-grey smoke. For some reason the gesture caused Valentine to take an instant dislike to the man.

"Put like that it sounds pretty rum, I know.....,"

"So how exactly would you put it then Sir? Or am I missing something, perhaps? Something you've failed to tell me?"

"She's, well, she's important to me Inspector. I was going to ask her to marry me."

"Last night?"

"No, of course not. But soon, very soon."

"But now she's found someone else I presume?"

"Yes." Valentine couldn't believe his luck, it was all going swimmingly.

"How long have you known Miss Ross?"

"Since the winter. We met in the library in Newport. She works there."

The policeman leaned back, making the chair creak, all the while keeping his eyes fixed firmly on Valentine, giving him another disconcerting grin before he spoke again.

"We're both men of the world, Lieutenant, but you must admit it was an extraordinarily long break-up scene, if I may say so. From the time you left Shanklin to the time you returned was, what, six or seven hours? That's a very long time to say 'adieu', surely."

"We talked Inspector, a lot. And argued. And talked some more. The time went very quickly. I tried to get her to see sense and forget this other chap. Change her mind, but she wouldn't have it. We're finished. It's all over now." He did his best to look suitably dejected, brushing an imaginary speck of dust from his uniform, whilst from outside the noise of lorries arriving and troops spilling out, drifted into the hall.

"I'm sure you realise the importance of this investigation, Lieutenant."

"Of course I do."

"We know about the pipeline and to have an enemy agent roaming the island, more than likely knowing about it as well, just isn't on. Is it?"

"Certainly not!" He knew he was being tested. "The Germans must not find out. They must never know."

"Exactly. So is there anything else that you might want to add to your statement which you think may be of importance, anything at all?"

"Not that I can think of. Has the man who was shot talked yet?" He asked casually, keeping the all important question until last. "Surely his information is vital."

"No, but he will, I assure you. He's quite badly shot up as a matter of fact, lost a lot of blood. A number of witnesses said how quick you were to help him."

"I tried to stop the bleeding, that's all."

"You did well, Sir. He's very important as you say. Some of the eye witnesses did mention that you and Lieutenant Merryfield appeared to be laughing at the men and that's what angered them. Is that correct?"

"We'd never set eyes on the pair, so why ever should we laugh at them? I don't understand."

"Neither do I Sir, that's why I asked."

It was time to leave. "Well, unless you have any more particularly pressing questions, Inspector, I do have a very important job of work to get back to."

"No, I think that's all, Sir. We know where to find you if we need to. Thank you again for coming in."

"My pleasure. What else could I do? This man must be found Inspector, I would imagine him to be a very dangerous man in every sense of the word."

"You're not alone in thinking that Lieutenant, and I assure you we're doing our best. We have an excellent description of him."

"Tell me," said Valentine, lifting his cap from the desk, standing ready to leave. "Is this a civil or a military investigation, or both?"

Inspector Stretch also got up and slowly came and stood in front of the desk. "Because the shooting involved two civilians, the barman and his quarry, shall we say, strictly it's a civilian matter. Yet, because of the secrecy surrounding the pipeline, we're working very closely with your security people. I understand that when he learnt of the possible security breach your boss, Sir Donald Banks, went through the roof."

"Understandable when you consider what's at stake, surely?"

"Of course. But rest assured, Lieutenant, no stone will go unturned." He tapped his pipe, decisively, into a metal ashtray that was already brimming with charred tobacco. "Nice to meet you Lieutenant," he said, giving the young man a look that betrayed nothing of what he was thinking. "Remember, if you think of anything else you'll let me know, won't you."

"Of course, Inspector," replied Valentine, looking away unable to hold the man's stare, but relieved now that a good foundation had been laid for Charlotte's disappearance, yet suddenly feeling very tired after last night's exhausting episodes and so little sleep.

On his return to the pumping station, Valentine reported to his immediate superior officer, Captain Mummery, keeping him abreast of what was happening, only to discover that Roger had already done the ground work and the news was the hot topic of conversation at the pump site. Both of them were looked upon as heroes for capturing at least one suspected Nazi agent. If only he could have felt like a hero, and not a villain, he might have been able to enjoy the acclaim.

Because of the relentless pressure of work, Valentine wasn't able to meet Roger Merryfield until lunchtime. For most of the morning his mind hadn't been on his duties at all. He kept reliving the awful events of the early hours. Ethan's lifeless, staring face; the knife; Charlotte's revulsion at her own actions. There were so many unanswered questions. Roger was right, there was obviously more to her than met the eye.

"I'm anxious to hear how you fared with the lovely Charlotte," he said as they ate their sausage and mash. "There wasn't time earlier." But one look at Valentine's worried expression and the dark circles under his eyes told him what he wanted to know. "Look old boy, are you sure you know exactly what it is you're getting yourself into?"

"It's too late to back out now, even if I wanted to, which I don't."

"Oh dear! I don't like the sound of that."

"It's better I don't tell you, Rog'. The less you know the better. Not that I don't trust you, you understand."

"I'm pleased to hear that at least."

"But if anything should come of last night, well, you can't talk about what you don't know, can you?"

"True enough."

"Having said that, however, I do need your advice."

"Oh yes? You remind me of myself when I go

cap in hand, on the scrounge, to my dear old Pop. So, what is it?"

"Charlotte's got to get away, tonight. Right away."

"Away? How far away? Europe, I suppose." He was reading between the lines.

"No, wrong direction."

"Really? Ireland then?"

"Possibly."

"First of all she's got to get off the Island, of course."

"Exactly."

"Ah! I see where you're coming from now. You're talking a naughty 'ask no questions hear no lies' type get away. Is that it?"

"Precisely."

Roger was about to come out with an amusing reply but thought better of it. It was obvious his pal was in some sort of trouble and he took another mouthful of sausage and chewed on it thoughtfully. "I've a distant cousin who's employed by the Harbour Master's office in Southampton," he said eventually. "I could give him a ring. See if he's got any bright ideas."

"That would be marvellous. I knew you'd come up with something."

"Would it matter if it was somewhere further away than Ireland? It all depends on what's in dock at the time."

"I hadn't thought of that. Not really I suppose."

"Alright, I'll see what I can do, when I've finished these disgusting sausages."

Within an hour and a half Roger had a reply. "There's a four and a half thousand ton, ancient, coal fired, cargo steamer leaving Southampton tonight for Venezuela. Sailing under a flag of some obscure South American banana republic or other, but the captain's the type who doesn't ask questions. Any good?"

"Is that all? Sounds awful."

"Yes, that's it."

Now that the solution had presented itself he didn't know how to react. "I don't know."

"Well you'd jolly well better hurry and make your mind up, this isn't a cruise line we're talking about here, you know. If you want it, and my cousin's risking his neck doing me a favour remember, I have to let him know within the hour."

"But how would she get to Southampton?" Another problem.

"Good old Roger's thought of that too. Honourable cousin, who asks no questions, but expects his palms well and truly greased, will arrange a pick up in Newport docks tonight when the tide's right."

"But how much is all this going to cost me?! I'm skint as it is."

"The Captain wants £200 sterling, and that's without the palm greasing."

"Dear God!"

"Yes, you could always borrow it from him of course, or, and I know I'm going to regret this, there's always yours truly."

"You're a pal Rog'," he told him, "and your cousin's pretty decent too. Must run in the family."

"Hmm. He's not too bad for a grammar school oik."

"I went to grammar school, I'll have you know."

"Ah, but then you're different. And there's a war on." It was an admission of friendship. "Now, do you want this or not?"

"Yes," said Valentine, seizing the moment. "But Venezuela's an awfully long way away, isn't it?"

"So, write! This war can't last for ever and then you can fall into each others arms as Mr. and Mrs. Valentine Gray." It was meant to be a light hearted remark but it didn't sound amusing at all. "Listen old boy," he began seriously, keeping his voice down so the men working nearby wouldn't overhear. "I don't know what the lovely Charlotte's been up to, nor do I want to know, but if she's on the run from the Germans, or whoever else for one reason or another, and stolen your heart along the way then bully for her. That's what I say. Bully for her and bully for you, too. I hope you'll be very happy. Just make sure of one thing."

"And what's that?"

"Whenever you need a best man, remember me."

"I will Roger," he said offering the man his hand. "And that's a promise. You're the very best of pals a chap could wish for."

"You do realise that this could be a very dangerous journey, don't you, flag of convenience or not. There's still lots of Admiral Donitz's U-Boats floating around the Atlantic, you know. Just to cheer you up."

"Needs must I'm afraid Roger. Needs must. But she cannot stay in this country a moment longer."

"That settles it then. I'll telephone again and get all the final details and tell him it's all systems go for later tonight. Oh....." he said, stopping from turning away. "You wouldn't like me to make a reservation for two by any chance, Lieutenant?"

"Please don't tempt me. God help the poor girl, that's all I say. God help her."

The M.G. sat silent and still in the darkness of a side turning next to a disused warehouse on the west bank of the river Medina, a little way outside Newport town centre. A stiff breeze whipped against the soft roof and a steady, cold drizzle rained against the little car, creating rivulets of water that streaked down the misted windows like the tentacles of an unearthly creature, determined that it shouldn't escape. At least there were no air raids tonight, but out in the Solent away from the shelter of shore, waves were already mounting, cresting grey and threatening in the darkness. Any ship brave enough to venture out into the open waters of the Western Approaches would be in for a rough night. Yet, these concerns were far from the minds of the motor car's occupants, who were sat holding one another's hands, speaking in restless, short bursts knowing their time together was rapidly ebbing away.

"What time's high tide?"

"Twenty three fifty six," Valentine told her. She was playing nervously with her hair, twisting it around the fingers of one hand, just as she had on another occasion in the rain, a life time away.

"What time's the boat coming?"

"I told you. Ten minutes after midnight. We've twenty minutes."

"So little time," she was clearly very anxious. It had been a difficult day putting on a performance at the library, pretending nothing was wrong, yet knowing that things couldn't possibly be worse. And now, hiding in the dark like a fugitive ready to be whisked away to what may just as well be the other side of the world, and God knows what. She squeezed his hand. He was the one thing, the only thing, in her life she could depend on and now she was about to lose that too. But not for long, surely. The war couldn't last for very much longer and then they'd be together forever. "I did everything you told me to," she said. "The house is nice and tidy, and all locked up."

"Good, well done. Bringing a suitcase of Ethan's things was a stroke of genius. Even his toothbrush."

"I'll drop it over the side when we get into deep water."

"Along with the radio transmitter case."

"Yes, that too."

"I'll be glad to see the back of that thing, I couldn't risk being seen dropping it off the end of the pier myself. Think what the police would say if they'd discovered me with it."

"Don't. I want to forget it all. Everything that's gone before is gone for good now. Finished. Now I want to start afresh."

He stopped her fidgeting and ran his fingers through her hair for the last time. "Write to me via Roger. You've got his home address in Dorset, haven't you?"

"Yes, but I don't understand why I can't write to you directly."

"Because when Mrs. Thomas returns and reports Ethan missing, the police will instantly link you and me together, and you never know..... it's not worth the risk. The sentence for aiding and abetting the enemy is looking down the barrel of a gun and I'm not keen on that! He'll pass everything on, I know he will. I trust him completely."

She squeezed his hand again and kissed the palm.

"Dear God, yes, I'm still the enemy aren't I, although I don't feel like it. Oh Valentine, whatever's going to become of us?"

"Relax, you'll be fine."

"Why couldn't I simply catch the ferry like everyone else?"

"Because, A you need a pass which you don't have and B, they keep track of all the passengers coming and going, and when they check to see if Ethan left together with you, what will they discover but that you left alone, which will naturally arouse suspicion."

"Boy, you're good. You should be the spy, not me."

Time was running out and he looked at her, conscious that he still knew so little about the woman he was prepared to take such crazy risks for. "What did you do before the Nazis forced you to work for them?" he asked.

"I was a school teacher, specialising in English. I was due to go on and teach at the university in Berlin. They were so proud of me. They wouldn't be now though," she sighed. "Do you know, I've not even told you my real name?"

"Charlotte's not your name!? Come to think of it, no I suppose it isn't."

"No, its not. It's Martha Kowalski."

"I've heard that name before."

"It's common enough. I was born in Poland and brought up in Germany."

"They made you change it, of course. I'm not sure I could ever get used to that now. You'll always be Charlotte to me. My Charlotte."

"What's in a name? I'm still the same me inside."

"My poor angel."

"No!" she exclaimed, suddenly drawing back. "That is one name you must never call me. Ever!"

"I didn't mean...... ."

"Angel is my code name," she told him gravely. "The Nazi's thought it would be amusing as my step father's name, in Polish, means angel."

"You poor girl. I think you've suffered more than I'll ever understand."

"Please," she asked, her head resting against his chest. "Let's not talk about the past. I hope that the past and all it contains is now finally resting in peace. Just hold me close in these last few moments we have together. This is how I want to remember you. My brave soldier, my righter of wrongs, my knight in khaki." Never had anyone ever spoken to him with such tenderness. They were words he would not forget.

They sat quietly, content just to be close, knowing, yet not giving voice to the inevitable; that it would be a long time before they could hold one another again.

Valentine suddenly jumped. "Money! I've forgotten about money. What a chump. Have you got any?"

"Yes," she replied calmly. "A little. Enough to keep going for a while anyway."

"What will you do when you get there?"

"Teach English I suppose. I'll be alright. I've come this far on my own, so a bit further won't make that much difference. I'll get by."

"I should have been more thoughtful."

"Don't be silly. You've done more for me ......"

Suddenly they both saw what they'd been waiting for. Piercing the watery darkness came three flashes of light from a small boat, as it negotiated the narrow water way. Three, followed by three more. This was it.

Inside the soft topped car it was just possible to hear a change in the boat's engine speed as it slowed, to negotiate a position ready for the return journey, up the river to Cowes and out into Southampton Water.

The lovers knew they had only a matter of seconds left together and they embraced with painful intimacy.

Valentine knew the boat wouldn't wait and forced himself to move. "Quickly now," he said, leaning across, opening the door on her side.

"Oh Valentine."

"I'll get the cases."

Even in the darkness it was possible to make out the outline of the boat, which in a former life had been an inshore fishing vessel, with a high bow and a stub, square wheel-house. It bobbed up and down in the swell at the end of an old, short, wooden jetty just yards from where the car was parked. The throb of its engine filling the night.

Valentine raised the collar of his rain coat against the penetrating drizzle and pulled his cap down firmly as Charlotte joined him at the rear of the M.G., tying a head scarf on as best she could.

"I'll take Ethan's case and the transmitter," he almost had to shout; "you carry yours." He led the way towards the boat. Someone jumped from the ship and ran towards him. "Come on mate," said the man, his features lost in the darkness, "I'll take one of those. Let's get a move on. I shouldn't want to be found here."

Carrying a case the man leapt aboard and took the rest of the cases.

The pair held each other close, their faces wet with rain, and kissed with intensity.

"When all this is over will you marry me, Charlotte?"

"Yes I will. Of course I will. There could never be anyone else for me, not now. I don't know where or when, but one day I will marry you, Valentine Gray. I promise."

"My darling girl."

"Come on now, let's be having you!" It was the skipper.

"You will write, won't you?"

"How could I not?" She stepped onto the shifting deck, unwilling to let go of his hand. "Years from now we'll look back on this night and remember it as the start of our new life."

"I don't know what I'm going to do without you."

"You must be careful not to make the police suspicious when you talk to them. You must protect yourself!" Her voice was only just discernable above the appalling conditions.

"Try not to worry about it." When suddenly in the darkness of midnight she saw his face crack with the embryo of a mischievous grin. "Maybe I'll tell them a little Wight lie."

With that the skipper pushed the throttle forward, Charlotte's fingers slipped through Valentine's for the last time, and he watched as the vessel moved out into the centre of the river and away.

He couldn't see, but she remained on deck clutching a corner of the wheel-house, her face streaked with a mixture of rain and tears, mouthing words that only she could hear before the wind plucked them away forever.

Oblivious to rain and wind, darkness and time, he stood on the very tip of the jetty, long after the beat of the engines was lost in the night. Nothing mattered now. Nothing mattered anymore. Nothing at all.

Valentine returned, soaked through, to the car, his mind almost paralysed by a mixture of fatigue and emptiness. How long would it be before those magnificent eyes looked so lovingly into his once again? Surely, just as soon as the D Day invasion was under way, Hitler would be sure to surrender and life return to normal. He vowed to take the first available ship direct to Venezuela and marry her there and then, and until that day, the postman was going to be very, very busy.

He flung open the door, just managing to hold it against the wind, and jumped in, only to get the shock of his life. A circle of cold steel, from the end of the barrel of a German Luger, dug deep into his left cheek, almost knocking a tooth loose. "One move. One sound. And your brains will be plastered all over the car."

He didn't need to turn to see who it was. The man's voice gave him away immediately, and there was a smell, an unwashed, damp smell, earned from living outdoors and running in fear of your life. "What have you done with the girl?"

"She's gone. She's safe. You can't touch her now."

"I don't care about her, she's nothing. Amateur. It's you I want. You can help me."

"Help you? Never!"

The gun dug deeper until his cheek felt as if was about to rip open.

"Oh, I think you will. If you don't and the police catch me I'll have to tell them all about your little night time assignation, and I'm sure they'll be very interested to hear of your relationship with an enemy agent."

"You filthy..... ."

"Shut up!" He brought the gun barrel down sharply against the side of Valentine's head.

"How did you know we were here?" he asked, as soon as the pain eased.

"I've been watching 'Angel's' address and when you turned up in the middle of the night behaving like a thief, I knew something was up. But now," he said menacingly, jamming the gun barrel into the English man's face again. "You're going to help me."

"Go to Hell!" It was difficult to talk with a mouthful of German weaponry. The man ignored him.

"While you were saying your sweet goodbyes I was checking over this old warehouse here. It'll do me until dawn, when I want you to bring me food and clothes, and then I'll tell you what you're going to do to get me off this island."

"You must be raving mad, I'd rather die!"

"Shut up and listen!" he said, forcing the gun barrel in ever further. Valentine still hadn't been able to turn and look at the man, but he knew him. "In a minute I'll go and take cover in the warehouse, then before dawn you're to bring me some food and dry clothes, and make sure they're the right size. Remember, if the police find me I'll sing like a nightingale in your Berkley Square, before they put me in front of a firing squad. And then they'll come after you. So if I'm caught it's your death warrant too! Be back here before dawn, come alone, and drop the things just inside the door. I'll be watching, waiting."

He gave Valentine no chance to respond. Suddenly the vehicle was filled with wind and rain as the passenger door flew open and the man deftly slipped out of the compact little car, slamming the door shut before disappearing into the darkness.

Valentine didn't move for a moment but sat frozen behind the driving wheel, unable to assimilate what had just happened. Gingerly he felt his head and cheek, gently trying to massage life back into the damaged flesh. It didn't feel as if it was bleeding, but there'd surely be a lovely bruise there in the morning. Everything the man said was true; that's what made it all the more terrible. He couldn't tell anyone otherwise his association with Charlotte would be exposed and then what would happen?! And what about PLUTO? Hundreds of thousands of men and women were depending on it remaining a secret. "Dear God and now it's all down to me." He automatically grabbed hold of the steering wheel, squeezing it as hard as he could, as delayed shock took control of his weary body and began to shake it violently. But, gradually, the moment passed and he just managed to throw open the door before being sick, until his stomach had nothing left to surrender. As he pulled the door closed again and wiped a still trembling hand across his mouth, he knew there was only one thing to do, and one person to trust.

It was almost 03.30 and the night sky was already showing early signs of the approaching new day. The weather had calmed. It had stopped raining, but there was still a strong blow, bringing in thick banks of low cloud from the west, as the little M.G. pulled to a halt two hundred yards or so from the warehouse. The passenger door opened and Valentine stepped silently out, turning to have a final word with the driver. "You're O.K. with what you've got to do?" he whispered.

"Yes", replied Roger. "Do be careful yourself, old boy."

"Oh, I'll be careful alright. His sort aren't worth dying for." He quietly clicked the door shut, watching as the car pulled away.

The last three and a half hours had been a nightmare. He'd just been fit enough, after the confrontation with the agent, to drive back to Shanklin, wake Roger and explain what had happened and what his proposed plan of action was to be. The two young men had applied themselves to what the circumstances demanded.

As Valentine soundlessly made his way towards the warehouse, keeping close to the shadows of surrounding buildings, he allowed himself a smile at the recollection of the way Roger had dealt with a bolshie Home Guard officer on duty at one of the road-blocks outside Shanklin. The poor man would be eating humble pie for a long time.

The warehouse was only a few yards away and the sound of the M.G.'s engine was clearly audible in the stillness. If he could hear it, then so too could the Nazi agent. He removed the automatic

Walther, screwing the silencer firmly in place. There could be no room for error, though the chances were he was even more exhausted than Valentine, having been on the run for well over twenty four hours.

He had a clear view of the car parked out front and made his way, crablike, hugging the building, until the door he'd noticed earlier was only a few yards ahead. He watched as Roger got out, purposefully leaving the engine running, pulling his cap low and lifting the collar of his rain coat.

Roger went around to the boot and removed a sack, making his actions as obvious as possible. He walked over to the warehouse door and pulled it open with one swift, determined movement, unsure what was on the other side, and dropped the sack directly on the step. Without closing the door he walked quickly back to the car, jumped in and with an exaggerated rev' of the engine drove off, leaving Valentine alone.

Except for the stiff breeze everything was silent. The minutes began to tick by as Valentine's heart beat began to increase, until he could hear it in his head, thumping out its cardiovascular warning. He raised the firearm in both hands, at arms length, steadying it against the brickwork, pointing it eighteen inches above the level of the sack.

Just when he thought the man wasn't going to show, there was a hand clearly visible in the semi gloom and, without hesitation Valentine fired two quick, successive rounds. The twin popping sounds only just perceptible. He waited for a reaction. But there was none. He waited for what felt like an eternity before cautiously moving forward, still with the Walther held at arms length, making towards the door.

Then he saw what he'd prayed he'd see. The body of a man slumped back inside the entrance. Standing over him it was clear he'd been hit in the chest and throat. Death would have been instantaneous.

The threat to both Charlotte, himself, and the all important PLUTO line had been successfully eliminated.

For the second time in twenty four hours Valentine now had another body to hide. He began to drag the corpse, many times the weight of Ethan Thomas, further inside the abandoned building, when, suddenly a solution presented itself. In the semi darkness he walked over a wooden trap door recognising the distinctive sound of a hollow underneath. Searching for the opening, he lifted up the door and, not seeing or caring what lurked beneath, unceremoniously bundled the German's lifeless body inside. It landed with a heavy thud, as simultaneously the door closed down firmly over the top of it. There it would remain secretly entombed, for no-one could ever know what had just taken place.

Without further hesitation Valentine collected the sack which contained nothing more than his service raincoat and, closing the warehouse door, made his way quickly back to the point where he'd left Roger, who was waiting in the car.

"Thank God! I was beginning to get worried."

"Just take me home Rog'. I'm absolutely exhausted."

It took three days from the time Mrs. Thomas reported her son missing before the police linked his disappearance to that of Charlotte Ross. With the Island still on a high state of alert for the enemy agent, Lieutenant Gray was quickly brought in for questioning. According to D.I. Stretch, the two incidents had somehow become connected. That Gray's name should show up twice was beyond mere chance.

Valentine had already laid the foundations of a perfect alibi and was fortunate that Charlotte had reported for work and been seen by a number of people.

"Some say she appeared very agitated Lieutenant."

"I'm not surprised Inspector, obviously she was planning to run off with Thomas."

"Did you see Thomas when you called there that night?"

"No," he hesitated. "No, I didn't."

"Are you quite sure you didn't?"

"I'm sure, Inspector. Quite sure. I presume he was asleep."

"A number of people have said how surprised they are that such a beautiful, young girl ran off with Ethan Thomas, presuming they have indeed run off together. Apparently he wasn't exactly God's gift to women kind."

"Well there's no accounting for taste is there Inspector? Charlotte wanted to finish with me because she was obviously deep into a relationship with him. I'm just glad she's out of my life, that's all. The two timing little hussy."

"And you've no idea where she, or they, may have gone, because the funny thing is there's no record of either of them having left the island?"

"None at all. Nor do I care. I know she came from Norfolk, maybe they've gone up there."

"Yes, it's a possibility. We know that's where she came from, the library service told us that much. Any idea where exactly?"

"No, although she did mention Norwich once or twice."

Stretch was about to continue but was interrupted by a young constable approaching the desk. "Excuse me Sir."

"What is it?" he demanded impatiently.

The policeman whispered something in his ear, being careful he wasn't overheard.

"Oh No!" Stretch's fist came down hard on the desktop, causing the various items on it to jump wildly. "Are you absolutely certain?"

"Yes Sir. The news has just come in."

"Damn it!" And he threw his pipe across the desk. "Where's my Sergeant?"

"He's out, Sir. They all are."

"Oh dear," said Valentine. "Bad news?"

"The agent from the pub. The one that was shot."

"What about him?"

"He's just been found hanging in the hospital toilets."

"Oh no! And he was your best prospect too."

"Don't they know how to guard prisoners properly these days?!" He shouted after the constable who was already making a hasty retreat. "Now the balloon will really go up."

"This other man's got to be found now. God alone knows what he's learnt. This is very, very serious."

"Do you think I hadn't thought of that?" The blue eyes were flashing with frustrated anger.

"However did he manage to hang himself in a toilet for heaven's sake?"

"Apparently he'd stolen a bed sheet, made an impromptu rope and strung himself up. Obviously as guilty as hell." The implications for the continued security of PLUTO were obvious, and, with more pressing matters taking precedence, Valentine was quickly dismissed.

"If there's anything I can do, I hope you'll let me know, Inspector."

"Thank you Lieutenant. If there is, you'll be the first to know." He gave Valentine a piercing stare. "We didn't quite finish our little chat, did we?" he said, "but there'll be other occasions. One day the truth behind all this will be known. Of that you can be sure. There always comes a day of reckoning."

"What are you suggesting? I'm not sure I like your tone."

"What am I suggesting?. Why nothing. I'm simply stating a well proven fact. Please stay on the island," he said, finally turning away. "Good morning, Lieutenant."

The search for the missing Nazi agent continued for the next few weeks as security was tightened to the maximum level, without interrupting the ongoing work, along all points of the fuel line and at both pumping station sites. Every point of exit around the entire island was watched day and night; every boat and pleasure craft searched; every creek and inlet guarded. A description of the man was circulated throughout the South of England, yet as everyone believed, if the man had managed to escape across to the mainland or Ireland, France or even the Channel Islands, then it was a lost cause. He'd slipped through the net.

With such an enormous use of precious manpower there was nothing for it but to call off the search. It was just as if he had disappeared into thin air, leaving the secrecy of the PLUTO project hanging precariously by the slimmest of threads. What did the man know? Was Berlin already in possession of the most important secret of the entire war? Should the D Day invasion plans proceed? Questions that kept the lights burning late in Downing Street, and questions that played heavily on Valentine's conscience. There was always the very strong possibility that the agent had radioed information prior to meeting his death.

Valentine himself was interviewed again by D.I. Stretch regarding the disappearance of Ethan Thomas and Charlotte Ross. The police, however, could produce nothing even remotely incriminating and the file, though never truly closed, was laid to one side as an unexplained riddle of war time England. Except in the sceptical mind of Detective Inspector George Stretch for whom the case remained wide open.

Chapter Seven

It was the second morning of the ongoing interview with the Reverend Valentine Gray at Newport Police Station. They had managed to secure the same interview room.

In his years on the force D.I. Preston had seen many a felon reduced to tears - some in repentance, others irked at being caught and tearful at the thought of a stretch behind bars. But, having sat through the second half of the Reverend's tale to learn that he had been the one who had buried Ethan Thomas, and to watch as the burden of guilt the man had carried for over forty years lift from his shoulders like a forgiven sin, was something he'd never witnessed before.

Talking it through had caused Gray to relive every moment, every painful circumstance just as he knew it would. Every emotion, every memory, every private and personal detail had come flooding back with a vengeance. The sights, the sounds, the smells. Moments, precious periods in a life no amount of years could ever erase. But now, it was all in the open. Now it was no longer buried, rotting like the ugly corpse of Ethan Thomas. Yes, there would be repercussions and consequences, possibly serious, yet no longer was it the crushing burden he'd never shared with any other living soul. Finally, he'd been liberated.

Eventually he was quiet and slumped back in the chair and looked at Preston.

There was no doubt now, in Preston's mind, that the vicar's story was true. The forensic report agreed that the man had died as a result of a knife to the chest, and there had been verification from the M.O.D. and the Island Library Service. No-one could fabricate a story like that. Why ever would they? A search for the original police records had revealed that they had been destroyed in a fire towards the latter days of the war, caused by a stray V2 flying bomb, but from what he'd heard and the extraordinarily passionate way the story had been related, left him with no uncertainty that he was looking at a truthful man.

"It's quite a tale, isn't it," said Valentine.

"But surely you haven't quite finished. Whatever happened to Charlotte? Do you know?"

"Oh yes, the postscript. Charlotte sailed for Venezuela on a ship called the Maracaibo Star bound for La Guaira. I know that she was safely put aboard and the ship left Southampton that night on the tide. And, I also know the ship arrived safely in La Guaira, but she wasn't on it. She'd vanished. Vanished into thin air."

"Don't tell me she didn't write."

"I'm sorry to say that is exactly what happened. She didn't write once. Not one single letter. As soon as practical after the end of the war I was so determined to find her that I journeyed to Venezuela myself. Lloyds of London told me the Maracaibo Star was originally registered in Argentina, but more than likely sailed under a flag, any flag of convenience during the war years and, as far as they could say, sailed out of La Guaira. Eventually I found the ship, but by then it had been sold off and decommissioned, if that's the correct term, and the Captain, who apparently was Brazilian, proved to be untraceable.

I contacted our Consulate there and they were very helpful and sympathetic, but you must remember this was immediately after the war and she was simply one of thousands of missing persons. It was like looking for the proverbial needle, but in a thousand haystacks." He sighed. "From that night in Newport to today, I haven't heard a single word of Martha Kowalski alias Charlotte Ross, which naturally can only make me believe that something happened to her. A beautiful, lonely woman on a ship full of men? I must have been crazy to agree to it. The other alternative is, of course, that I was told a complete pack of lies. She was a professional secret agent and somehow found her way back to Germany. The evidence does point in that direction. And yet,

I know she loved me. I know she did. She wouldn't have left me high and dry without a very good reason. But what, after all these years, I shall never know." He sighed once again, and sat up straight. "But now it's your turn to tell me something Inspector. Exactly where do I stand in the eyes of the law? I'm ready to face the music I assure you. Quite ready."

"Technically, yes Sir, you are an accessory after the fact," Preston broke to him. "But the war? Any lawyer would plead extreme mitigating circumstances. There isn't a court in the land that would convict you, foolish though you were. It never does to cover a wrong with another wrong, Sir. They both catch up with you in the end."

"So it would appear, Inspector. I had visions of being hauled off to prison in handcuffs."

"There's no danger of that. I'll have a word with my Superintendent, but I don't think you'll be breaking up rocks under the noonday sun just yet a while." He smiled for the first time.

"So what happens now?"

"Now, we've got to get a condensed version of all that you've told me down on paper, in the form of a statement, just the relevant details, D.C. Willard'll help you, which you will have to sign. And that, unless I'm much mistaken, will be the end of the matter."

"I see." This wasn't what he expected at all. "And Ethan's body?"

"When the morgue has released it and any loose ends, as it were, tied up, he'll be cremated."

"I thought as much. Now I wonder if you would be good enough to arrange something for me Inspector. Something that's been on my mind for some time."

"If I can."

"I buried Ethan Thomas once, in a very deplorable way, but now in my capacity as a clergyman I'd very much like to give the poor man a proper Christian burial. I think that's the best I can do. Would such a thing be possible, do you think?"

"I can't say definitely but I see no reason why not. I think it's a very decent gesture. But I'll have to come back to you on that."

"Good. And that's it, then?" His relief was unmistakable.

"Yes, that's it. You're free to go. We have your address and contact number and as I say, I'll be in touch."

The two men from different worlds and different times shook hands. Except for a written account of events it was all over.

When eventually that was completed, typed up and witnessed, Valentine soon found himself back at the hotel, packing ready for the return journey.

At the end of the working day, Inspector Preston called in on his step father. As expected there had been no improvement in the old man's condition.

"You must try and forget this unhealthy fixation with Gray," said Roy, after filling him in with developments. "This man's not a murderer."

"I tell you he is! - whatever he's told you it's all a very cleverly thought out - packet of deception, especially prepared - for the likes of you."

"Dad, really."

"I'm sorry Roy but - it's true. He's cunning and - clever. I remember he was back - then. D.C.S. Cartwright and I were - convinced he'd murdered both of them - and was involved with the - spy business. But we - had no proof at all."

"Well history has proved you wrong there. The German's had no idea about PLUTO or our invasion plans."

"Maybe, but on - the disappearance business - I know that a beautiful girl like she was - wouldn't run off with a - bloke like Thomas and - leave the handsome soldier - at home. It doesn't add up - one bit."

Ray sat on the bottom of the bed annoyed suddenly for feeling unsure. "What about the mother, Mrs. Thomas? Do you remember anything about her?"

"Only that she was very - fat and uneducated. - But poor woman, where was her - son? She was beside - herself. He'd just vanished. - She showed me a picture of him. - But looking back now, - and I've plenty of - time to think lying here day - in day out, Gray - was just playing with me. He - saunters in all dressed - up in his uniform and tells - me some cock and bull yarn - about breaking up with her. - All night they talked he - said. Ever known that?!"

Roy didn't respond.

"No. It's not normal - I tell you if she hadn't - shown up for work the next - day, I'd have arrested him - on suspicion of murder. He's -guilty Roy and you're letting - a guilty murderer, a double murderer - walk free. You're making a - terrible mistake."

"I wonder what really did happen to her?" he said, determined the old detective must be mistaken.

"Ha! I could tell you that."

"Martin?"

"Hallo Dad. You're back then. I did call."

"Yes, that was nice of you."

"I was concerned about you. Good time?"

"Er, yes. It was just something that had to be attended to. Long overdue."

"Church work was it?"

"Sort of."

"You're being unusually secretive. It's not every day you get involved with the cops."

"One day I'll tell you son, but not today, and certainly not over the telephone."

"But you're O.K?"

"Oh yes, quite well. Quite well. I might be going back again in a little while, just for the day."

On a bright June morning some weeks later, following a telephone call from Inspector Preston, Valentine journeyed down to the Island once again, this time to conduct a brief service for Ethan Thomas.

He was met again at Ryde Pierhead by Constable Willard and driven to the crematorium on the outskirts of Newport, where they met the Inspector. As far as it was known no family existed, so no mourners were present.

After a short word of remembrance, prayer and scripture reading, the coffin containing the remains of Ethan Thomas slowly disappeared through the red velvet curtains on route to it's final resting place. It was, without doubt, the most peculiar funeral service Valentine had ever conducted.

While they were walking slowly back to their vehicles across the crematorium car park, where mourners were already arriving for the next funeral service, Preston said something that took Valentine's breath away.

"There's something I haven't told you Reverend."

"Oh?"

"You remember you told me you were interviewed once or twice by a detective at the time when everyone was looking for the elusive spy."

"I remember."

"Detective Inspector Stretch was his name. George Stretch."

"Yes, I remember him well. He smoked a pipe incessantly."

"Well, he's my stepfather."

Valentine stopped dead. "Your stepfather?!" He repeated, clearly shocked. "Well, well. What a coincidence. And, is he..... ?" He asked cautiously, beginning to walk on.

"Yes he's still alive, but only just. It was the pipe smoking that's killing him. He's not expected to live very much longer."

"I am sorry to hear that. It's terrible to see one's loved ones suffer. But what a remarkable coincidence that you should be related to him and, obviously, following in his footsteps. What a small world. Please do remember me to him when you next see him."

They shook hands once again.

"Safe journey, Sir."

"Thank you, Inspector. Goodbye."

A little while later Valentine stepped aboard the ferry, just as Thomas's ashes were being scattered in the crematorium grounds. 'So that's the end of that,' he said, mentally drawing a line under the whole episode which had been awakened by the chance reading of an item in the newspaper.

That night Roy Preston couldn't sleep. Plagued by the look on Gray's face at the news of his connection with Stretch. Hearing his stepfather's voice sounding again its awful, gasping warning.

'You're making a terrible mistake - Roy. A terrible mistake.'

Chapter Eight

The years immediately following the war had been difficult for Valentine, as they had been for thousands of men and women returning home from the forces and trying to pick up their lives where they had left them.

Having witnessed so much unnecessary death and suffering, he was left questioning his very existence. There had to be more to life than merely a day to day struggle for survival. There had to be a purpose. That was when he turned to the Bible and among its pages discovered the peace and meaning he craved.

Within two years, following an unsuccessful period in industry, he'd been accepted at Oak Hill Bible College, in North London, to train for the ministry. That was where he'd met his wife, Ann.

Seated now at the breakfast table, using an antique silver meat skewer that had belonged to his grandfather, he slit open, one by one, the pile of Christmas cards that had dropped through the letter box. But, no matter how sincere the greetings he was unable to rid himself of a chasm-like emptiness. Ann had passed away on December 23rd and Valentine always treated the day as a day of remembrance.

As he read the year's batch of cards, his mind was at her bedside, caressing a weak, damp hand until it finally stopped moving altogether. Every year it was the same.

Hidden amongst the cards was a letter. The envelope was hand written and posted on the Isle of Wight. Aroused, he carefully opened it. It read:

'Dear Reverend Gray,

I'm sure a letter from me was the last thing you expected at Christmas as I haven't been in touch since our last meeting here during the summer. Since then there has been an interesting development in the case which I would very much like to discuss with you.

As you were good enough to come to the island last time I would like to reciprocate on this occasion and, unless I hear to the contrary, will be with you around midday on the 23rd when I look forward to meeting you again.

Yours sincerely,

D.I. Roy Preston

'Good heavens! Now what! Can't they let sleeping dogs lie'. He was angry suddenly. 'It's over for goodness sake. Over! With all the rapes and murders in the country hasn't he got anything better to do.' He stood up abruptly. It couldn't have arrived on a worse day. The chair toppled backwards and crashed on the floor, but he left it there and strode over to the window and stood gazing at, but not seeing, the heavy frost that had formed during the night.

A pair of sparrows on the frozen bird bath were pecking at the remains of some crusts he'd put out earlier. The scene helped calm him. 'All the way just to see me? It must be important. But whatever could it be? An interesting development?' He crossed the room, snatching up the letter. 'The 23rd! That's today! Good Lord, he'll be here at lunch time. The letter's dated the 18th. It must have been delayed in the Christmas post.' He lifted the chair and sat down again. 'Fancy coming all this way to see me just before Christmas.' He glanced at Ann's photograph. 'But why now?'

Shortly before two pm there was a knock at the door of High Park House.

"Inspector." The greeting was polite but cautious.

"Reverend Gray."

"How nice to see you again. Do come in."

"And you, Sir. I was concerned you might not have received my letter and I purposely didn't want to go into too much over the phone."

The six months or so since their last meeting hadn't changed the policeman at all. He still carried a burdened air and the lines on his features hadn't softened, yet as he entered the house and went through into the lounge there was a look about him of anticipation, excitement even, which certainly hadn't been there during the summer. The observation encouraged Valentine into thinking this surely wasn't the expression of a man bearing disagreeable news.

"I only received your letter this morning," began the vicar, "so this is rather a surprise."

"I hope it's not inconvenient."

"Not at all. But you must forgive me, I'm not being at all hospitable. Have you eaten?"

"Yes thanks, I had a sandwich on route. I'd love a coffee though.

"Good idea. Coffee for two. I won't be a moment."

The visitor sat back in the floral patterned armchair and stretched out his legs. It was good to get off the island sometimes and see something different, something new, and this wasn't a part of the country he was familiar with at all, but he liked what he'd seen so far. The wide open green, dotted with clusters of mature trees and surrounded by well maintained residences; the lights of the Christmas tree standing tall beside the village pond, twinkling in the afternoon glow as people, wrapped up well against the cold, hurried past clutching parcels and shopping ready for the holiday. Inside the house a coal fire gave the neat lounge a very pleasant feel. Taking in the photographs and pictures, the upright piano, books bulging from an overcrowded bookcase and a multitude of Christmas cards on every surface, all left him feeling that he'd done the right thing in coming. To say what he had to say over the telephone would have been wrong, cruel even. Yet, as he sat there listening to the clergyman rattling cups in the kitchen, he couldn't stop his mind from drifting back to his stepfather's bedside on the night he died, just fourteen days earlier, and to some of what the sick man gasped with his last remaining breath. 'Get Gray - lock him up.' Nothing would change the old man's unshakable conviction that Gray was a murderer, and, seeing the man again after a few months, Preston found he'd awakened doubts which he knew now to be ungrounded and yet, what was it about him? The house and contents were all that one might expect a middle class suburban vicar's home to be. But, was it all a front? A façade? Could there be lurking behind it a man with a secret? If he was so burdened with the Ethan Thomas incident as he said, why wait until the body was discovered before coming forward. Something, something intangible, wasn't quite what it should be.

Brushing the idea aside he took out a packet of cigarettes, but then thought better of it as the Reverend entered carrying a tray. They talked for a short while of life on the Island, and work, and family plans for Christmas, when Roy told him of his stepfather's recent death.

"I'm so sorry, Inspector. He was a clever man. Very good at his job I seem to remember. My deepest condolences to you and your family."

"Thank you" said Roy. "He'll be sorely missed."

As Roy sat back from placing his empty cup on the coffee table between them, Valentine knew he was about to explain the reason for his journey. This was no social visit.

"I'm sure you're wondering Reverend......"

"Please do call me Valentine."

"Thank you. I'm sure you're wondering, Valentine, exactly why I've come here to see you today?"

"Indeed I am. You said there had been an interesting development and yet I was under the impression it was all wrapped up, as they say."

The Inspector delayed for a moment. He knew what it was he wanted to say, having rehearsed it often enough on the way up, but now that the moment had arrived, the words refused to flow so easily.

"When," he began, cautiously. "When we parted I set Constable Willard a special assignment."

"Oh?"

"You told me, Martha Kowalski alias Charlotte Ross, never arrived in La Guaira."

"Which is exactly right. I went there myself to make quite certain she hadn't."

"That's right. But I'm now in the position to tell you categorically that she didn't sail to Venezuela at all."

"Whatever do you mean? I know she did." Mention of her name brought him to the edge of his seat and he carefully deposited his half empty cup on the table.

"Yes, she did sail on the Maracaibo Star bound for Venezuela. But a few days out the ship developed serious engine trouble and drifted for days unable to radio for assistance, because of a very real threat of German U-Boats picking up her signal which would have rendered the ship a sitting target."

"But what are you saying?"

"What I am saying is that the Maracaibo Star made an unscheduled stop before sailing on to La Guaira."

"But however did you discover this after all these years?"

"As I say, Constable Willard was given this assignment...... ."

"What assignment?!"

"I'll be honest with you Sir," and he paused. "I was very moved by your story. It went around and around in my head for days afterwards and going on what you told me of Charlotte, Martha, it didn't make sense that she would..... would drop you as it were, and what you said made perfect sense."

"And what was that?"

"That something must have happened to her."

"Yes, yes it must have done, it's the only logical explanation."

"So, as I say, I set Willard the task of finding out exactly what."

"Really? I don't know what to say."

"To be frank Sir, the young man deserves all the

credit. This isn't our usual way of working but, when I told him your story, he was very understanding and he really put himself out to try and discover the truth. Working nights and weekends, and often through interpreters and, because of time variations dealing with other countries, it meant that he had to put in a lot of unsociable hours."

"I had no idea." He was stunned.

"He's done a fantastic job. A real piece of first class detective work, so much so that I can now tell you what really did happen to Miss Ross after she left you that night."

"But however did he do it? I tried and tried but it got me nowhere."

"He managed to trace a member of the Maracaibo's crew."

"No!! Well, fancy that." This was amazing news and he slowly eased himself back in the chair, profoundly shocked. "But how very kind of Willard to do this for me. I really must ..... ."

"I haven't finished yet."

"Please continue, my goodness me, yes. I'm fascinated."

"So as I say, the ship drifted well off course, unable to radio for help, when she was sighted by an American cargo vessel, bound for Virginia, which took her in tow to the nearest port, which was Hamilton, Bermuda."

"Bermuda!!?

"Yes. The ship underwent repairs and then sailed on to La Guaira some days later."

"Well."

"The man, the crew member, distinctly remembers the very beautiful English lady, or......"

"Or a lady he took to be English."

"Right. And he told Willy that they definitely sailed from Hamilton without her."

"Without her?! Oh my Lord! ...so...so she got off and, and presumably stayed there!"

"That's right."

"Well. After all these years the truth is finally known."

"But." Now it was Roy's turn to sit on the edge of his seat."

"But what?"

"I think you should prepare yourself for another shock Sir."

"What do you mean?!" He sat up sharply.

"We have just learned from the police department on the island that Martha Kowalski, alias Charlotte Ross, is alive and still living in Bermuda."

Preston prepared himself for the man's reaction. His years of policing had taught him a great deal about human nature and he'd seen just about every response to shocking news in the book. Anger, disappointment, violence even. Yet, sitting opposite him in the warm and comfortable lounge, he began to think the vicar hadn't heard the bombshell at all.

The words hit Valentine hard and for a moment he couldn't assimilate what he'd heard. When he finally spoke his voice was that of a man with an inner reserve.

"How ironic. You weren't to know, Inspector, but today is the anniversary of my wife's death."

"I had no idea. I'm so sorry."

"That's alright, how could you know? It just struck me as ironic that on the day I remember the passing of my dear Ann, you should bring me news of.... well you know, don't you? Charlotte was my first love."

Unhurriedly, the clergyman eased himself out of the armchair and crossed to the window overlooking the green. It was already growing dark and a cold, damp mist was descending across the wide expanse of green, hanging over it like a curtain, creating an unreal picture. Though, some way off, it was still possible to see the lights of the Christmas tree reflecting on the undisturbed surface of the pond. As he watched, a pair of ducks circled above it for a moment before dropping down to an uncomfortable landing on the ice. Life was full of surprises. Some of them painful.

Eventually the clergyman spoke. "You're absolutely certain," he began, without turning from the window, "that she's still alive?"

"Yes certain. She goes under the name of Martha Kowalski."

"To me she'll never be anything but Charlotte."

The ducks were slipping and sliding on the ice anxious to be off and away.

"Is she married?"

"Not as far as we know."

"Then I will go to her," he said decisively, and swung round. "Immediately, in the new year." He went and stood with his back to the fire.

The policeman smiled. "I guessed that's what you'd say."

"I must know why she never contacted me, Inspector. I must know." He wiped his hand across his face. The news was beginning to have a delayed reaction. "I want to hear it from her own lips."

"Come and sit down, Sir. There are a number of things I must go over with you."

"There's more?!"

"Only details."

Valentine resumed his seat as Roy took out his cigarettes. "Do you mind?"

"No, no."

"I have already spoken to the police on the island and explained the situation, well, as much as they need to know, and that you would probably be going out there." He inhaled deeply, allowing the smoke to fill his senses.

"That was well anticipated."

"I put myself in your position. How could I not go? As I've said already, this isn't our usual modus operandi, but we do still have an interest and we, or more likely the Bermudian Police Authority acting on our behalf, will need to question her at some stage in the not too distant future."

"Question her?" he repeated. "Is that really necessary?"

"I'm afraid so."

"Is there any chance then that she could be arrested and tried?"

"After all these years there isn't a court in the land that would even give it a hearing, but we'd still like to try and tie up a few loose ends, as it were."

"I see." Valentine was clearly uncomfortable.

"I won't be accompanying you, but you will be met at the other end by a member of their C.I.D. who'll take you to Ma.....Charlotte's address."

"So does that mean they've spoken to her already?" The idea worried him.

"No, no. She hasn't been approached at all. But in future she may need to advise the police before leaving the island for any reason. How you may, or may not wish to proceed is entirely your own business". He removed a folded sheet of paper from his jacket pocket. "This is her address in Bermuda and the name of the man I spoke to, who'll sort out accommodation and point you in the right direction."

Valentine took the paper and read it through. How strange to see her name again after all this time, today especially, and he ran his finger over the letters. "The Lord giveth and the Lord taketh away. Blessed be the name of the Lord."

"I beg your pardon?"

"Nothing Inspector, nothing. Only the musings of an old man."

"Let me know exactly when you plan to go and I'll make sure there's someone there to meet you."

"I don't know what to say, you've been so kind. And Constable Willard as well. I'm deeply obliged, tell him, for all his hard work and perseverance. I shall write and thank him personally."

"I'll tell him, he'll be pleased." Preston made to go. "Which only leaves me to say it's been very nice to see you again Sir, and I wish you all the best in your future quest."

"Off so soon? Surely you'll stay and have some tea?"

"No, thanks all the same, I've a long drive home."

"And to think you came all this way just to bring me the news. What can I say? Thank you so much, Inspector."

"It's my pleasure," adding, "how could I possibly tell you over the phone?"

"How indeed?"

The two men moved out into the hall and Valentine stood on the step and watched as the Inspector walked to his car.

"God bless you Inspector," he called, "drive carefully. And a Merry Christmas."

"Thank you. God bless, er, you too." 'Why is it I can't feel at peace about you?' he thought and said, "let me know what happens."

"Oh yes I will, I promise."

Preston unlocked the car door, threw in his overcoat and climbed in after it, pleased with the way the meeting had gone. The engine burst into life and the wipers quickly dealt with the haze, and he turned, caught in the ochre glow of the street lamp, giving the scene a parting glance as he pulled away.

But to Valentine standing watching, suddenly the car became a boat; the street a river; the mist a chilling drizzle and he waved as Charlotte was taken from him forty years earlier. It felt as if he was standing on the wooden jetty once again. Rain coursing down his face, wind whipping at the folds of his coat. His heart being torn in two.

He stood there, quite still, arm outstretched, when suddenly he realised he wasn't waving farewell, but a greeting. This wasn't a parting, but a reunion.

"But why didn't she write? I must know. I must!"

Chapter Nine

For Valentine, aeroplanes and flying could never hold the same level of excitement that trains held for him. Not that he was, by any measure, an experienced air traveller, on the contrary. Other than a week in Majorca with Ann when Martin was eighteen, and a church conference in the Holy Land some years later, he'd never ventured further into the delights or the not so delightful aspects of flying. Yet, as the British Airways flight, direct from Heathrow eight hours earlier, positioned itself over the waters of the Atlantic ready to land on the tiny, fish-hook shape, coral island of Bermuda, he felt his pulse quicken as his ears popped, and he craned his neck to catch an initial glimpse of the place the brochures had described as paradise.

Christmas had been enjoyable with the family. As always, he'd spent Christmas day itself at Martin's, in Bishops Stortford, with his wife Susan and the twins. But all day his mind had been on other things, other events in another time, and he hadn't realised how strange his behaviour had become, until Martin approached him after lunch, when they were alone.

"So, what's on your mind, Dad? You've been somewhere else all day." Naturally he'd planned to tell his son he was going away, but thought it best to wait until Christmas was over.

"I'm sorry son. I hope I haven't spoiled things for everyone."

"Of course not, but I can see you're not quite yourself."

"I've a lot on my mind at the moment, that's all. Do you remember I went down to the Isle of Wight earlier in the year?"

"Yes."

"I was there for a while during the war, you know."

"I remember you telling me."

"Well, something cropped up while I was there last time and as a result contact has been made with an old friend."

"But that's good, isn't it? Meeting up with old comrades in arms."

"I don't know, that's just it."

"So, what's the problem?"

"Well you see," Valentine said cautiously, "the friend is a woman." He watched his son as he absorbed the news.

"Dad, if I read what you're saying correctly," he said, "that's just wonderful!" He leaned across and gave his father a friendly smack on the knee. "I'm so pleased for you."

"I know what you are thinking, but things aren't quite as - as one would wish."

"What's the problem? She's not married, is she?"

"No, of course not! No, she's not married, but she does live a long way away. In Bermuda, as a matter of fact."

"Bermuda! Well! So you are going to visit her then, and renew your acquaintance?"

"I plan to, yes. Very soon."

"Dad, I'm genuinely delighted for you. Delighted. I think it's great. And Susan will be overjoyed too, I know she will."

"Unfortunately, it's not quite as uncomplicated as it might be. And you're reading far too much into it."

"Oh go on. The course of true love and all that."

"Look," he said, beginning to regret telling him at all. "Let's just say I'm going to visit an old friend and leave it at that."

"As you wish. But whoever she is, she must be someone really special to get you to go all that way, and see if I'm not right. Once you get under the palm trees with the soft sand and a warm breeze. Ha! You wait! Just you wait and see."

Now, as the aircraft circled for its final approach, Valentine caught his first glimpse of variegated, turquoise waters, caressing powder-pink sands, and thought of the difficult letter he'd written, announcing his intended visit and the surprising reply under the circumstances.

The transatlantic airliner taxied to a halt alongside a cluster of airport buildings and the passengers began to alight, stepping down into the brilliant mid afternoon sunlight, pleased to be free of the confines of the cabin and breathe clean, sweet smelling, tropical air. Valentine followed the line of fellow travellers as they moved inside and collected their luggage, passing quickly through Custom and Immigration Control and out into the bustling reception area for new arrivals.

"Reverend Gray?"

"Yes?" Startled, he looked to see who had called his name, and a tall, dark man with a bushy moustache and closely cropped hair smiled down at him. He was wearing Bermuda shorts, knee length socks, topped off with a traditional navy blue blazer.

"D.S. Outerbridge. How do you do?" he shook the vicar's hand with a strong, firm grip.

"You policemen never fail to amaze me. How could you possibly spot me amongst all these people?"

The man laughed and gave the visitor a friendly pat on the back. "Once the English vicar, always the English vicar, Sir."

"Oh. That obvious am I?"

"I'm afraid so."

"Someone else said that to me once."

The man picked up Valentine's suitcase and they moved outside in the direction of the car park.

"D.I. Preston on the White Island has asked me to take care of you."

"The White Island, yes." The name sounded rather nice, exotic. "It's very kind of you to bother."

"No problem. I've booked you in at the Palm Reef; you'll have a good view of Hamilton Harbour from there. I thought we'd get you checked in and then I'll take you to Martha Kowalski's address."

How strange to hear her name used in such a matter of fact way.

"I greatly appreciate you taking the time out of your busy day to come and meet me like this, but I've decided to call on her tomorrow morning. I can always take a taxi."

"Just as you wish, Sir. This is Bermuda, there's no rush."

The leisurely drive from the airport at one end of the island into the centre along winding, narrow roads was like taking a leap back in time, and had it not been for the huge differences in the fauna and flora the clergyman could well have been back on the Isle of Wight during the forties. Even though it was early in the year, and still winter, it was quite warm, forcing him to loosen his tie, and by the time they pulled into the hotel's forecourt he'd definitely decided not to call on Charlotte until the following morning.

Valentine carefully replaced the receiver to the bedside telephone. His heart was still thumping against the wall of his chest and his breathing came in short bursts. He remained sitting quietly on the edge of bed until the tightness in his chest had subsided.

How was it possible that she could have this effect on him after forty years? The moment she'd said hello his head had started to spin. Her voice hadn't changed at all; matured perhaps, but still unmistakably Charlotte, and sitting there, his mind played and replayed, like a gramophone record stuck in a groove, all the words he'd just heard.

'Your letter was such a shock. I thought you were dead. I wrote a thousand times. After all these years. It's so strange to hear your voice again. We've so much to talk about. A lifetime to catch up on. I can't believe you're here on the island.' She had sounded thick with emotion.

He checked the small alarm clock. One hour and he'd see her face to face. How would she handle the news of his marriage or the discovery of Ethan Thomas? 'A thousand letters' she'd said. It's obvious now what happened. He lowered his head in silent prayer.

It was mid morning when the taxi pulled off Middle Road and turned into Sousa Estate. This part of Devonshire Parish was built up with varying styles of comfortable middle-class dwellings, and after weaving their way around the narrow labyrinth of roadways, they came to a halt at the end of a cul-de-sac. The driver pointed to a house on his right.

"There you are, Mister Sir. Valley View," the young man was cheerful enough. "You want I should pick you up again?" he asked, looking in the rear view mirror.

"I don't know. If I do, I'll call you."

"I'm cool."

Valentine paid the man with unfamiliar dollars and climbed out, watching as the car reversed, feeling strangely isolated and vulnerable, when he suddenly realised he'd come empty handed. A little gift, flowers, anything! But it was too late now. How careless. Not a good start.

It was a pleasant looking, pink washed, single storey house on a slight incline, fronted by a small lawn and surrounded by flowering bushes and shrubs. How beautiful it must be during the summer if it looked so colourful at this time of year, with the sunlight dancing off copious, different coloured flowers, most of which he'd never seen before. To have brought more flowers would have been a complete waste.

He stepped up to the door, when a vivid red bird sitting atop the white roof, singing for all its worth, caught his eye, and he felt his spirits lift. He took a deep breath filled with the heady, blended scents of the garden, and rang the bell.

The door opened immediately.

"Valentine!"

The sight of her standing framed in the doorway was like suddenly turning the clock back, except the years hadn't been kind. She was wearing an attractive, pink dress, leaving him in no doubt that she'd retained her figure, but the once raven hair had given way to the purest white, and it had been cut short, very short. Those dusty black eyes that could have stopped a man's heart with a single flash, even though they spoke a silent greeting now, had lost their fire and were ringed by half-moons making them appear even darker still.

"I'm, I'm sorry I'm late." He'd been planning what his opening gambit would be but now as he stood there, his mind was a blank. Just the sight of her after so many years and he was as tongue-tied as on their first meeting.

"But you're not late. Besides, I've waited almost forty years. A few minutes longer won't have made any difference." As soon as she'd finished she could have bitten her tongue; it was hardly the ideal welcome, but then didn't he deserve it. "Please do come in," she followed quickly, "I saw you arrive from the window." Her remark hit home. Perhaps this was going to be even more difficult than he'd envisaged. "I remember you used to look out for me in Newport."

"Yes, I remember," she told him, somewhat offhandedly.

He crossed the threshold and she quietly closed the door behind him and they stood together in the narrow hallway. Brilliant light, beaming down from a window set in the roof, showed that she was well tanned from years of living in the sun, but deep strokes around her mouth and brow added on far more years than had actually elapsed. Yet even so, for her age, she was still a strikingly beautiful, poised woman and he bent and lightly kissed her on both cheeks. She made no objection. Just a touch, and the intervening years vanished beneath a surge of memories.

"It's been a long time, Charlotte." It felt strange to be so close again.

"Yes it has. But you haven't changed you know," she sounded nervous suddenly. "Not a bit."

"Ha! I don't believe that."

"It's true. Silly, but somehow I imagined you still in uniform."

"Do you know, I still have my old uniform. Full of moths now, of course, but I just couldn't throw it away."

"Too many memories, perhaps?" She was keeping her distance.

"Yes, too many memories."

"Come through into the conservatory. It's nice,

overlooking the garden." Years of living in a privileged expat society had left their mark, creating in her a very English foreigner. As she led the way through the bright little house, their footsteps echoing on the rich, dark, Bermudan cedar flooring, and out into a colonial style conservatory, filled with plants and cane furniture, Valentine realised he found the subtle change in her most becoming.

"It gets extremely hot in here during the summer months, but at this time of year it's really very pleasant." She sat down, indicating an armchair the other side of a low table between them, which was already prepared with a jug and glasses. "There's a sliding roof panel which I draw across when it gets hot, otherwise all the plants wither."

"It's very pleasant, as you say."

"You're not too hot, are you? I know what it's like when you first arrive."

"No, I'm just fine."

"Lemonade?"

"Thank you." He watched as, with an unsteady hand, she filled two tall glasses. "It's so good to see you again, Charlotte," he told her gently.

"I call myself Martha these days. I have done ever since I arrived here. It is my name after all."

"To me you'll never be anything but Charlotte."

"Well," she glanced up at him, catching his eye, but then quickly looked away. "You'll have to get used..... ." The jug slipped in her hand suddenly, spilling lemonade over the table simultaneously as she let out a stifled wail of a sound, just managing to drop the glass jug on the table before burying her face in her hands and breaking into distressing, pitiful sobs. Her whole body shaking with grief. With forty years of pent-up hurt and anguish.

He reached out and put a hand on her arm, not knowing what to say, but she shook him away, the same time as something fell to the floor. He picked it up, realising at once what it was, and slumped back in the cane chair.

Charlotte composed herself sufficiently enough to speak. But when she did, her voice was hard and full of bitterness. "Enough of this ridiculous pretence! Just tell me one thing. Why didn't you write? I must have written you a thousand letters. Each one more pleading than the last. But they all came back. Every single one. You hadn't even the decency to open them!"

"But, Charlotte."

"Then suddenly, out of the blue, you decide to write and nearly give me a heart attack, and you breeze back into my life as if it was forty years ago and nothing's changed. You cruel, heartless bastard! Well, let me tell you, everything's changed. I've changed. I don't know why I ever agreed to see you again. I must have been crazy. I thought I was over you, more fool me. You ruined my life. Do you hear me? Ruined it!"

"Charlotte! Listen to me. Please."

"Well? What lies are you going to fill me with

this time?" She was again on the point of tears, and dabbed nervously at the corners of her eyes with a handkerchief.

"Charlotte," he spoke her name softly. "I never received one of your letters. Not one."

She looked him directly in the face.

"Yes, it's true," he said. "As God is my judge, I never received a single letter."

"But I wrote via Roger Merryfield's address, just as we arranged. Hundreds of times."

"But Roger died."

"What?!" The implications were obvious. "When?"

"Three weeks after the D Day landings."

"Oh no!" The truth sucked at her breath. "So.....
."

"Yes. The silly fool was demonstrating his prowess on a motorbike he'd found in Normandy, when the brakes failed and he went straight into a brick wall. He was killed outright."

"Oh, that's terrible."

"I contacted his father, who himself was a widower, but the poor chap was so distraught at losing his only son, he kept telling me there were no letters when obviously there were, until, in the end, he became so annoyed he told me to clear off and leave him alone."

"I can't believe I'm hearing this." She shook her head in utter disbelief. "Dear Lord, tell me this isn't true."

"I'm afraid it is. At the time I naturally thought you hadn't written at all."

"But how could you ever think that? You knew what you meant to me."

"I didn't know what to believe. I had no idea where you were or even if you were still alive. I even went to Venezuela after the war looking for you."

"You did? Oh! Are we going to go on suffering the consequences of war for ever?"

"I've gone over this a million times in my mind, but I can only think Mr Merryfield made arrangements with the Post Office that all Roger's mail should be returned to sender and forgot to tell me. I learnt he died himself a few years later."

"But why ever stop his son's mail?"

"I've no idea. People do strange things following a particularly painful bereavement, sometimes."

"Oh Valentine, I'm so sorry for what I said to you just now." This time it was she who reached out to him, and he took hold of her offered hand. "But, you must see my position."

"Of course I do, now I know the truth."

"I thought you had either been killed or had stopped loving me. Found someone else. I was..... well." And she sighed deeply at remembrance of the time.

"We've a lot to talk about, Charlotte."

"I've a lot to tell you too, believe me. But I kept all the returned letters, every one of them. I even wrote to the Royal Engineers to see if they knew what had happened to you, but they couldn't be definite, only that they had no record of a death under that name. Which was worse, from my point of view."

"Why?"

"Because then I knew for certain you'd stopped loving me."

"Oh dear," he squeezed her hand gently. "Oh dear. We have so much to talk about."

"I even thought of journeying to the U.K. myself, but what would have been the point if you didn't love me. Presuming I was to find you in the first place of course. But, the big question is, why now? Why, and how, have you suddenly appeared after all these years?"

"Of course, you don't know."

"Don't know what? What is it? Tell me."

He looked down at what he'd been clutching in his hand all this time. "Here, this is yours."

"Where did you find it?"

"It was on the floor."

"Do you recognise it?"

"How could I forget?"

"It's been my most treasured possession. All I had to remind me of the love of my life. There's been no-one else you know. I could have married a number of times, there was never a shortage of suitors."

"I can well imagine."

For the first time since his arrival, she gave him a genuine smile from deep within. "But I couldn't, I just couldn't." She pinned the silver brooch back onto her dress. "I used to bury myself in my work, and besides, as soon as they knew about ..... ."

"About what?"

"It doesn't matter. Some other time. There was one particular man I very nearly married, quite high up in the government he was. A very nice, attentive, caring sort. We even planned a wedding date, but I had to say no because I didn't love him the way I loved you. I'd tasted real love and I knew that everything else would just have been a shadow. It would never have worked. He was very upset."

"I can well imagine he was."

"Now tell me, what is it I don't know? No more shocking news, please. I'm not sure I could handle any more in one day."

"Oh dear. There's no gentle way to say this. It's Ethan Thomas."

Just mention of the name made her gasp and sit bolt upright. "What about him?!"

"They found him."

"Oh no!" And she listened intently as he brought her up to date with events many thousands of miles away on the Isle of Wight.

"Have the police contacted you at all?"

"The police? No. Why ever should they?"

"They will do, I'm afraid. I gave them the story back in England, not knowing, of course, that you were still alive, but now that they know where you are, they are bound, at least, to question you."

"For something that happened all those years ago? And in war time?"

"I think you should prepare yourself, anyway. You may even find they'll restrict your movements."

"Whatever do you mean?"

"On and off the island, I meant."

"Well, I certainly won't be going anywhere for a while, so it doesn't matter. As if I haven't got enough to worry about already."

"What sort of worries?"

"Nothing. It will keep."

They talked for the remainder of the day, pausing only for lunch, when Charlotte had to admit that nothing was prepared. So an unpretentious salad appeared along with a couple of glasses of wine, as they continued to exchange almost forty years of news.

"I notice you still wear your adopted mother's ring."

"I've never taken it off," she said, giving it a turn. "It's wearing thin now, but I still feel I let them down, even after all this time."

"The chances are they were part of the holocaust even before you left Germany."

"I think, deep in my heart, that's what I've always known."

"It might be possible to find out. If you'd like me to, that is?"

"I think so, yes."

"I'll see what I can do. Let me have their details sometime."

He went on to tell of the hunt for the spy, and the aftermath of her disappearance coinciding with that of Ethan Thomas, and the subsequent police investigation which eventually arrived at the conclusion he'd hoped for, in that they'd run off together.

"Poor Mrs. Thomas. How did she take it?"

"I don't know. I purposely stayed clear, playing the part of the jilted boyfriend."

"The whole thing was terrible, wicked. I still have nightmares about it."

"I'm afraid war makes people do things they wouldn't normally dream of."

"Did they ever find the other man?"

"No," he lied, believing it best that she didn't know he'd killed the man himself. "After a while the search was called off." Talk of one body was more than enough.

"So with 'Mercury' dead that was the end of it?"

"Yes, and he clearly hadn't talked, so as you say, that was the end of it all. That chapter, anyway."

Charlotte spoke of the terrible storm that hit the Maracaibo Star soon after leaving Southampton, and how they had battled for days with a defective engine which eventually died, leaving them to the mercy of the wind and waves and the fear of discovery by German U-Boats.

"I've never been so terrified in all my life. The rusty old ship was being thrown around like a toy, creaking and groaning like it was about to break up. The wind was so strong, it felt as if it would rip the clothes off your back, with spray as fierce as nails. I was told to lock myself in my cabin, but even there in the bunk I had to hang on for dear life. By night we weren't allowed to show a light at all, and by day, even though we were sailing under a flag of neutrality, we just lived on our nerves. The Captain was petrified of being discovered by a rogue submarine. I remember thinking how strange it was to be sitting at sea, a helpless target waiting to be shot at by my own countrymen. I'm no mariner, but it was obvious what a dangerous position we were in. Very little sleep, unable to keep any food down, scouring the horizon day after day, and then on top of that I was nursing a broken heart having just said goodbye to you. The whole experience was one horrible, terrible nightmare. I remember one poor crew member had a ghastly accident and actually died. He was buried at sea later, when it calmed down. I can still picture the Captain and crew standing around together on deck as the canvas bag slipped silently over the side. It could have happened to any one of us."

"However could I have put you through such misery?" he said, feeling the full force of her recollections, as if the storm had blown itself out only yesterday.

"I knew you did it for my own good. They shot spies back then, remember. Even reluctant ones. But then, after a few days, a friendly ship was sighted and we discovered what it was to feel the joy of being rescued." She told of how they were towed to into Hamilton dockyard and her immediate love affair with the island and the snap decision to stay.

"At that time although my papers were false they were good enough to satisfy the authorities, who helped get me established with accommodation and such like, desperate as they were for teachers with most of the men away at war." She continued, that there followed a number of moves over the years to various schools around the island, until finally being offered the position of Headmistress at an all girls school, which she held until retiring quite recently. She pointed to a photograph of the school signed by members of staff.

For Valentine's part, he told her of the brief article in the newspaper and the string of extraordinary events, and the sterling efforts of a young policeman on the Isle of Wight, which eventually led him to Bermuda. He relived the remainder of his war years, his promotion to Captain, and the period of life before his move into the ministry. Then he spoke of his marriage, and Martin, and their happy life together until Ann was struck with cancer. All the while, Charlotte sat listening to his every word, building a picture of a life which the hand of fate and the passage of time had denied her.

The shadows began to lengthen and Valentine looked at his watch. "Gosh, it's gone five o'clock, I must be thinking about telephoning for a taxi."

"Before you do," she hadn't finished with him. "I must say this," and paused, before continuing, "today hasn't turned out quite the way I expected Valentine, and I've come to a decision whilst you've been talking."

"Oh dear. Is it something I want to hear?" He was half joking, but the atmosphere between them changed, suddenly becoming tense.

"I'll ask you that when I've finished."

"Alright."

"There's something I haven't told you," she automatically lifted her chin in a resilient gesture. "There's no easy way to say this, but I have a brain tumour."

"Oh Charlotte!" It was the cruellest blow of all.

"That's why I retired a little earlier than perhaps I might otherwise have done."

"I am so sorry."

"I'm due to have an operation in a little under a month's time, that's why I agreed to see you this afternoon. I was going to give you a piece of my mind, but, as it is, well, everything's different now, isn't it?"

"It certainly is."

"The op' naturally isn't without risk, and so I've decided I would very much like to spend the interim time with you. Would..... that..... Would that be possible? Could you conceivably stay a whole month? You're retired too, you told me."

Valentine felt as if he'd received a powerful punch to the solar plexus. The conservatory was swimming.

"I don't have the faith you obviously have," she continued, her voice falling to little more than a whisper as her head bowed. "But I feel as if God in his divine mercy has looked down on my years of heartache, and in what may well be my last few remaining weeks, is allowing me a brief glimpse of what life might have been had we ever married. And, for that I thank Him from the bottom of my heart."

Valentine awkwardly eased himself up and out of the low cane armchair and decisively pushed the little table between them aside. He lowered himself to the ground, oblivious to the shooting pain in his knees, until he was kneeling directly in front of Charlotte.

"What on earth are you doing?!"

He took both her hands in his, and kissed the palms one at a time, then cupped them gently together. "Martha Kowalski, alias Charlotte Ross, or whatever your name is." His voice was shaky. "I vowed I'd marry you, one rainy night in England,

and you promised you'd marry me. Do you remember?"

"Yes." Her reply was only just audible.

"Well, I'm sorry I've been a long while in fulfilling that vow, and I know I'm on the wrong side of sixty-five, but God willing I'm good for a few more years yet."

"Oh, Valentine."

"Charlotte, my darling Charlotte, would you do me the honour of becoming my wife?"

For answer she gave him a smile. Her face suddenly alive with an inner radiant glow of happiness.

"Yes I will, Valentine. I will, a thousand times yes. But there's something I must tell you first." And still holding his hands as if her announcement might suddenly pluck them away, she turned. "You see my retirement photograph on the wall?"

"Yes?"

"Tell me what you see underneath it."

"Another photograph," he answered, puzzled, "of a young man in a graduation gown."

"Look at me," she told him. She put her hand to his face in a loving manner. "Valentine, that handsome young man is your son. Our son."

Chapter Ten

It was the dogs that woke her. Deep within the recesses of her mind she heard them barking far away. It wasn't the lonely cry of stray mongrels one might expect to hear at night. But aggressive snarling and snapping that grew closer as sleep subsided and reality returned.

The barking continued to build and was accompanied by voices. Men's voices. They weren't the ordinary voices of men returning from a night's drinking, but determined voices thick with demanding shouts of command. They were joined by the sound of motor engines. Heavy, powerful engines, the sort used by large trucks. Then, dominant suddenly over all, came the unmistakable tramp of infantry marching in unison over the cobbled, stone streets.

Martha turned over and switched on the bedside lamp. It was only half past two. Still not fully awake, she sat up and realised she was shivering. But why? It was September and not at all cold, when suddenly she let out a cry. She was shivering with fear. Something was terribly wrong and all the while the noises grew louder and closer and more menacing.

She slipped out of bed, putting on her dressing gown and slippers and went to the window of the apartment, being careful to move the curtain aside only as much as absolutely necessary, afraid of what she might see. But there was no mistake. Even by the dim light of the street lamps it was still possible to make out, further along the narrow street, a large number of troops gathering in ranks, with important looking officers strutting about, shouting orders, the light catching the brass buttons of their uniforms. They were supported by a line of covered trucks and a pack of Alsatians, all pulling on their chains, snarling and barking at anything that moved.

Martha felt a cold shiver run down her spine and was about to close the curtain when she noticed lights at other windows across the street, with figures looking equally fearful. She snapped the curtain tightly closed as the door opened and a short, plump woman, in her mid sixties, with dark hair and a trustworthy face, wearing a grey housecoat over her nightdress, entered.

"What is it Mama?!" cried Martha. "What's happening?!"

"Come away from the window," the woman's voice was firm and steady, belying how she felt within. "Whatever's happening it doesn't concern us."

"But what's it all about? There's so much noise." The two women embraced. Martha was taller than her adoptive mother and, over the top of her head she saw the man she'd only ever known as father, leave his room across the hallway. He was carrying a shot gun.

"Papa?!" she queried, breaking away, "whatever are you doing?"

The man turned. He was of average height and build, yet completely void of hair on his head.

"I have a right to protect my family," he told her.

"No, Aniol," cried Malkah. "No good will come of it."

A whistle sounded from down in the street and for a second everything hung in a pregnant stillness.

"Achtung!! Achtung!!" A cold and authoritative metallic voice suddenly broke the silence, booming out from a loudspeaker. "By order of the High Command, all Jews are to leave their homes at once to be re-housed in another area. You have ten minutes to pack one suitcase per person. This directive also applies to the elderly and infirm. No-one is excused. No furniture is permitted under any circumstances, all your needs will be met in your new homes. Pets must remain, they will be cared for. I repeat, ten minutes, when all residents must assemble in the street for processing. Anyone resisting or caught hiding will be considered an enemy of the Reich, and shot! Heil Hitler."

Immediately there followed sounds of soldiers running over cobblestones accompanied by shouts and cries, as they forced their way into buildings along both sides of the street. The dogs were aggravated even further and began to bark uncontrollably, working themselves into a frenzy, as doors were broken open and troops swiftly networked out onto the many different levels of apartments, in what had, at one time, been a respectable quarter of Berlin's suburbia.

"Dear God in heaven!" Malkah stifled a cry. "It's started."

"What's started Mama?! What's it all about?!"

"I've been waiting for this."

"But where are they taking us?"

"We must all do exactly as we're told," Malkah announced, firmly taking the lead.

"But what new homes?"

"I don't know, Martha. But I do know that to oppose them would be an act of gross foolishness," and she turned to her husband who looked foolish himself dressed in pyjamas, a shotgun ready at an obtuse angle. Thirty years earlier then yes, maybe they would have put up a fight. But not now. Resistance would be suicidal. "I admire your bravery my dear," she told him, "but this isn't the time for heroics. Somehow I think there'll be time enough for that later."

"I don't see why I shouldn't.... !" But he cut himself short. He knew his wife was right and reluctantly rested the weapon across the top of a chest of drawers and moved back into the bedroom to start packing. "And don't fill your case with books," she called. "Take sensible clothes and plenty of underwear." But he had already decided what was going in his suitcase. An insurance policy, some cash, passports and a treasured copy of the Torah wrapped in a prayer shawl, along with his Capel. It was a question of priorities he convinced himself, and the word of God, along with a little self insulation would always come before any plans the Führer may harbour for the new Germany's Jewish population.

Knowing the military would be true to their ten minute ruling, the woman hurried Martha into action. "Come along now. This is no way for a school teacher to behave."

Mention of her responsibilities brought the girl to her senses and she pulled a suitcase down from the wardrobe. "But whatever's going to happen to us?"

"I don't know, but we must do our best not to upset them. Are you alright now?"

"Yes"

"Be quick then. I'll go and pack, too."

Minutes passed, when suddenly the door of their apartment burst open and two young soldiers rushed in, like a tidal wave, brandishing rifles with fixed bayonets before them. "Schnell! Schnell! Everybody out. Quick! Quick!!"

The terrified occupants rushed to see what was happening, then just as quickly turned back to finish getting ready. There were only precious seconds remaining.

The two men immediately proceeded to pass through the flat on an indiscriminate tour of destruction. Running their rifles along shelves, wiping them clear of clocks, books, whatever stood in the way. Kicking over furniture, smashing mirrors, stabbing upholstery with their bayonets, until, within a few moments, the family home was reduced to an unrecognisable shambles.

One of the soldiers marched into Martha's room just as she finished dressing. "Outside, Jew!" he yelled. "Quick!"

"How dare you just walk into a lady's bedroom!" It was the look of contempt on the man's face that made Martha's blood boil. "Just who do you think you are?!"

For a second he felt shocked and didn't know how to respond.

"Well, don't just stand there like an imbecile. Get out and let me finish dressing." He was on the point of turning when his masculinity took over and he strode over to the girl and struck her across the face with a bare hand. "You filthy Jew! How dare you talk to a soldier of the glorious Third Reich like that!"

The blow knocked Martha against the wall and she could taste blood in her mouth, but she tossed her head defiantly.

"Makes you feel good, does it?! Hitting defenceless women?!"

His companion meanwhile had rounded up Malkah and Aniol and was goading them at the point of his bayonet into the hall, oblivious to their cries. They were dressed for travelling; Malkah unable to stifle a moan of despair at the sight of her ravaged home. But the whole ordeal had left her husband confused and he looked bewildered beneath the rim of his homburg. All three now stood and watched as events unfolded.

"Oh, so you like a bit of rough do you!" The soldier was still in Martha's room. "Well I'll show you rough!" He brought the butt of his rifle down catching Martha on the side of the head, sending her reeling across the room, ending up sprawled across the bed, unconscious.

"No!!" screamed Malkah, lurching forward, fear suddenly bulging in her eyes.

"Shut up or you'll get the same!" Her guard dragged her sharply back. The soldier in Martha's room meanwhile had unbuttoned his tunic and was twisting her senseless body around, dragging it forward until her legs dangled over the edge of the bed.

"No! No!" pleaded Malkah. "Please no! Have mercy!"

His wife's dreadful cries awakened something in Aniol, and he saw his opportunity and made a grab for the shotgun, still resting on the chest of drawers beside them, in the hallway. But the young man was too quick and as the old man's hand stretched across the wooden surface, he brought his bayonet down on it, pinning it to the hardwood with a sickening thud.

The professor let out a terrible cry, collapsing to his knees, his hand still riveted to the chest-top, blood already oozing out onto the polished surface.

"What have they done to you?!" screamed Malkah. "Oh you silly old, brave fool." She dabbed as best she could with a handkerchief at the open wound, left stark and gaping as the soldier yanked the bayonet free. ""Serves you right! Now get outside. Both of you! Schnell!" He hauled the old man to his feet, still clutching his hand and quietly moaning, and pushed him roughly down the hall. "You too old woman!"

Malkah was torn between helping her husband and leaving Martha, when an immaculately dressed Major walked in as casually as one might stroll into a restaurant for a late supper.

"What is all this commotion?" He spoke mildly. But it was a question to which he neither wanted, nor expected, an answer. The soldier snapped sharply to attention. "It'll give me a headache for certain." It took him only a matter of seconds to absorb the scene. "You". he addressed the professor. "Where is your suitcase? You'll need it, you know. Woman," he said, moving down the hall. "Outside. Are these yours?" He kicked one of a pair of leather suitcases.

"Yes Sir," Malkah told him, and was about to speak further but didn't get the chance. "Take them both downstairs," he ordered the soldier. "Now."

"Herr Major."

"And what have we here?" The soldier in Martha's room had re-buttoned his uniform and was standing at the foot of the bed just as she was coming round, rubbing the side of her head and groaning.

"This Jewess was putting up a fight, Herr Major, and I..."

"You want to be very careful young man. You can catch a lot of nasty diseases from them, you know." He looked down at the body on the bed, realising immediately what a stunningly beautiful girl she was. Indicating a chair that had fallen over, said. "Pick it up."

"Herr Major."

"Did you have her?" he asked coolly,

"Nein, Herr Major."

"Join the others downstairs."

"Ja, Herr Major. Heil Hitler."

When the soldiers' footsteps had left them alone, he repositioned the chair and sat down, crossing his legs, watching as the girl recovered herself.

"It was very foolish of you to put up a fight," he informed her, eventually. "I presume that's what took place?" His voice was cultured, cold, as if the night's drama was nothing more than a scene in a low budget show.

"I didn't like his attitude." She knew she had nothing to lose.

He waved his hand dismissively. "Conscript riff-raff. What can you expect?"

"We're still human beings, Jews or not."

He inclined his head, combining it with a twist of the lips in a mocking grin. "What is your name?" he asked.

"Martha Kowalski," she told him, still feeling dizzy and rubbing her head.

"And what does Martha Kowalski do when not upsetting high-spirited young soldiers?"

"I teach languages."

"Do you indeed. I'm impressed. May I?" Without waiting for her consent, withdrew an elegant gold cigarette case and lighter and in a well rehearsed exhibition, lit a cigarette, sending the smoke spiralling lazily upwards.

"And which languages does Martha Kowalski teach?"

"Polish, English and French."

"Brains, as well as beauty."

"The man you just sent downstairs used to be a professor of languages at the university. He taught me well."

"The old man?"

"Yes, the old man."

"Which only proves appearances can be deceptive."

It was like listening to the voice of a viper.

"So tell me why Martha Kowalski isn't wearing the yellow Star of David the Jew King, on her coat as required by law, unlike her obedient parents?"

"Gentiles don't have to wear a star."

He took a long and deliberate drag on the cigarette, exhaling the ice blue smoke through his nostrils. "Please don't play games or insult my intelligence. You know that and I know that. I asked you why you aren't wearing one."

"I told you. Gentiles don't have to. And I'm a Gentile."

"You're full of surprises, Martha Kowalski. Your papers," he said sharply. "Show me your identity papers."

As Martha obediently eased herself up and fetched her handbag, he removed his peaked hat, placing it on the bed, revealing a head of blonde, cropped hair. He was pure Aryan stock, the product of a bloodline dating back generations. Blue, piercing, calculating eyes, a sharp chiselled nose and dimpled chin. He ran an intelligent, quick glance over her paperwork.

"Sit." He watched as Martha lowered herself onto the disordered bed, the mixed sounds of dogs, soldiers and terrified residents rising into the still room and filling her with apprehension of what the couple must be enduring.

"So, explain to me how, why, you, a Gentile, live here. And," he added, "speak English. Let me hear how good you are."

"And, how would you know how good I am?" She fired back quickly, instantly switching from German.

"I myself lived in England some years ago."

"As you say, appearances can be deceptive."

"Answer zer question."

Martha's head still hurt, and she couldn't understand why the man was so interested in her, but at least he hadn't knocked her about.

"The couple, they're not my real parents." The noise outside the window had risen abruptly to sounds of mass panic. "Will they be alright? What's happening to them?"

"Zer sooner we finish zis conversation, zer sooner we'll find out. Proceed." His pronunciation certainly did not mirror the standard of Martha's.

"My real parents were both killed in a road accident when I was small. Malkah and Aniol took me in as their own daughter and I've been with them ever since. They mean the world to me. They're the only family I have."

"And your parents were not Jews?"

"No. Neither of them."

"I see. And yet you choose to identify with zer couple?"

"I told you, they're my family. They've been both mother and father to me. I love them."

"There's just you? No brothers or sisters?"

"Only my brother. Jan."

"Where is he?"

"Warsaw. He's a dentist."

"That must be difficult at the moment."

"I haven't heard from him for some time."

The Major thought for a moment, flicking ash onto the floor. "Go over to zer window."

"But why?"

Without responding he stood up, dropping the cigarette and stubbing it flat beneath his heel. "Let me help you," and he took Martha's elbow in a new found show of respect, helping her to her feet and moving towards the window, when she caught the sickening scents of nicotine and Eau de Cologne.

"Your accent is very good, you know. In fact it's almost perfect."

"I was well taught," she answered defiantly. The Major had his hands on the curtains but suddenly, instead of drawing them open, he pulled hard sending the curtains, runners and pelmet all crashing to the floor in a cloud of dust. Martha gave a scream, expecting he was about to hit her. He didn't. Instead he just looked at her in the combined light of the bedside lamp and confused flashes coming in through the glass. She was trembling now, but fought hard not to show him how frightened she was.

Without taking his eyes from her, he spoke again. "You're very beautiful," and he ran the palm of his hand down her hair where it gleamed in the light. Just his touch made her cringe. "Someone as beautiful as you should be spared all," and he nodded in the direction of the street, his eyes still fixed firmly on hers. "Zis. Describe to me what you see."

"I don't understand."

"Tell me, Martha Kowalski, what you see happening down in zer street. I want to hear your English."

She turned and gazed through the glass almost in disbelief at the scene of confusion taking place just below where they were standing, sending a bolt of terror through her like a knife.

There were dozens upon dozens of people - residents, neighbours of all ages - dressed for an undisclosed destination, carrying suitcases, being herded like cattle into groups by soldiers - who were clearly enjoying themselves. She saw frightened children clinging to their parents, screaming, having been plucked from their beds and dragged outside where dogs barked and snapped angrily at their heels. Trucks that had moved up the street were being unceremoniously loaded with human cargo, their drivers anxious to move off. It was like watching a modern exodus. But what really sickened Martha, as she steadied herself close against the glass, was the noise. As if sensing her feelings, the Major suddenly leaned over her and swung the window wide open, filling the room with sounds straight from the jaws of hell. She was unable to utter a word. Just when she thought it couldn't get any worse, it did.

An elderly couple were trying unsuccessfully to lift themselves up onto the tailgate of one of the trucks, being bawled at by a soldier, who made no attempt to help when the old man lost his footing and fell, tumbling backwards onto the cobblestones, knocking his hat off. The light was sufficient enough for Martha to recognise the bald head immediately, and she let go a scream and watched mesmerised while the soldier kicked at Aniol's old, frail body.

"No! No! Tell them to stop!" she pleaded, immediately changing back to German, yet unable to turn away from the sickening, hypnotic scene.

To her surprise the Major acted promptly. Shouting down to the soldier, as loud as he could, his voice only just audible above the appalling din. "The old couple there! Put them in my private car."

The startled soldier indicated his acknowledgement and helped Aniol up and led the pair away.

The Major closed the window.

"Enough. Come and sit down," he said, and guided Martha back to the bed.

"Thank you for that," she admitted, reluctantly. "But what will happen to them?" She was on the point of tears. "That was terrible to watch. Is that any way to treat human beings, no matter who they are?"

"First things first, Fraulein. For now they will remain in my car, until I order otherwise," and he sat himself back on the chair. "I think it's time I introduced myself. I am Major Konrad Bracher. I'm with the Abwehr, Military Intelligence. This isn't my usual 'cup of tea' as the English say, but I just had a hunch about tonight. I must apologise for the exuberance of the young soldier who assaulted you earlier, but as it is, it might turn out to your advantage."

"I can't imagine how."

"Let me present you with an interesting choice, Martha Kowalski," and he lit up another cigarette. "Firstly, you could walk out of here within the next few minutes and join the old couple you love so much, and experience along with them whatever it is that awaits them."

"Which is what exactly?"

"Come, come Martha, we're both intelligent enough to know that their future doesn't look, well, too rosy, as the English like to under estimate. On the other hand, you could come and work for me."

"Work for you?" After what she had just witnessed the thought disgusted her. "Doing what?"

"Doing whatever it is I order. But in return I would guarantee the safety and wellbeing of your loving parents."

"That's blackmail!"

He shrugged his shoulders. "Call it by whatever name you wish, but you must admit it makes good sense. Work for me and they live. Go with them and you all suffer. And, the old professor doesn't look as if he could take much more," he searched for the right word, "excitement. You don't need me to remind you that the Führer isn't too favourably disposed towards Jews or those who associate with them, so look upon this as a golden opportunity for an unselfish act on your part. Which surely is but little in return for what they did for you."

The viper had bitten its prey.

"I presume this work, as you call it, involves me giving you my body?" The Major smiled. "Fraulein Kowalski, beautiful though indeed you are, I have far more serious things for you to involve yourself with than the delights of the flesh. What you do in your own time, of course, is no concern of mine, but I can assure you sex is not the issue here."

She thought for a moment before speaking again. Her head was still hurting and her brain wasn't thinking straight, but what choice was there?

"So, what next?" It was her way of capitulating. How could she ever let Malkah and Aniol suffer at the hands of these demons?

"Very good. A wise decision." He stood up, collecting his hat, positioning it at a rakish angle. "Now we must go and say goodbye to the old couple ..."

"Goodbye?!"

"But yes of course. They will be looked after well, I assure you."

"But how can I trust you?"

He shrugged again. "You can't. But then you have no choice but to trust me."

"But how will I know they're well?"

He paused in the door and thought for a moment, tapping his dimple with a forefinger. "Let us do what they do in all the best English romantic novels," he said. "When you've finished your training ….. "

"Training?!" she echoed, fearful of what she was agreeing to.

"Training, yes. Why, I have great plans for someone who can speak English as good as you, Martha Kowalski, great plans. Now I presume the woman wears a ring, so when you've finished your training I'll have her send you her ring as a sign of her well-being. How does that suit you?"

"You must take me for a fool."

"Oh no, Fraulein. A fool is something I do not take you for. Far from it." He moved into the hall and stood next to the blood-stained chest of drawers. "Collect your things quickly and we'll go. And to think I nearly didn't venture out tonight. What luck."

Chapter Eleven

Charlotte quickly opened the door and was rewarded with Valentine's beaming face.

"Good morning my dear," he began, "What a beautiful day."

She stepped out into the sunshine, greeting him with a lingering kiss. "Good morning to you, my darling. Did you sleep well?"

"As a matter of fact, no. Who would after the news you gave me last night. But do you know, I've never felt better," and he linked his arm in hers. "I feel as if I've been given a new lease of life."

"We can walk around to the back garden this way," she told him, leading him round the side of the house across the lush lawn. "I know exactly what you mean."

"And what about you? Did you sleep well?"

"Well, yes. Too well in fact. Unfortunately I had dreams all night. Not very nice dreams, either. Reliving the days back in Germany. I'm afraid it's left me with rather a bad head."

"Would you rather I left you in peace today? I don't mind."

"I won't hear of it. Besides, do you honestly think I'm going to let you out of my sight a second time?" She gave his arm a squeeze. "I'm so happy, Valentine. I feel as if the sunlight has pierced my very soul."

"How blessed we are to have been given a second chance."

"I remember you used that word once before."

"It's true. But I'm concerned about your headache."

"You mustn't be. I'll be fine if I have a restful day. I'm supposed to rest anyway, so that'll give me an excuse. Give me an opportunity to show you all my photographs, right back to when Valentine was a baby."

"That sounds so strange. Not only do I discover I've another son, but one who bears my own name."

"What a shock he's going to get."

"Oh dear. Don't you think he'll be pleased?"

"Oh no!" she exclaimed. "He'll be delighted. I've always told him how much I loved his father, but then, to actually have you here will be simply wonderful."

"When's he home again?"

"The Coast Guard agreed to give him time off so that he could be here when I have my op' next month."

"Hmmm." It was the one black cloud . "I hope he won't be disappointed when he meets me."

"Don't be silly, why ever should he be?"

"I don't know. Ageing English vicar. Then I must contact my family, too." He laughed as they stepped into the conservatory.

"Why do you laugh?"

"Something Martin said before I left. He said that once you got me under the palm trees I wouldn't be able to resist your charms."

Charlotte laughed. "Well, exchange the palm trees for the conservatory and he wasn't far out. But you told me he doesn't know about us."

"No, he doesn't. Not the details anyway. He soon will though. But tell me something my dear," he began. "I remember you mentioned that you had a brother."

"How clever of you to remember. Yes, Jan. He was three years my senior. Trained as a dentist, but couldn't settle in Germany and went back to Poland just as soon as he was able."

"Do you keep in touch?"

"How wonderful that would be. My dear Jan. No, sadly we lost all contact when the Germans invaded in '39. I tried to find him through some mutual friends immediately the war was over, which was difficult enough after all the bombings and the country in a state of utter confusion, but he'd vanished - disappeared completely. I was assured his house was still intact and yet there was no trace of him at all. And no-one knew anything. I had no choice but to lay him to rest in my heart as another casualty of Hitler's Third Reich. I'm certain."

"How very tragic."

"Yes. Another sad chapter of my life."

"Funny thing, I met a Polish dentist during the war."

Really?"

"Washed up on the beach. The poor chap had escaped from Jersey."

"Then it certainly wasn't Jan. Coffee?"

"No, I suppose not. Thank you. I thought I'd take you somewhere special for a celebratory lunch. If you are up to it, that is."

"Oh, how lovely. Thank you darling. Oh, I'll be alright and I know just the place."

During lunch in the beautiful pink building of the Princess Hotel in Hamilton, overlooking the sheltered blue waters of the capital's harbour, they began to discuss wedding arrangements, soon settling on the quietest of ceremonies at a Registry Office. There not being the time to obtain the necessary church licence before Charlotte had her operation, and Valentine wasn't a resident. Due to the circumstances they took the difficult, but agreed decision, that their respective families wouldn't be told until after the event, as knowledge would only delay matters. Instead they planned a church blessing and celebration, involving everyone, as soon after Charlotte's operation as possible. This brought them to the question of where they were going to live.

"Let's get the hospital bit over first," said Charlotte, "there'll be plenty of time for that later."

"As you wish, my dear." But her reluctance disturbed him. "You haven't really told me much about your illness."

"Gosh, where can I begin?" She said, turning to watch as the pianist resumed his seat after a break and started to play. "It's been ongoing for some time. They tried all the conventional treatments, that's when I lost most of my hair, but that didn't work, and so now surgery is the only alternative. Unfortunately, the tumour's buried quite deep apparently, and difficult to get to, but if I don't have it removed they tell me I won't be here at Christmas."

"Oh, no!"

"I'd already decided to have the op' and now that I've found you, or rather you found me," she smiled, "I know I made the right decision. Ten months or a year with you Valentine isn't enough. I want you until I die at a ripe old age."

"That sounds a very sensible attitude."

"I have to be positive. Especially now."

"Yes, especially now," their hands touched across the table.

"How do you feel in yourself?"

"Not too bad. I have to take handfuls of tablets every day, I'm sure I must rattle, and I do tire easily. I get very tired sometimes, actually."

"You should have told me. I feel guilty now at dragging you out like this."

"Hardly dragging. Do you hear me complaining?" Her eyes flashed with a spark of their old fire. "Believe me, you're exactly what the doctor ordered."

The remark made him laugh, injecting a lighter note into the serious news. The main course arrived and they talked of happier things, when suddenly, Charlotte stopped and rested her knife and fork.

"Valentine. This tune . Do you recognise it?"

"Sorry," he said, shaking his head. "Should I?"

"You of all people should. It's called 'My Funny Valentine'."

"Well, fancy that. Maybe you should serenade me."

"Maybe I should. I know it well enough. I have the record at home. I must have played it a thousand times and shed an ocean of tears over you. It was some time before I even learnt to smile again. You were my waking thought each morning and my last vision at night." Her words were like an arrow to his heart. "I saw your face everywhere," she continued, reliving the memory. "I heard your voice; your footsteps. I could taste your lips against mine. The touch of your hair."

"Oh, my dear girl. Whatever can I say?" Suddenly a tidal wave of guilt engulfed him as he looked past her dark eyes, reading the harm the years had bequeathed, and found himself wanting her pain to become his. To share the weight of all those unfulfilled desires she'd carried for so long. "There's so much I have to put right."

"I'm just pleased one of us, at least, found happiness."

"With Ann you mean?"

"Yes."

"Yes we were happy. And, do you know, I feel she'd be happy for us both now, too. In fact I'm certain of it."

"She must have been a lovely person. I wish I'd known her."

"Well, at least you have something to be very thankful for," he said, emphasising 'very' and trying to lift the moment.

"And, what's that?"

"That I didn't sing to you."

After lunch, they sat on the terrace drinking coffee and watching as a huge American cruise liner negotiated a course to the Front Street dockings.

"This is a very lovely island, Charlotte. I can well understand your falling in love with it all those years ago."

"I seriously contemplated returning to Germany after the war, but the country was in chaos and I'd already started a new life in this safe and beautiful corner of the world. Not to mention a young son and what would be best for him. Looking back though, I know I made the right decision. I've been very happy here. We both have. It's changed a lot since then, of course, but..... look!" And she pointed up at a bird a little smaller than a seagull, enjoying the same colourings, but with a long forked tail. "My first one this year. Do you know what it is called?"

He shook his head.

"A Longtail. The Bermudian Longtail. They return every year during the first week of February. That's the first one I've seen. How lovely. It's a promise that summer isn't too far away."

"And what a summer it's going to be for both of us my dear."

"Oh, I hope so Valentine," and she leant over and squeezed his arm, "I do hope so. I'll be so relieved when this operation is over and out of the way."

"You know, when I was younger," began Valetine, "I once asked a wise old man how I will know when I've met my wife."

"And, what was his response?"

"He was very quiet for some time. I remember thinking he couldn't have heard me, but eventually he lifted his head and looked skyward just as we are now, and answered, 'you will never stop thinking about her. She will occupy your thoughts every hour of every day. Everything will fade into insignificance beside thoughts of her and her wellbeing.' "

"And is that how you feel now?" she asked, well knowing what he would say, but needing to hear it nonetheless.

"Oh yes," he confirmed, his face breaking into a tender smile, "that is exactly how I feel and have ever since I knew you were still alive, and I am convinced everything will work itself out, my dear. You wait and see."

"Let's hope you are right."

The carefree Longtail was conspicuous against the clear blue sky and they watched it gracefully rise and fall on a breeze from the ocean, its long tail flapping like twin ribbons with minds of their own, until it was out of sight.

It was the smell of ether mixed with disinfectant that upset him. It wasn't an overpowering smell, but ever since having a tooth removed as a small boy he'd always associated the smell with pain and suffering, and now, as he sat in the waiting room of the King Edward VII Memorial Hospital on the outskirts of Hamilton, he found memories of the scent were turning the clock backwards.

How extraordinary the last ten or so months had been. From the quiet, ordered existence of a widower in Hertfordshire, to having his life thrown upside down by the chance reading of a few lines in a newspaper, to sitting in a hospital on a tiny island in the middle of the Atlantic Ocean, accompanied by a son he never knew existed, whilst surgeons fought to save the life of his new and long lost wife.

It couldn't all have been for nothing though. Surely it wasn't meant to end on an operating table? Yet, who could know the mind and purposes of the Almighty? Was this a punishment for what they had done to Ethan Thomas?

Suddenly Valentine felt overwhelmingly tired, as if everything he'd experienced had taken place within the last twenty-four hours. It left him feeling drained and mentally fatigued, but as he looked across at his son, seated opposite, he promptly saw the answer to his question. Whatever the outcome, it hadn't been all for nothing. Certainly not. What a fine young man he was. Tall, broad shouldered and good looking. Charlotte said that he looked as he himself had when they met during the war. 'I can't see that. The nose perhaps, but no, he's his mother's son. Dark hair and those deep, dark eyes. My son. I can't believe it. Good position with the U.S. Coast Guard, a pension. He'll make a fine husband for some lucky girl. He's leaving it late though, already in his thirties. What will the church say about it all? Who cares what they say. I've a new wife and a new son, that's what really matters.'

He glanced at the wall clock. It was almost ten in the evening. Charlotte had already been in theatre for over five hours and now the hospital was growing quiet at the end of the day, and cleaners began to move around, oblivious to the thoughts and concerns of the English clergyman.

'Twenty-two-hundred, Roger. Time for a swift one before they close? Those were the days. Dear old Roger. You and your stupid motorbike. You promised to be our best man.'

"Are you O.K. Dad? You look far away."

"I'm tired," he said, "just very tired."

"Why don't you take a turn on one of the visitors' beds? I'll call you if anything happens."

"Yes, I think I will. That's a good idea, son." How peculiar to give a stranger so precious a title.

The compact private room was spotlessly clean and he stretched himself out on top of the covers, not bothering to remove his shoes.

'Does everything have to smell of ether?' He saw Valentine's face again, just as he had that first meeting at the airport, instinctively knowing who he was, even before Charlotte called out. Directly he'd seen his parents standing waving, he'd dropped his bags and walked straight over and flung his arms around his father, hugging him tightly. Both of them too choked to say anything.

He should have been at the wedding, but then if he'd been there it would only have been right to include Martin and Susan. But it would have taken days and days to arrange all the flights and time off work, which would only have delayed things when time wasn't something in plentiful supply. No, they'd made the right decision and he smiled to himself - stretched out on the bed - at the recollection of Martin's reaction to the news over the telephone and listening to the whoops and cries of delight emitting from the other end. Valentine had forgotten about the time difference and got them out of bed. The news that he had another son would have to wait though. The wedding and operation was enough for them to absorb for now.

Charlotte's lengthy telephone call to the east coast of the United States also went well, once the initial shock of knowing his father had as good as been resurrected from the dead, and, finally married his mother. But it was a joy to his heart, knowing how much she had always loved the man and that now she wouldn't be facing an uncertain future alone. The two Valentines had tried to speak, only managing a brief greeting and a promise to catch up when he came home. When Charlotte finally replaced the receiver, she'd almost floated back into the lounge on a cloud of euphoria. "He can't wait to meet you, darling! He's overjoyed and wishes us a wonderful day."

What a wonderful and happy day it had been, too, and how lovely she'd looked. Yes, she could still turn some heads as they had posed for the obligatory photographs under a 'moongate'. The 'moongate' being one of those traditional stone, circular arched constructions that miraculously defies the laws of gravity.

Who would have thought that at sixty seven he had found love again, and to have married on his birthday, too! What a gift.

They had spent their wedding night at the Sonesta Beach Hotel, and after a sumptuous meal retired, exhausted, to their room overlooking the sheltered, little, rock fringed bay They had sat for a while on the balcony, sipping champagne in the moonlight, watching reflections skipping along the top of the waves like excited fireflies. How romantic it had all been, and he laughed to himself at the memory of her seductive voice. "Turn the light out, Valentine." "Whatever you say, Mrs. Gray." 'Ah, there's life in the old boy yet!'

He felt for his new wedding ring and examined it by the light on the bedside cabinet. What fun they'd had choosing them; first one design, then another. Those days before the wedding had been so happy. It had been a busy time because they felt they needed to get to know one another again, and, every day brought some extra and interesting titbit of the separation years into conversation. But it was also a time of uncertainty and, as Charlotte's operation drew close she found she began to rely more and more on Valentine's strength to sustain and encourage her.

They fell into the habit of taking a gentle walk in the morning, Charlotte using the opportunity to show Valentine as much of the island as possible, and to meet some of her friends. Then following lunch or a picnic, Charlotte would rest in the afternoon until Valentine made tea at around four-thirty. They usually stayed in for supper, although they occasionally ate out. But it was all over much too quickly, like the turning of a page of a novel, and, as he lay staring at the antiseptic ceiling, new, important and worrying questions were already forming in his mind. What did the future hold for them both? Would she make a complete recovery? What if she didn't? Which side of the Atlantic should be their home?

'Funny, the police didn't contact her at all. Maybe they've dropped it. Changed their minds. Academic now, anyway.'

His body was crying out for sleep, but with a nervous system locked in overdrive, adrenalin continued to course through his veins, squashing all hope of rest. How could anyone sleep at such a time anyway. He checked his watch; almost eleven, that made it nearly six hours in the operating theatre. Poor girl. Poor surgeons. He closed his eyes, not in sleep, but in prayer.

He was on the point of wondering if he should get up, when there was a knock at the door. It was his son. He put his head round, his expression full of urgency. "Dad! The operation's over and they'll be taking her to I.T.U. in just a few minutes."

"Thank God." Valentine swung his legs onto the floor, suddenly filled with a fresh burst of nervous energy. "How is she?"

"I don't know, they haven't said. The nurse just told me the doctor wants to see us."

"Oh."

Together they made their way down the long corridor, following signs for 'Intensive Therapy', their hurried steps disturbing the stillness, and were met at the door by the consultant surgeon still in his operating greens. He looked exhausted, his skin an unhealthy shade of pale. The long gown and reduced light combining to give him a ghostly, almost supernatural, aura.

"What news doctor?" Once inside the office young Valentine's patience evaporated.

"I'll come straight to the point," he said, wiping a hand across his face. "We now know the full extent of the tumour. We knew it was bad, but we didn't know quite how bad until we opened up." He was choosing his words carefully. "There is no easy way to say this, but I very much regret to say that the operation wasn't a success. Things were far more advanced than we feared. I am so very sorry."

"But what do you mean!?" Charlotte's son stepped forward.

"Just a moment." Valentine spoke calmly. "Are you saying that my wife is dead?"

"No, Mr. Gray. But I'm afraid she hasn't very long. Only a matter of hours, probably. No more."

"Oh Mom!"

The Reverend slowly stood up when, for a fleeting second, he had a glimpse of himself standing there in front of the desk, floating like a spectator. He became conscious suddenly of an energy flowing through his weary frame. Not a nervous, energetic energy, but a peace not of himself. Like a warm, reassuring glow.

It was the news he feared most and yet, in his heart of hearts, it was the news he had expected. Such happiness as they'd enjoyed during the past month couldn't possibly last. They had kissed and prayed before the operation and now at least they could say their goodbyes. Now he needed to be strong for Charlotte, for Valentine and, for the time being at least, for himself too.

"Come along son," he said, "we must go to her."

He extended his hand. "Thank you doctor for all you've done. I know you did your very best."

"She's in no pain Mr. Gray," he reassured him, "but she may slip in and out of consciousness, due to the medication."

"I understand. Thank you doctor."

A different hospital, a different time, a different end, but still the same feeling of utter hopelessness.

With an efficient air, the young nurse removed the blood pressure cuff, checked the monitor which continued to bleep out its irritating noise every few seconds, and wrote something down on the chart, before adjusting the flow of the colourless liquid intravenous drip. "I'll leave you alone now," she said, giving the forlorn looking man a compassionate half smile. "I'll be back now and then to check on your wife." Before leaving she adjusted some of the flowers and cards from friends and well wishers that almost covered the table at the bottom of the bed.

Charlotte was propped up in a semi-raised position, her head a mass of bandages as thick as a turban. Her skin had adopted a damp and sickly yellow pallor. Dark shadowy crescents had appeared under each eye, as if underlining her infirmity and, as she tried to focus on her visitor, her eyelids quivered with an agitation all their own. The fingers of one hand raised themselves in recognition.

"Hello darling." Her voice was dry, delicate. The speech slow.

"My darling girl. How are you feeling?" It sounded such a trite thing to say in the circumstances.

A corner of her mouth twitched with the suggestion of a grin. "I've felt better."

Valentine took her hand in his, it was clammy and frail, but he felt her grip him in return. He sat down on the black plastic chair beside the bed, still clutching her as if hanging onto life for as long as possible. Charlotte followed his every movement with her eyes, unable to move her head.

"It was nice of you to let Valentine come in first," she said, her voice not without its former dignity.

"They would only let one of us in at a time."

"Poor boy," her lips trembled, "it breaks my heart to see him so upset."

"He's a fine young man and he loves you very much."

"Yes, he is," she took a slow breath and let out a sigh. "I wonder how many children you and I would have had?"

"Lots and lots, I'm certain," he said, punctuating her fantasies with the shadow of a smile, "who knows?"

"We would have been happy, wouldn't we?"

"We would have been deliriously happy," he reassured her, at the same time drawing close when her eyes were closed for a moment, thinking she may have lost consciousness as the doctor warned. But, her eyes slowly opened again and she continued voicing her thoughts.

"I'm sorry to keep you up so late. You'll be very tired in the morning."

"It's not important, please you mustn't worry yourself. I'm fine, truly. You're the important one."

"They shaved all my hair off, you know." She looked at him, waiting for a response but he couldn't speak, the lump in his throat growing bigger by the second. "I know I'm dying, Valentine. They told me the end is very close."

He felt the grip on his hand tighten and he bit his lip until it hurt. "You're very brave my darling one. But I'm worried you'll tire yourself talking so much."

"I'm alright," she told him, "it helps to talk. But I'm not brave. No. The night I landed on the Isle of Wight by submarine, that was brave. I was still terrified though."

"A submarine?!" It was the first he had heard of it.

"Sounds foolish now doesn't it? But at the time it was real. Oh, so very, very real." She rested a moment, thinking. How strange to suddenly be taken back to the years they knew before, in a single sentence. "I knew about your PLUTO line."

"You knew?! I always wondered if you did."

"But I never told Berlin. It was too obvious what it was for."

"One word, and single-handedly you would have changed the course of history. What an amazing thought."

"I was on your side remember, not theirs."

"I'm so proud of you." He ran his hand down her pale cheek.

"Will my good deeds outweigh the bad we did to poor Ethan, do you think?"

"We must all look to what Jesus accomplished at Calvary when he took our sins upon him, not at what little good there might be in ourselves."

"I doubt the 'Pearly Gates' will open for me."

"Heaven will be full of forgiven people Charlotte, not good people."

"You're a good man, Valentine Gray. You would have made me a good husband. You would have been a good influence."

"And you a good wife, my darling."

"Maybe. Yes I think so." She ran a dry tongue over cracked lips and he reached up to the bedside locker for the glass of water and dipping his finger in, moistened her lips and lifted the glass allowing her a few sips.

"Thank you dear." Her eye lids became heavy suddenly and gradually closed. He became conscious again of the regular bleep of the heart monitor. The staff nurse reappeared.

"Everything alright Mr Gray?" She spoke in hushed tones.

"I think she's resting."

"This will happen more and more frequently, I'm afraid."

Valentine nodded, not letting go of his wife's hand. "Yes, I understand. Thank you."

"I'll be back in a little while."

It was four or five minutes before Charlotte opened her eyes again, and when she did her thoughts were only for her loved ones.

"I haven't had time to alter my Will. I've left everything to Valentine. Will you forgive me? I haven't left you anything."

"Really Charlotte. You've already given me a thousand memories which are far more precious than anything else could ever be."

"My signet ring," she offered, just managing to raise a hand. "Poor Malkah's ring. It's hidden beneath a plaster. Take it. Wear it. Think of me sometimes, when you're quiet and alone. Will you do that?"

Valentine couldn't hold back any longer and began to weep freely.

"Please don't cry for me my darling. Instead remember the good times. And thank God that he allowed us to meet again after all these years and enjoy the very best of love together. These past few weeks have been the happiest of my life."

"For me too," he could only just speak.

"Think how I would have felt lying here if we hadn't met again. I'd still be blaming you. Instead, I love you even more now than I did forty years ago."

Suddenly, her eyes glazed over and though her lips continued to move no sound came. Then all conversation ceased.

Valentine sat up and prising his hand free, wiped his eyes. It was all too dreadful.

Young Valentine went and sat with his mother. The trauma of watching her fight for life, mixed with the prospect of living without her, was too much and he soon came back into the waiting room looking pale and exhausted.

Valentine immediately went back to be with her, gently taking her hand once again. When she spoke her breathing had deteriorated. Her voice reduced to little more than a whisper.

"Pray I see the dawn, my darling. Just one more time. When I was a child my mother used to sing me a song about the dawn....., the light chasing the darkness away....., I used to sing it to Valentine when he was a baby... ."

"You don't have to talk, my love," each painful breath was like the twisting of a knife in his heart.

"He was a fine baby, you know."

"I remember the photos you showed me."

"I had hoped to see him married and present me with some grandchildren, but it wasn't to be..... . It's time he settled down."

"I'll take care of him my love, you needn't worry."

"Yes, I know you will...... I know."

"He has a whole new family now."

The nurse returned, this time only for a moment, and was gone.

"One thing I've learnt," continued Charlotte, "is that life is short..... too short. If I had known that, I would have done things differently."

"You mustn't tire yourself my darling," and he kissed the back of her hand again and again, holding it close to his cheek, drawing in its softness.

Charlotte held him with eyes that had captivated his heart a lifetime ago and slowly, and with obvious difficulty, her face stretched to the beginnings of a smile, and with a voice suggesting a tune said, "My funny Valentine, you are my favourite work of art..... each day is Valentine's day."

Charlotte Gray died at 05.57. Her bed had been turned towards the window to catch the first bright rays of the new dawn, and she passed from this life into the next holding the hands of the two most important people in her world, her two Valentines.

Her husband prayed aloud, still unwilling to let go of her hand. "Lord, in thy infinite mercy, receive into thy kingdom the soul of this my love. My darling, precious Charlotte. Amen."

"Amen," repeated Valentine, as father and son embraced.

At the request of the school governors, where Charlotte had been headmistress, her funeral was held in Hamilton Cathedral some days later, filling the great building to bursting point with over four hundred girls, their parents and members of staff and many personal friends. She had obviously been deeply loved.

Valentine contemplated taking part of the service himself, but in the end decided against it for fear of breaking down. At the stirring sound of so many young voices raised in 'The Lord's my Shepherd', his throat soon closed up and he could only listen, wondering if somehow in the ether of the great universe Charlotte was listening too. Valentine, his faced streaked with tears, gave his father a sideways glance thinking much the same.

Charlotte was finally laid to rest on a hill top overlooking the wide reaches of the Atlantic

Ocean, fanned by the warm winds of the Gulf Stream. Looking east to the Isle of Wight, to Germany, to the former life and time that had ultimately reached its sad conclusion.

Before walking away from the grave, Valentine stooped and picked up a small pebble from the pile of freshly dug soil and popped it into his pocket. A little piece of Bermuda would be going home with him, along with a collection of unopened letters, tied together with ribbons going yellow with age.

Chapter Twelve

The bedside alarm clock gave a warning click and Roy Preston quickly stretched out and switched it off, before it could ring and disturb his wife. It was time to get up.

"It's alright. I'm awake," she said, turning towards him.

"I've been awake for hours," he told her, yawning and rubbing a hand across a fresh growth of stubble.

"Why's that?"

"I don't know. I've got something on my mind and I just can't leave it alone."

"One of your cases, I bet. I hope the Force realises what a dedicated man they've got in you."

"Dad was convinced the Gray chap was a murderer. Even on his deathbed he said he could smell the man's guilt."

"I was there too, remember."

"He was very rarely wrong, you know. Had quite a reputation."

"So where's the man now? Done a runner?"

"No. I know exactly where he is. Overseas. But

he'll be back soon. Dad was right though, there's simply no proof. Not one single scrap."

"What do you think yourself?"

"I've always believed he's innocent. He told me an utterly convincing story and yet, I can't put my finger on why I can't just leave it alone. He even wrote and told me he'll be away longer than expected."

"Not many guilty criminals write you letters, I wouldn't have thought."

"Or is it the action of a very clever, guilty man?"

"Well, you'll never find out lying there all day, Sherlock."

With his stepfather's last words still ringing in his ears, Preston threw back the sheets and slid out of bed.

"I feel very guilty at dragging you all this way to meet me son, but after talking with you on the phone and thinking things over in the aeroplane, I've decided there's something I must attend to while it's still fresh in my mind. It'll never get done at all, otherwise."

An announcement over the tannoy system at Heathrow Airport, briefly interrupted the conversation. "Susan and I are concerned you're doing too much, Dad. You've been through a great deal in the last few months, what with the wedding and operation and then the funeral on top of it all. I think you ought to come home."

Valentine sipped his coffee, the caffeine helping to clear his mind after the long flight. "No, I appreciate your concern, believe me I do, but my mind's made up. It's still early in the day and I can take a train and be on the Isle of Wight soon after lunch." He didn't let on how tired he felt. This was just something that had to be done. To neglect it would be wrong.

"But, why ever go back there?"

"It's all connected with my visit last year."

Martin looked at his father across the small table in the cafeteria. Suddenly, he felt as if he didn't know him any longer and it troubled him. So many things had happened in the last year that remained a puzzle. "To be honest Dad, I feel there's a lot you're not telling me," he said. "Suddenly, you're up and gallivanting off to Bermuda, to meet someone none of us know anything about. And then, you're married. Then it's over, tragically of course, but now you're no sooner home again than you want to rush back to the Isle of Wight. Just what exactly is going on?"

Valentine shook his head. He was right of course, but this was not the time to begin telling him the whole lengthy saga.

"I'm afraid you're going to have to trust me, Martin. I promise you, with my hand on my heart, that I'll tell you everything, and believe me, there's a lot to tell, just as soon as I get back. I'll only be there one night, then it's straight back home, I promise. Why don't both of you come to lunch on Sunday?"

"Are the police still involved?"

"No. Well, indirectly."

"You're sure you're not in any trouble? You haven't broken the law?"

"No, of course I haven't. Believe me. Everything is..... well, I'm broken hearted, but not in any kind of trouble."

Martin noticed his father's tearful eyes. "Of course I believe you. I'm just concerned, that's all." The man had been through more than he was letting on. "You miss her badly, don't you?"

"Yes I do." It was the first time he had heard himself admit it. "I do miss her. I feel our relationship ended before it had really begun. It was like a cruel taste of what might have been. A teaspoonful of a banquet. Perhaps it would have been better if I hadn't tasted it at all - from one point of view." Valentine looked at his son. What would he say when he learned he had a half brother? "I hope you don't think I've behaved foolishly in all this, Martin. I was worried you may feel that, because I married Charlotte, I didn't love your mother."

"Don't be ridiculous! No-one's questioning your love for Mum at all. But that was a long time ago. I told you, Sue and I were delighted for you. A second chance of love and all that. Great stuff. It's just a shame..... ."

"How I wish you could have met her."

"That would have been nice. But at least you have the memories. They'll be all the more precious now."

"Yes, there's always the memories. And the photographs," he said. Then, pushing his thoughts aside. "You can help by taking most of my luggage home, if you wouldn't mind. Oh, and before I catch the train I need to call at the duty-free shop."

"The duty-free? Don't tell me you've taken to drink!"

The suggestion made him laugh, something he hadn't done in a while, and the air between them brightened. "No, of course not. I need to get a little something, that's all. Perhaps you could help me choose."

Newport Police Station on the Isle of Wight was as busy as ever, with uniformed officers and plain-clothes men and women hurrying this way and that, in the never ending conflict of right versus wrong; good over evil.

The Reverend Gray was told he would have to wait and was shown into a stuffy and sparsely furnished interview room where he sat patiently reading the previous day's Telegraph. Presently, the door opened and one of the men he'd come to see walked in.

"I'm sorry to have kept you waiting so long, Reverend. Always busy, I'm afraid. How nice to see you again. Thank you for your letter."

Detective Inspector Preston dumped a pile of files on the table and held out his hand. He still wore the same harassed expression.

"And it's very nice to see you again, too, Inspector."

"My, you look well, I can see you've been out in the tropics. How did it go?" He sat himself down across the other side of the fixed table and lit up a cigarette.

"I won't keep you, Roy, but I did promise you I'd bring you up to date. I haven't forgotten your kindness to me in motoring all the way to Hertfordshire to tell me you'd found Charlotte, so the least I can do is return the courtesy."

Roy Preston appeared to relax at the sound of the clergyman's steady voice and considerate manner. "Excellent," he said, but in a way that suggested a whole lot more.

"Charlotte," Valentine continued, curbing his emotions, "Charlotte, I'm sorry to say, is dead."

"And after all that." Roy's reaction was surprisingly controlled.

"Yes, after all that, as you say."

"I'm so sorry."

"Thank you. It was a brain tumour. They tried to operate, but it didn't succeed."

"I am so sorry."

"However, before she died we did manage to get married. Only a mere forty years later than perhaps we should have done. I've brought you a copy of the death certificate. I thought perhaps you may want to see it. I know you like to tidy up any loose ends." He placed the paper on the table top where Roy gave it a cursory glance. Valentine was on the verge of telling him of his new-found son, but decided against it.

"It's only fair to tell you that I knew about this already, Sir."

"You knew? How? I didn't put it in the letter."

"We've been working very closely with the Bermudian Force and they kept me informed of events while you were away."

"So you knew..... about the wedding?"

"Yes. And Mrs Gray's operation."

"I see." Valentine stood up abruptly and began to move about the room.

"This has been the most unusual case I've ever been involved with, but now that Mrs Gray has passed away, well, that's the end of it. I hope you do believe me when I say that I'm genuinely sorry it all had to end like this."

"Yes, I do believe you Inspector," he said, choosing not to look directly at him. "But I didn't know you had us under surveillance. I feel as if my last moments with Charlotte have been spoiled somehow."

"You most certainly were not under surveillance. Even watched would be too strong a word. They just kept an eye on you both. That's all, Sir. Nothing more. You have my word."

"Eye or not, they were acting on your instructions."

He nodded. "That's policing, Sir."

"Well, I'm not impressed."

"You've no reason to feel like that at all. But I am a policeman, first and last. You must remember that."

Valentine didn't respond, though unconsciously worried the pebble in his pocket.

"You may be interested to know that D.I. Stretch, my stepfather..... "

"What about him?" he said, quickly turning round. "He died, you told me."

"Yes, that's right, but he always believed you were guilty."

"What?!"

"At one point, back during the war, he was even convinced you'd done away with both Ethan and Charlotte."

"That's absolutely ridiculous! Well, he's certainly been proved wrong then, hasn't he?"

"Yes. And I'm very glad he has been, Reverend. For once he was obviously wrong. Very wrong."

Valentine resumed his seat, beginning to feel the effects of many hours of travelling, and conscious suddenly of tightness in his chest.

"Are you alright?"

"Yes. But I'm annoyed. It leaves a very nasty taste."

"I'm sorry, but it was either that or take her in for

questioning. And under the circumstances I don't think that would have been very appropriate, do you?"

"No, maybe not." The thought of sitting in a police station whilst Charlotte was interviewed was too terrible to contemplate.

The two men talked for a few more minutes, until, "I'm so sorry, but you will have to excuse me, Reverend. I'm in the middle of a particularly nasty G.B.H. case."

"I understand. You didn't know I was coming, after all."

"Hmm. But I greatly appreciate you taking the time to call in like this, I'm just so sorry things worked out the way they have for you."

"The good book says there's a time for everything. Unfortunately though, some times are much easier to handle than others, you know."

Preston had to admit the good book was probably right. The meeting was clearly over and he stood, collecting his files. Life moved on. He extended his hand across the table a second time. "It's always a pleasure, Sir, and again, my deepest condolences."

"Thank you. Yes, my little adventure is over and now I must try and return to some semblance of normality. Tell me," he asked the detective, "is Constable Willard available? Only I'd very much like just a few moments of his time, if it's at all possible."

"Yes, I'm sure he is. I'll go and dig him out." He left the interview room wondering why the Reverend hadn't mentioned his newly discovered son.

Ten minutes later, Constable John Willard entered. "Reverend Gray. This is a pleasant surprise. What brings you to the Isle of Wight?"

The two men talked of the investigation into the Maracaibo Star, before Valentine produced a small parcel and placed it on the centre of the table.

"What's this?"

"A little something to show my appreciation, John. I know all about the work you put into tracing Charlotte and, had it not been for your perseverance, we would never have met again. An important part of my life, a very important part of my life, would have remained lost. It's the least I can do to say thank you."

The young man's face lit up. "It's the best watch I've ever owned. What can I say? But, I will have to declare it."

"Of course. But you've earned it. Now", he said, as he stood up, "I must be off and let you return to your duties."

"You must at least let me run you back to the ferry."

"The ferry?" Valentine checked his watch, it was only half past three. "Yes, do you know I might take you up on that. I had planned to stay overnight, but there's still plenty of time for me to get back. Thank you."

Willard spoke to someone at the front desk before taking him to an unmarked car parked behind the station.

"Do you have time for a run down to Shanklin, Reverend?"

"Shanklin. Why?"

"Only there's something I think you might be interested in. I learnt a lot when I was looking for your Charlotte. Local history's becoming a bit of a hobby of mine. The boss says it keeps me out of mischief," he smiled cheerily, "he might be right, too."

'Your Charlotte.' Just the mention of her name and he was back at her bedside. The distinctive smell of ether in his nostrils; the grip of her hand; the early rays of dawn falling across her face with a radiance that had lingered until the monitor announced with its high pitched warning that the end had finally arrived. He felt for her ring. It was all he had.

"Yes, alright, if it won't take too long. But, do you have the time?"

"I'll make the time. It's not every day I get presented with a new watch."

The journey to Shanklin didn't take long and all the way there Valentine relived the countless times he'd made a similar journey in the M.G. Making sure there was no lipstick on his face and straightening his uniform, before entering the Mess. All, a lifetime ago.

The car pulled to a halt near where the old pier had once stood on Shanklin seafront, which was now almost deserted. Valentine failed to understand why the Constable had brought him all this way.

"You must be wondering why I've brought you here, Reverend?"

"You're reading my thoughts."

"See that rock over there?" he said, at the same time pointing through the windscreen to a large, grey lump of granite, standing roughly five feet high on the Esplanade, some way on from the car.

"Yes. What about it?"

"Let's go over and read what it says."

Detective Constable Willard read the inscription as they stood in the weakening sunlight, a stiff breeze coming off the water ruffling his neatly brushed hair.

" 'This plaque marks the site from which the PLUTO oil pipeline left these shores for France at the time of the Allied Forces Landing at Normandy in June, 1944.' " The young man looked at Valentine standing beside him and was about to comment on the impressive memorial, but one glance at the man's face told him to keep quiet. The vicar's gaze was of someone in deep, concentrated recollection.

The pair remained there, quite still. The only sound that of the sea and a lone gull circling overhead.

D.C. Willard had learnt a lot in the course of his search; the many stories of war and threat of invasion; the bombings; the sheer hard work, sweat and ingenuity of the pipeline engineers. It must all look very different from what it did in the early forties. Now the old boy would be remembering the friends and personalities. The loves, the losses.

After some minutes Valentine lifted his head, looking skyward and took a deep breath before turning to his companion.

"I am so thankful to have been here, John," he spoke slowly but with conviction. "Just to know that what we did all those years ago hasn't been forgotten, is..... is like a ray of sunshine to a weary soul. Thank you so much."

"You're very welcome, Sir."

"But now, sadly, I think it is time for me to take my leave."

They drove north, following the coastal road, passing through the old villages of St. Helens, Nettlestone and Seaview, eventually dropping down into Ryde and out onto the head of the pier, where the ferry was on the point of departure.

"You'll just have time to buy a ticket."

"John, what can I say? Thank you again. It's been greatly encouraging , greatly encouraging."

"Next time you come I'll take you to the museum. There's still a lot more to see."

"I'm sure there is. Next time, perhaps."

"Thanks again for the watch."

"My pleasure."

Valentine stood on deck, quite oblivious to the wind, as the ferry pulled away, unable to take his eyes off the island that was gradually drawing further and further away.

Would he ever return? It was unlikely, he thought. The skeletons in the cupboard had finally been laid to rest once and for all. Who would have thought that the clandestine events, during one solitary night of the turbulent war years, could have had such far-reaching consequences. With every turn of the ship's screw he felt the gulf between those years and his new life grow deeper and wider. Yet, he knew he'd never forget, however far away he might be. How could he? Every unique and precious memory leading him to where he was today; the widower of two loving and wonderful women and the father of two, fine and handsome sons.

Gripping the polished handrail, steadying himself against the movement of the ferry, he continued to stand there, watching the island grow smaller. A number of lights were already appearing, in the fast approaching twilight, from windows across Ryde, like little pockets of hope, and he extended his arm in a final wave, changing it suddenly to a salute, drawing himself up to attention, the strong breeze quickly wiping away any moisture from his eyes, not thinking nor caring who saw his final act of remembrance and respect.

"Goodbye, dear friends," he said. "Rest in peace." Slowly, lowering his arm, and with a final look at the receding outline of the island against the darkening sky, went and found himself a seat inside. The last four hours had been a strain.

It hadn't been easy to leave Valentine Junior, as he now liked to be called, since it was clearly going to take him time to come to terms with his mother's death. They had been very close and he planned to stay in Bermuda for a while to sort out her affairs before having to return to work in the U.S. The reverend smiled to himself, as he chose a seat next to a salt-encrusted window, at the recollections of their goodbyes.

'How did Churchill put it?' he thought. 'This isn't the beginning of the end, but the end of the beginning.' Surely this was the end of the beginning of a lovely relationship. He yawned suddenly, as a wave of tiredness swept over him, magnified by the rocking and pitching of the boat, glad that he was finally going home.

On his return to Hertfordshire the silence of the house struck him afresh, not helping to lift his spirits, and he retired early.

The following morning, after a hearty breakfast, he settled down to tackle the pile of post, awaiting his home coming, which the faithful Mrs Hemmings had laid out on the dining room table. Most of it went directly into the bin, but there was one letter which particularly caught his attention. It was postmarked 'West Berlin'. A response to a letter he'd written from Bermuda to the 'Holocaust Missing Persons Bureau'. It read as follows:

'Further to your letter regarding news of Herr Aniol and Frau Grunberg. From our records we can confirm that they left their residence in the Berlin town, moving to a ghetto area, where from they were later transported to Poland and died together in Auschwitz some time during April 1943. We trust this is a adequate answer to your enquiry.'

This meant that Charlotte's adoptive parents were both dead before she had even arrived on the Isle of Wight, just as she'd always feared. The whole tragic saga was purposeless. Or was it? Would she have survived if she'd stayed in Germany with such close Jewish connections? If she hadn't come to England they would never have met. Or would they? Could fate have possibly found another way of bringing them together? So many unanswered and unanswerable questions. But, at least, there were still her letters.

Sunday lunch at High Park House had been cleared away. Susan's offer to wash up had been declined and Valentine ushered both her and his son into the lounge. The twins had been left with neighbours, and the three made themselves comfortable.

"That was a lovely lunch, Dad."

"Thank you. But we all know that I haven't invited you here solely for lunch. I feel I owe you both an explanation for my .....," he searched for the right words, "unorthodox behaviour these past few months." He paused, giving the couple an opportunity to comment. But other than a fleeting glance at one another they remained silent and expectant.

"Well, I've decided to have the spare bedroom redecorated," he began tentatively. It wasn't what they had expected. "Because this time next month I shall be having a relative of ours, from America, come over and stay for a while, and unless I'm very much mistaken he'll become quite a regular visitor."

"I didn't know you had any relatives in the States, Val," said Susan.

"No, neither did I," added Martin, wondering where this was leading. "What's his name?"

"It's funny you should ask that right away son, because his name is the same as mine."

"Gray, you mean?"

"No, Valentine."

"So, where's the family connection then?" queried his daughter-in-law.

"I think, perhaps, I'd better start at the beginning," said Valentine, purposefully avoiding his son's look. Then, as the shadows lengthened, they listened - fascinated.

"However," he said, when finally he'd told them all they needed to know, "there's something I must attend to, for my own peace of mind at least. I know that Charlotte had a brother and I believe we may have met by chance in 1944. I really feel I ought to try and discover what became of him. The chances are he's long since gone, of course, but in a strange way I think it will be good for me. Give me a project to focus on."

Chapter Thirteen

With the assistance of the British Dental Association, Valentine was able to contact the Polish dental authorities, and within weeks had the information he wanted. A post-war address for Jan Kowalski. At least he had returned to Poland - if it was the same man.

The flight to Warsaw took only a couple of hours, but all the way Valentine battled to convince himself he wasn't wasting his time. Could the broken body of the man on the beach that night really have been Charlotte's brother?

The address was in a run-down area of the city east of the Vistula River, a few miles from where, years earlier, the great Russian army had sat and watched for 63 days whilst the city and its inhabitants were annihilated by German troops. It turned out to be an apartment, in a small, dilapidated block, occupied by a young couple. But once he'd been able to make himself understood it became apparent they couldn't help. Enquiries in the remainder of the building and adjacent dwellings were equally fruitless.

The local authorities proved helpful enough, but were unable to tell him anymore than he knew already. That Jan Kowalski had briefly lived at the address between 1946 and 1947. They couldn't help at all with a pre-war location, as all records had been destroyed.

A visit to the Registrar of Deaths also led nowhere and after three days he decided to return home. Disappointed, but not unduly surprised.

From his hotel he booked a flight and, with a few hours to spare, decided to take a stroll; calling in at a chocolate shop to find something for the twins.

It was a small, traditional shop full of enticing handcrafted confectionery and, as soon as the proprietor became aware that he had a customer from England, was anxious to prove his mastery of the language.

"You welcome Sir. English people very welcome. All chocolates home made. Very nice. Very nice."

Sitting in a rocking chair in one corner of the shop, wrapped in a blanket, was an old man. Dark glasses couldn't conceal his unmistakable blindness and every sentence the owner shared with Valentine, he translated for the man, his father.

Before long the conversation turned to the reason for Valentine's visit.

"You are taking holiday, Sir?"

"No. As a matter of fact I'm trying to trace someone."

"Who is this?"

"I doubt if..... . He was a dentist. Lived near here. A man by the name of Kowalski. Jan Kowalski."

The information was relayed to the old man, who after a moment nodded, smiled and said something.

"My father is asking what it is you ave want to know."

"He knows the man?!"

"Oh yes Sir," and he spoke with his father again.

"He says he remembers..... because..... he made him some of, what do you say? Pretend teeth."

"False teeth."

"Yes, the false teeth. You must excuse my English Sir, I am learning still."

The old man was smiling and pointing enthusiastically at his discoloured dentures.

"No, you're doing very well. But don't tell me those are the actual teeth?"

"Oh Yes Sir. Very fine quality."

"Goodness me! But does your father know what became of him?"

The father did know.

"Father says that one day there was a sign on the dentist's shop door to say 'business closed'."

"But are you sure he's not referring to before the war?"

"Oh no Sir. This was 1946. War finished. Germans Kaput!"

"And the dentist was closed?"

"Yes, nothing more. No more dentist. Gone. Finish."

The father spoke again.

"Father says there was some, er, quiet talking...... ."

"A rumour?"

"Yes, a rumour. Very good. There was a rumour that he was in love with a girl in England. Someone he met during the war years."

"England? Is he sure? Whereabouts in England?"

The old man's answer came as a shock.

"He thinks it is probable that he went back to where the Nazis' made him to work. Your English Channel island."

"He went back?!!"

"Yes Sir," he said, surprised by the man's reaction. "To the Jersey island."

As soon as Valentine arrived back in England he telephoned Directory Enquiries. It was a long shot but it paid off handsomely. There were two Kowalski's on the island, but only one with the initial J. It was too much of a coincidence. This had to be Charlotte's brother.

There followed a difficult few days as he toyed with what to do next. Presumably Kowalski believed his sister had died during the war. The man had a right to know the truth. But, how would he handle it?

Valentine decided on writing a brief letter of introduction. A difficult letter none the less.

Within a matter of days he received a reply, along with an invitation, and subsequently arranged a flight to the island of Jersey.

Jan Kowalski lived in a large, double fronted residence, built into the hillside, overlooking the sweeping sands of St. Brelade's Bay, to the south of the island. As the taxi approached along a narrow, tree lined lane, the mid afternoon sun was gradually surrendering its radiance to the fine mist of autumn rolling in off a grey-green sea, damp and consuming, covering all but the tallest rock formations, leaving them floating like dumplings in an unappetising soup. The clergyman drew his coat closer.

There was always the possibility that the man was not Charlotte's brother after all. Any doubts Valentine may have harboured were immediately compounded when the front door was opened by a man, a little older than himself and of average height, but with matured fair hair and bright, piercing blue eyes. Unlike Charlotte's altogether.

"Mr Gray," he began in a friendly fashion. "How very good of you to come all this way. I found your letter quite intriguing." There was a hint in his voice of the old country. "How very nice to meet you."

"And you Mr Kowalski. Thank you for the opportunity."

"Please do come in. Here, let me take your suitcase."

The house was expensively decorated and furnished; the large Persian rug in the centre of the entrance hall not going unnoticed.

"Do come through into the lounge. You must be tired after your journey."

Outside the mist thickened and continued to coat the island in shrouded hues of twilight.

Jan switched on a lamp, highlighting expensive looking paintings on oak panelled walls and offered the Clergyman a cigar to go with his whisky and soda. He declined.

"Now," he said. "I have many, many questions all itching for answers, especially about Martha, or Charlotte as I believe you prefer to call her."

"That's right."

"But first, you must explain how you found me. A real piece of detective work, surely."

"It's a great relief to know that you recognise the name. It puts my mind at rest immediately."

"At rest. I don't understand."

"I now know that you are indeed Charlotte's brother."

"But of course I'm Charlotte's brother. Son of Malkah and Aniol. Who else could I possibly be?"

"I couldn't be one hundred percent certain of that until I'd met you. I even went to Poland to try and find what became of you. I have so much to tell."

"Poland. Did you indeed. So, what led you here?"

"Can you believe I met someone who was still wearing a set of dentures you made in 1946." The thought of the yellowed teeth made him laugh.

"Dentures? Oh yes, dentures. My God, isn't it about time they were replaced? Ha! But what led you to Jersey? Tell me. I'm fascinated."

"Someone told me you'd fallen for an island girl and came back."

"Ah yes. Of course. The lovely ..... Molly." Jan twisted uncomfortably in the leather armchair. "But Molly passed away. Tragically."

"I'm so sorry."

"Suddenly."

"How very sad for you, especially after all you'd been through."

"What do you mean?"

"Your escape from here, when the island was occupied."

But Jan looked blank.

"Please don't tell me it wasn't you washed up on the beach that night. I've gone over this a thousand times in my head. It had to be you. How many other dentists from Warsaw escaped from Jersey? The coincidence is just too great."

"Yes, yes of course. Forgive me Mr Gray, but we are talking a long time ago remember. The escape," he said, draining his glass. "Dear me yes. How awful that was."

Valentine studied the man; the chiselled nose, the dimpled chin and instinctively knew something was wrong. Terribly wrong. He was saying one thing but, at the same time his eyes were giving an altogether opposing message. But whatever was it? He wore the expression of someone whose mind was on other things altogether.

"How could you possibly forget your broken legs and the way the surgeons fought, all night, to save them," said Valentine. "I see you've lost your limp, too."

"Yes. Yes. What a night! I'll never forget it. I'm sorry, my memory isn't quite what it used to be. The limp is much better now, of course, after all these years."

"Alright," said Valentine, leaning forward. "Let's stop playing games shall we? Just who exactly are you?"

"Whatever do you mean? I've told you who I am, Mr Gray. Malkah and Aniol's only son. Martha's only brother."

"The Jan Kowalski I knew didn't break his legs. He had no limp."

The man sighed. "Oh my dear Mr Gray," he said, "I really didn't want this to happen." Immediately he opened a drawer in the small antique cabinet beside him. "Believe me. I didn't. I had hoped we were going to have a nice little chat and send you on your way. But now you leave me with no choice."

"Whatever do you...........?"

Suddenly Valentine was looking down the barrel of a German 9mm Luger.

"What ever's this?!"

"Oh you English do so like to ask the blatantly obvious."

"You can't just......."

"Don't you dare tell me what I can't do in my own home! Sit back in the chair! It's you that's invaded my life remember. But I'm damned if I'm going to let you spoil it. I've lived here for a long time now and for however many years I've got left, I intend to remain here. In peace and quiet."

"Who exactly are you, for goodness sake?"

"Yes," he said after a moment. "I believe that's a reasonable question. You deserve an explanation. Before I kill you."

"What?!!" Valentine was suddenly too terrified to move.

"Please, dispense with the theatricals Mr Gray. I've seen hundreds, literally hundreds of people die in my time, so one more, I assure you, will make no difference whatsoever. My name is Konrad Bracher. Have you heard the name before?"

But Valentine's brain refused to work.

"I wasn't sure how much Charlotte had told you."

"You knew her?"

"I discovered her, shall we say. She worked for me."

"She worked for you? When?"

"During the war. I was her handler."

"Yes. Yes. I remember now. You forced her into working for you."

"Oh I wouldn't say forced, Mr Gray. She was a sensible girl. She knew there was no reasonable alternative."

Valentine couldn't help but finger Malkah's ring.

"Do I recognise the old woman's ring? How very touching."

"But what about.....? You're not Jan Kowalski."

"Indeed I'm not. I'm so glad you have finally managed to deduce that."

"But where is he? What's happened to Jan?" Should he call out?

"Mr. Kowalski had to close his business in rather a hurry. A sudden and unexpected decline in the number of patients."

"What do you mean? You killed him?" Was the house empty?

"Removed, would be my choice of word."

"But why?! I don't understand any of this. Why are you pointing a gun at me? Why for goodness sake?!"

"Come, come Mr. Gray. You're an educated gentleman. We're both old soldiers. Put two and two together, as you English say. I used to be with

Military Intelligence. The Abwehr. When it was obvious the war wasn't going quite the way the Führer imagined, I started to look for a way out. An escape plan. I'd done things, you understand, that, well... . Suffice to say things that would be frowned upon today.

I managed to remain incognito when the Allies took Berlin, but I knew my luck couldn't last. I'd have been discovered sooner or later. Then, one day I received news from one of my agents that Charlotte's brother had suddenly appeared in Warsaw. Early in 1946. He'd fallen into my lap. The poor deluded fool went back to help rebuild Poland, he told me. After the Jewish uprising and destruction of Warsaw there was nothing left to rebuild! So, I simply took his identity," he shrugged. "It was a perfect plan. A little hair dye, dark glasses. My Polish was passable. I became Jan Kowalski. And what better place to enjoy my newly found freedom than the tax free haven of beautiful Jersey."

"You vile, wicked apology of a man."

"Oh please Mr. Gray. Be happy for me. I look upon it all as an exercise, and a very successful exercise up until today, in self preservation. What could be wrong with that? It's in man's nature to fight for survival. And don't think I'm alone here, either. There's many a comrade on these islands, I must tell you. But enough of me," he waved the Luger nonchalantly. "Tell me about yourself, and

Charlotte. I'm not widowed incidentally, in fact I never married, but Kowalski did mention a girl. How very clever of me to remember her name. He told me he planned to earn some money and marry her."

"I'll tell you nothing."

"Charlotte was a highly intelligent girl I remember, and very beautiful. She would have made an excellent spy. First Class. But her heart wasn't in it."

"Of course her heart wasn't in it, you held her parents hostage."

"Hostages they were not Mr. Gray. Let me assure you of that. They quickly went the way of all Jewish flesh," and he gave Valentine a deprecating smirk.

"You disgusting barbarian!" Suddenly he felt his chest tighten, breathing was becoming difficult.

"But what of Charlotte? You hinted in your letter that all was not well."

"Charlotte's dead. I'm glad she is too, to hear you talk like that about the couple she loved would have broken her heart."

"So she's dead. I wondered what became of her. I would say I'm sorry but, under the circumstances, somehow I don't think you'd believe me. But now Mr. Gray," he said, sitting up. "I regret it's time for you to join her."

"Are you completely mad?!" He gasped. "My family all know I'm here. They'll have the police crawling all over this place if I don't contact them soon."

"People disappear every day, Mr. Gray. You will merely become another unexplained statistic. I told you. I am not alone on this island. Even the taxi driver is a sympathiser. I have only to make a telephone call and within no time it'll be just as if Mr. Valentine Gray never existed. But we have talked enough. It's getting late and I have an appointment and, besides, I've told you far more than I should."

All across the island evening was surrendering to night.

"I'm sorry our brief acquaintance has to end like this. Your quest to do good has rather backfired. You should have stayed at home." He pointed the gun directly in the centre of Valentine's chest. "Goodbye Mr. Gray," he said, without even a suggestion of emotion.

"No wait!!" cried Valentine, trying to push himself away. "We can talk this through!" But the heavy chair wouldn't budge. "Wait! Stop!" he pleaded, suddenly dizzy with fear, and feeling the blood drain from his head. "Oh Jesus, help me."

"Until we meet again. In heaven or in hell."

There was a loud click. Followed by another. And a third. When suddenly the air reverberated with the foulest of Germanic oaths, as Bracher pounded the Luger repeatedly in the palm of his hand.

It was now or never. With Bracher's attention occupied, Valentine raised his foot and with a surge of adrenalin kicked out in the direction of the gun. The men watched as the old firearm was lifted high into the air. Turning over and over before starting its descent some yards away.

They sprang to their feet. But Valentine used his foot again, sticking it out. Not delaying to watch as Bracher tumbled to the floor with a grunt.

The gun landed with a sharp crack. Firing off a round that thudded into the skirting board across the other side of the room. Valentine snatched it up, swinging round, aiming at the Nazi who was already on his feet.

"You English pig! I'll get .... ."

Without hesitation Valentine fired. "That's for Jan!" he spluttered. "And for ruining Charlotte's life." He fired again. "And that's for Malkah."

Bracher staggered back with a look of incredulity as fire burst from the barrel for a third time.

"And that's for Aniol."

The man clutched his already blood soaked chest just as his leg caught the edge of a glass topped coffee table and he was pitched backwards, snapping the plate glass in two. Crashing to the floor - dead.

Suddenly the room was silent. The smell of spent cordite fresh in the air. Valentine looked at Bracher. He looked at the Luger still clutched in his trembling hand. He closed his eyes, allowing the gun to drop to the floor and, collapsing into the nearest chair, buried his face in his hands and wept.

Valentine Gray remained there for some time. Time when his mind transported him back. Further and further down through the years. Through the blackness of the night on Pyle Street, and another killing. He felt a shiver, and heard the voice of reason call out her warning. Go back! Stay away! But it was too late. His nostrils twitched with musty dampness, and he saw himself climbing the dark, creaking stairs.

Suddenly his head was full of yelling and shouting and sounds of a scuffle. He burst into the room to see Charlotte struggling with Ethan. Her dress was torn at the shoulder and he was calling her a dirty Nazi. Over and over again.

"Valentine! Help me!" yelled Charlotte. "Get him off me!"

"She's a Nazi spy I tell you!"

In two strides Valentine was on Ethan and hit him hard on the jaw. But he refused to let go of Charlotte. Hanging on to her for all he was worth with his only hand.

"She's a spy!" he shrieked as Valentine punched him repeatedly until finally he toppled backwards, pulling Charlotte with him. All three collapsing onto the floor in a heap.

Suddenly Charlotte screamed. Ethan let out a peculiar wheezing sound and went quite still.

"Oh my God!" she cried, pushing him off. "No! No! What have we done? What have we done?"

There it was once again. The knife she had been defending herself with, protruding from Ethan's chest like a monument to guilt.

"Yes, if anyone killed Ethan Thomas it was me," he conceded to Bracher's lifeless body. "It was all my fault. I can still see him attacking the woman I loved. I lost control, but it was all a terrible accident. Charlotte would never have killed him, poor chap. She only wanted to frighten him off. But it all went horribly wrong," he sighed and wiped a palm across his eyes. "For years I've buried the truth, like the body under the floor. But don't you understand? I had to keep it secret. I had to lie to the police. I couldn't risk being charged with manslaughter. How could I face prison? Not at my age. I even lied to my own family. May God forgive me. God forgive me."

It was some time before he was sufficiently composed for his thoughts to focus and he poured himself a brandy from the cocktail cabinet, helping to ease the pain in his chest.

Looking round for a telephone he dialled 999. A woman asked which service he required.

"I wish to report a shooting," he told her. "No, on second thoughts I want to report the execution of a Nazi war criminal. And you'd better send an ambulance - for me that is. I don't feel too good. And, oh yes, I insist on speaking to Detective Inspector Roy Preston on the Isle of Wight. There's something I need to clear up."

"What number are you calling from, Sir?"

"They're never going to believe this at home, you know. Never. Not in a million years."

"Hello Sir. Hello".

The end

Epilogue

It was the annual 'Liberation Day' Remembrance Service on the island of Jersey, 9th May 1981, when the island's residents gather in Liberation Square, St. Helier, to pay their respects to the memory of those who suffered so appallingly at the hands of the Germans during the five years of occupation, and give thanks for the liberation that followed in 1945.

The square was rich with the colours of numerous flags, veterans heavy with medals; military bands and ladies sporting expensive hats.

Amongst those present, seated in the warm sunshine, was the Reverend Valentine Gray, accompanied by Detective Inspector Roy Preston (who had become embroiled in the affair of the shooting and called to give evidence at the subsequent hearing), and Dr. Martin Gray.

Police investigations had quickly ascertained the truth of Gray's story, that the dead man was not who he had masqueraded as, but a former Nazi officer, and was wanted to stand trial for war crimes by the Jerusalem based Simon Wiesenthal Centre.

The case of self defence never went to court.

The local media made the most of the incident and, although no-one gave voice to the opinion in public, in the pubs and workplaces, it was widely agreed, and especially amongst those who had lived through the occupation, that the Reverend had rendered the Island a great service.

Standing on the perimeter of the throng was a middle aged man visiting from Russia. As his lips parted in the united 'Amen', he revealed a number of gold capped teeth, exactly like his father's.

AUTHOR'S NOTE

'The Story of Four Islands' brings together some important points of history.

In addition to the original Valentine Gray Memorial, where Charlotte and Valentine met, visitors to Newport, Isle of Wight, will find a shopping mall and a wall plaque which reads:

'Gray's Walk. This walk is named in memory of Valentine Gray. The Little Sweep. Aged 10 years. The body of Valentine Gray was found in an outhouse in Pyle Street in January 1822. Public indignation of the circumstances leading to his death resulted in the passing of 'The Climbing Boys Act' which prevented young sweeps ever again being sent up the inside of chimneys, and ensured them more humane treatment.'

Under the direct orders of Adolf Hitler, the Channel Islands were turned into the most fortified area in Western Europe with a view to protecting hundreds of miles of French coastline from Allied invasion. But at the cost of 'slave labour'. In 1942 German records stated that there were 3,270 foreign (Russian, French, Spanish Republican and Polish) workers on Jersey alone. They were treated as an expendable, sub-human workforce. Barely clothed, pitilessly underfed targets of extreme cruelty by all branches of occupation forces. At least 557 died. The 'German War Tunnels' remain open to the public.

The general overseer of the PLUTO oil pipeline, without which the Normandy landings would not have been possible, was Lord Louis Mountbatten who, in addition to his many other roles, was Governor of the Isle of Wight for fourteen years and concurrently Lord Lieutenant for five years until his death in County Sligo in 1979. Remains of the pipeline may still be seen.

At the request of the British Government during WWII, one tenth of the land of the islands of Bermuda was given over to the construction of U.S. Naval and military bases to aid in the Battle of the Atlantic where submarines were a constant threat. The island was a vital link in the safety of convoys of men and materials that eventually helped to bring down Hitler.